Fading Past

A novel

by
Mary Kathleen Mehuron

Copyright © 2015 Mary Kathleen Mehuron
FADING PAST
Éclair Press
ISBN-13: 978-1519100948
ISBN-10: 1519100949

Developmental editor: Janet Hubbard
Editor and formatting: Marley Gibson
Cover text: James M. Tabor
Cover design: Jonathan C. Hyde
Graphic artist: Serena Fox

This book recounts some of the true events of my life, but it is a work of fiction. In many cases, I have compressed events and time and created prototypes for the people to which I am often drawn. It should particularly be noted that the characters of Belinda and Nathaniel are amalgams made in my imagination and born from self-observation. Belinda is also based on the extensive research I have done about little girls who are abused by family members, and the outcomes that occur as a result of this abuse. Names, dates, places, events, and details have been changed, invented, and altered for literary effect. Nevertheless, before I could write much of this book, I first had to live it.

Dedication

For my three sons, who are the North Star by which I have navigated my voyage to a new life. My children, you inspire me.

"Time tends to romanticize and idealize. Relationships are not black and white, but given enough time and distance we see them as such."

~ Christopher Gutierrez
September 22, 1012

"Now from out our fading past, a scene which can forever last"

~ Garry Platt

You're invited!

45th Reunion
St. Agnes Academy and
Avalon Park Graded-School
Classes of 1969

Special guests: Bergen County Youth Theater North

PARTY IN THE TENT AT THE TOWN PARK IN
AVALON PARK

Saturday June 29, 2014 ~ 2:00 - 5:30 p.m.
Cost: $30 ~ includes lunch provided by
Rose DeRosa Catering
Reunion organizer: Deborah Guianti

Prologue

It's not like I didn't know it was coming, but seeing the number in print was another thing.

Forty-fifth?

It just didn't make sense to me, although I realized we had graduated from elementary school in 1969 and it was now 2014; the difference between the two numbers isn't hard to calculate, and I am a professional math teacher.

Still rattled by the invitation, I remained unconvinced. I picked up my calculator and punched the subtraction problem into it. Sure enough, the answer was displayed on the little screen: 45.

I flung the offending contraption across the granite top of my kitchen island. It slid quickly and still had speed when it reached the other side, flew off, and made a clattering sound as it hit the floor.

My journal was open on the counter next to my laptop. I jotted down, "Time is flowing by me like the water in a steep mountain stream across a boulder. It runs over, under, and around me at a mesmerizing velocity. The effect is dizzying. Almost as though I can feel the earth spin beneath my feet."

Next to these sentences, I wrote, "2014 − 1969 = 45."

Shifting back from my journal to my computer, I quickly composed an e-mail to my childhood friend, Belinda, who, at various times of my life, had also been an adversary.

I knew that I was being impulsive, but at this moment, I didn't care.

From: Mary Patricia Maddin <pattyt55@gmsvt.net>
To: Belinda Barnes <snakecharmer711@gmail.com>
Subject: Class Reunion
Date: April 7, 2014 at 7:38:46 a.m. EDT

You must have received your invitation via e-mail at the same exact moment I did. While it makes sense to assume that we would drive down together, I may fly alone into Newark instead.

The truth is, and this may sound a little harsh, I am not at all sure that I want to be in a car with you for the hours it will take us to get to New Jersey. I refuse to ride as your passenger because I want to get there alive. The last time I allowed you to drive, you texted at night, in bumper-to-bumper traffic, going seventy miles per hour. Yet I know how reactive you get when someone else is at the wheel. The idea of you gasping and hanging on to the dashboard every time I pass another vehicle makes me livid. One hundred and forty miles of it might incite me to commit murder.

Patty

The anger I felt toward Belinda after our most recent falling-out had not abated. The problem was that we could be close one day (my husband, Rich, uses the term "enmeshed"), and then I would say something that would send her into furious isolation. I refer to this as her *disappearing act.* It's like Belinda's nerves are closer to the surface of her skin than other people's. She keeps an ever-vigilant watch for the next slight she is sure is about to be inflicted upon her. If you spent enough time with her, you would eventually bump into a subject she considered painful. I do better with her than most. However, after our most recent episode, Belinda had gone so far as to unfriend me on Facebook. Given enough time and space, she tended to forget what made her angry in the first place, and knowing this, I'd marked my calendar to call her in three months.

We had already been estranged for weeks when I'd seen a post on the social media site from a mutual friend, informing everyone that Belinda had been in a serious car accident. I'd panicked. *What if she had died?* How on earth could I continue my life in a world without her in it? My efforts to connect with her had been

2

met with silence. I didn't even know the name of the man who had gone with her to the emergency room.

Another week had gone by before I'd discovered the extent of her injuries. After all the years and the miles we had walked across together, I'd been sick to my stomach with worry. It turned out she had been taken by ambulance to the hospital and released the next day. She'd also seen an orthopedist, who had scheduled her for outpatient surgery on her knee. She was still going to physical therapy twice a month when the invitation came.

I poured a second cup of coffee and called her. She answered in her raspy voice after only three rings. "I haven't peed yet."

"Call me back, but read your e-mail first," I said. "I was very emotional when I wrote it, so prepare yourself for that."

"Oh, terrific. What a wonderful way to start my day."

Belinda and I had met in elementary school when we were nine and I was the new kid in town. Previously, during almost a decade of my young life, I had lived in a community of tract houses where everyone's grandparents spoke English with a thick foreign accent. We were mostly Catholics of Irish and Italian descent. The third tradition represented was that of Jews from Russia and Germany. It wasn't uncommon for the grandparents to live with their children. Those who didn't visited on such a regular basis that I knew them all for a distance of two blocks from my house in any direction. Unanimously, they treasured us kids and tried to impress upon us the significance of being born in the United States. A common endearment was "Only in America!"

Every elder in the neighborhood, as far as I could tell, had escaped genocide, poverty, or starvation. They were haunted by what had happened to them and to their family members who had not made it to Ellis Island alive. We children accepted their eccentricities, which were sometimes glaring.

One old man down the block sunned himself outside in a green-and-white webbed lawn chair. Every once in a while, he would start to scream and rock back and forth until his son or daughter-in-law came outside to comfort him. There was no therapy, no Prozac, no name for post-traumatic stress, and, in the end, there was only God to turn to. Or whiskey. Or both.

Our people, *muintir s'againn*, pined for the beauty of their homeland in Ireland. Longing permeated every conversation, but they were certain about the future of their offspring: "With our good hair and good teeth, you children will be more American than the Americans in one more generation." They counseled us about the importance of education. In closed circles around a front stoop, they speculated about the seats of real power in the United States. Famous colleges were spoken of with a reverence that rivaled the hush in the parish priest's voice when he invoked the name of the Catholic Church on a Sunday morning.

My Celtic bloodlines awarded me respect from the old ones. They talked to my siblings, my cousins, and me about being a "direct descendant," but with their Irish accents, it sounded like "d*ye*-rect d*ye*-scendent."

They would pay tribute to me: "This beautiful little girl here is the d*ye*-rect *dye*-scendent of O'Tuathaigh, one of the nine septs of the Hy Niall. I hear all about her high marks in school. She's a good girl, too. Helps her mother. *Mary Patricia Toohey!* You remember you have the royal blood running through ya. You remember who you are."

With that, one of them might hand me a coin and send me running to the corner candy store for a treat. I knew my place in the *old* neighborhood. I was a Toohey and a Noonan of Cork. The Noonans had been very active in the Rebellion. My mother's side was of the sept of Ó Gallchobhair of Donegal, the most senior of the Cenél Conaill. Being of the Toohey and Gallagher families meant I was an important part of the community. It was my birthright.

Three days before I met Belinda, my family had moved to Avalon Park. We left our Irish legacy and migrated closer to New York City, to a town with bigger, classier houses. Classier meant newer and included spacious landscaped lawns. A train station was within walking distance, and Daddy could ride it right into Grand Central Station. In the old neighborhood, the men had formed car pools or had gotten together and chartered a bus to take them to work in the city. My father said he could spend less time commuting now and more time with his family in our new location.

The huge problem with the move to Avalon Park was that the Catholic school was already at full capacity. It was a very small church, unlike the colossal parish we were coming from. New students were put on a waiting list that included children from the surrounding towns. For the first time in my life, I would have to attend a public school.

From the day I had started kindergarten, children had been divided into two general groups: Catholics and Publics. The Publics, those who attended public school, were not going to heaven. The nuns were specific about the fact that only *we* were going. I never understood where the others went when they died. Yet when I dared to ask, the sisters told me to mind my own business. God would take care of it all when the time came.

My father's closest friend said repeatedly, "Every day of your life, get down on your knees and thank God you are Irish." If heaven and hell were what was at stake, I had to agree with him. I, born into being a Catholic, was therefore chosen. No wonder people talked about the luck of the Irish.

That year, I would discover that there were some who counted themselves as Irish even though they *were not* Roman Catholic. This would be one of many revelations I had while shifting cultures. New facts came at me so abruptly that I swore at one point I heard a seismic crack in the bedrock of what I had been taught and wholeheartedly believed during the first decade of my life.

At the end of that April, I walked alone on shaking legs to the new school. The *public school*. I wore an outfit instead of a uniform. That, in and of itself, felt unfamiliar. I was so very small making my way down the wide street, feeling like an impostor without my maroon plaid skirt and vest. When, on that first day, the teacher called on me to answer a question, I stood up straight in the aisle to respond to her, which was the way it was done in Catholic school. All the children tittered, and my face burned with shame. I looked around the room and counted the leers. My classmates *did* seem evil. The sisters of St. Joseph knew what they were talking about.

Belinda came up to me right after the class broke for recess. "Join our group."

She took my hand, and we ran outside to skip rope. Belinda knew how to set up a Double Dutch game. Two long ropes were turned in opposite directions, and the player skipped both simultaneously. Belinda could turn the ropes with flawless rhythm. Each girl would skip until she made a mistake or one of the ropes got caught around her foot. At that point, she would be eliminated and the next girl would get a turn. When Belinda was up, she jumped furiously on and on. We started to cheer for her, and all the other students and the teachers gathered around. When she finally did make the mistake that ended her run, she got a big ovation from the crowd.

The other girls were winded and lay down on the grass. Belinda stayed behind with me and taught me how to play a game called Snake. We linked arms and twisted ourselves around as much as we could while still remaining attached. Eventually, we fell to the ground laughing. The recess bell sounded. She stood up and dug into her bag and produced a brand-new pencil. It was coated with pink glitter. Belinda held it up like a magic wand. "It's for you," she said as she leveled her butterscotch-colored eyes meaningfully at me for a heartbeat. We went back into the school together side by side.

It was also Belinda who showed me that the only dividing line between the public school play yard and that of the Catholic school of St. Agnes was a single-lane road. It was an alley, really; certainly it was not enough to hold back the flow of children sharing bats and balls before and after school and during the coordinated recess time. This exchange was exacerbated by the fact that all extracurricular activities included both school populations. The graded school Catholics had catechism class in St. Agnes Academy every Tuesday afternoon. And, of course, all the families worshipped together on Sundays and holy days. Oh, the nuns would wave their arms around from time to time, pretending to object to the influx of public school children, but in the end, they accepted it.

I came to adore Sister Mary Vincent, who, with her shrewd sparkling eyes, summed up my heritage in five seconds. Flowing robes covered her arms, and she would wrap one around me while she told me her stories of Ireland. I gratefully leaned back against her chest, listening patiently. Sometimes, I could feel the beat of her heart against the back of my head.

Belinda was not one of "us." Her people were of *Welsh* descent. My grandmother referred to the English as "them devils," but she wasn't sure what to make of people from Wales. The composition of Avalon Park, New Jersey, I quickly learned, was different from that of the town I came from. Most people here were Protestants. Instead of Catholic Mass, Belinda's family went to something called the Congregational church on Sunday. I wasn't sure what or whom they worshipped there.

The phone in my kitchen rang, interrupting my memories. When I picked it up, I heard the sound of a match strike and a deep, sucking inhalation on a cigarette. With a loud exhalation, Belinda said, "I thought we had this misunderstanding all worked out. I am really looking forward to the reunion. I haven't had fun in a long time. The accident just leveled me."

"My problem is that it wasn't a misunderstanding."

Belinda took another drag on her cigarette. "I couldn't answer your voice mails or e-mails. I was in far too much pain."

She used a tone that was dangerously emphatic. It was warning me not to push her or she would hang up. Her implicit demand was that I buy into her claim that she had not been able to call me. All she wanted now was to move on and start planning our trip. It had always been important to her, after a disappearing act, that I pretty much pretend that nothing had happened. But forty-nine years of this suddenly felt like one too many.

"You couldn't call or text *me,* but you were in constant contact with other friends of ours."

"I'm adjusting to the medications. It's a real thing. Google it!" She bellowed the last part.

"Can you at least tell me why you stopped talking to me in the first place?"

"No."

"What do you mean, no?"

"I can't. I wish I could."

It made some weird sense that she didn't remember anything. Why would she cut me out of her life when she most needed my help? Maybe we could consult a doctor and figure this out, I thought. I even felt a glimmer of hope that the future could be different for us. But the hurt was still fresh, and I was cautious. We had been talking daily and debriefing each other on every small event. Overnight, she'd stopped returning my calls. Yet I knew she loved me. I knew it. If she could understand the wounds she'd caused, surely she wouldn't do it again.

"You were perfectly fine when you talked to Don," I said. "Who, by the way, you didn't give the time of day to when we were in school. He told me you were in pain, but it sounded like it was under control. He said you sounded fine." When she didn't reply, I added, "You could have let me know—an e-mail even."

Silence. I wanted her assurance that she wouldn't cut me off again and a plan for the future.

I pushed because it could be months before I would have her attention like this. "What do we do the next time I bump into something painful inside you or I am too blunt, Belinda? You know it's only a matter of time. I don't want to keep doing this. I go into mourning every time it happens."

Belinda responded in a surprisingly flat and bland tone. "I know it's my fault. I've destroyed all my other friendships. I won't even get started on my love life. I've decided it's not going to happen again. I see your point, I hear you, but the problem was the medications that were prescribed. They turned me into a zombie. I'm pretty much healed, and I'm weaning myself off them." Then she began to wail. "Really! I've had the hardest life of anyone I know. Why does this always happen to me?"

Her statement hung out there, and I didn't say a word.

"I guess by your silence that you don't agree with me."

"Everyone's life is hard at times. Offer it up."

"What is *that* supposed to mean?"

"Suffering is a part of life. Offer it up to God, with an intention. Pray for a homeless kid to get a meal today."

Belinda snorted. "This is a real thing with you people?"

I was offended. "I'm pretty sure you've heard me use that expression before."

Belinda wailed again, exhaling air and cigarette smoke. "But my father *died!* Grief is a process, and it takes time."

I counted to ten. "He died five years ago. He was eighty-seven years old. Your father was a heavy drinker and smoker for all the years I knew him. I think he lived to a ripe old age."

"I am overly sensitive." She went on in her bland voice: "I'm working on it with my therapist. Don't you think I'm embarrassed by how I get triggered? You are the closest friend I have. You know how my father's death floored me. The accident followed, and it was like piling on the trauma. Now that Dad's dead, we will never have a chance to... talk about it. I feel so... so..." She was genuinely overcome with sorrow and couldn't go on.

I felt a massive emotional tug inside my chest. Compelled to finish her thought, I said, "Conflicted?"

She started to sob. Her anguish reached through the phone line and wrapped around my heart. I continued: "Yes, our parents were the problem, the big *problem,* but they could also have been the answer. Now that they're gone, our questions will go unanswered. The obvious one being why we didn't deserve to be protected and loved."

She was sniffling now. "Yeah. Yeah, exactly. I'm having a hard time with that."

"I can understand." My hardened heart melted. "I have the same thing."

And, just like that, our most recent split was over. We had mended the rift with our shared heartache and would be going to our reunion as the best of friends.

Belinda and I had not been broken by our early years, but we had certainly been cracked and dented. We both have acknowledged without reservation that this is true. I refer to us as being uniquely flawed. I tell my sons that the most interesting people are those with deep fractures at the core. My childhood and Belinda's were hard, more so than many can even imagine. As children, we bonded over the shame we felt. We didn't know the correct terms for what was going on in our homes. She and I didn't discuss it at the time; we didn't try to name the bad things, yet we would validate for each other that what we witnessed on a daily basis was not normal. From a young age, neither of us knew how to get out of our situations, but we could discuss the possibilities.

We also kept each other's *secrets*. We practiced total, unquestioning loyalty. If you had met Belinda and Mary Patricia in those pubescent years, our personality differences would have seemed more relevant than our similarities. We were complementary; what one could not figure out, the other could. The very first thing we learned to assess was: Which one of our houses will be safe for us tonight?

1965 in North Jersey

Fortunately, both sets of parents found it easier to have Belinda and me together than apart. We were both helpful and polite. Once cocktail hour ended, the moms and dads weren't really aware of what went on in their homes, anyway. We cleaned up the kitchen, put the little kids to bed, and then did our homework. We did what was asked of us and stayed out of the way. We were also stealthy. Each of us had an older sister who was the black sheep of the family, and we made sure the attention stayed focused on them.

Belinda was fun and beautiful. Whereas I had a limp cap of hair the color of clay dirt, her long locks and eyes were the color of a jar of honey held up to the light. Her facial features were vividly defined, the tip of her nose was pushed up just enough to be adorable, and her chin had both a subtle cleft in the center and a dimple on the right side that appeared when she smiled. Belinda's skin had a glow to it all year long, and it became deeply tanned in the summer. She had the complexion I imagined might belong to a Gypsy, and how jealous I was of it, as I was stuck with the swine-pink pale flesh of the Irish. I wanted to spend every waking minute with her.

One night, I slept over at her house. My head was on her pillow and hers on a sleeping bag on the floor. She was so generous in this way. Not only did she insist that I sleep in her bed, she would press into my hand any possession of hers I openly admired. I quickly learned not to make comments about her nice things, because it wasn't fair to her.

When the evening grew late, she jumped up and went to a dress-up kit her mother had put together for her. There was a small bag with used makeup in it, and she pulled out a brown liner pencil.

"I'm going to draw something on your chin."

When she was done, she went over to the mirror and drew two eyes on her own chin. With a flourish, she added an upside-down nose. Then, she lay back down on the floor.

"Try to imagine that the bottom of my chin is actually the top of a little head. *Bonjour, mademoiselle. Comment allez-vous?*" Her chin jumped to life as a puppet head. It was magic.

I answered her, *"Je vais bien, Jeanette."*

Jeanette was Belinda's name in our French class. I used a squeaky cartoon voice when I spoke to her, and I jerked my jaw in a spastic manner: *"Jeanette, quoi de neuf? Est-ce que vous parlez anglais? Ça ne me plaît pas?"*

At this, she guffawed.

We experimented with different accents. Then we tried making our puppet chins into men. Each time one of us spoke, the other one giggled uncontrollably. My stomach and face actually hurt from the hilarity, which went on for nearly an hour. The spell broke when we heard her parents begin to have a loud argument. We knew from experience that it could turn ugly, and we held our breath. There was a loud thud of something slamming against a wall, and Belinda quickly turned out the light. From her place on the floor, she snaked her arm up under the covers and took my hand.

We woke up the next day as though nothing had happened and tried to leave before the adults began stirring. School was within walking distance. Volunteers were always needed in the library. The school student council and various clubs were forced to meet before school because of scheduling issues, and we could easily join one of the groups. If worse came to worst, there was an alcove outside where we could curl against each other to stay warm. To pass the time, we became avid readers and ended up winning a lot of awards for book reports.

On this particular morning, Mr. Barnes, Belinda's father, surprised us by getting up early. He shuffled blindly to the percolator and poured a mug of coffee. Then he pulled a metal ice tray out of the freezer and opened it with a crack. The cold cubes in his cup gave him instant access to the caffeine. He inserted a cigarette into the left-hand corner of his mouth and struck a match. He was somehow able to smoke even as he guzzled down the coffee. Only then did he grunt a hello in Belinda's and my general direction.

Belinda hunched her shoulders and bowed her head, avoiding any eye contact with her father. Emboldened by her withdrawal, he strutted over. With the cigarette still stuck in his mouth, he used the curve of his thumb to stroke the nape of her neck. "Mmmmm. Like gossamer silk, your skin."

She shook him off, and he stopped. When he started again, she seemed resigned to it. The stroking continued, and her father's eyes rolled back in his head. It was an expression on a man's face I would come to know well as a grown woman. On that particular day many years ago, it made me leap up from the table. I went into the half bath off the hallway and furiously began to wash my hands. Belinda was soon pounding on the door. When I opened it, she had her coat on and mine over her arm.

We ran toward the front door as he called to us in a broken, phlegmy voice. "Hey, girls! Don't do anything I wouldn't do." A bass-toned, mucus-obstructed chuckle followed, ringing in the air until we slammed the door on it.

It was hard for me to imagine anything Belinda's father *wouldn't* do. As the helpful friend of his daughter, I had become something of a fly on the wall at their house. The two of us were often asked to serve at their adult parties and clean up afterward. I had watched the man in action as he targeted a woman and moved from flirtation to outright sexual advances with each cocktail he consumed. One night, at one particularly infamous party, the man completely lost his mind. He was already a bit drunk by seven, when the guests began to arrive.

Belinda's house was always a pigsty. Her mother tried to make a joke about the chaos and filth, saying, "When you get married, you have to choose which things you are going to be good at.

Housekeeping was not my first choice." She shrugged her shoulders with a theatrical wink. If Mrs. Barnes brought a fresh load of wash into Belinda's room, she piled the clothes on top of those already on the floor. Empty bottles were thrown back into their cardboard cases, but those boxes were left stacked high against the kitchen walls. Every piece of furniture was littered with random objects and trash.

In order to have people in her house, Mrs. Barnes had to make space in the living room and dining room. One afternoon, she enlisted her children to haul the debris in garbage bags to the already bursting garage. I helped them throw the bags on top of the existing rubbish. I swung a bag back, then used my forward momentum and aimed. It landed on the top.

While there was now room to move around the house, I couldn't help but notice that there were still stacks of debris along the perimeter. One of the piles was covered with a linen tablecloth. No one seemed to mind. Mrs. Barnes turned the lights down low and lit many candles, bathing the rooms in a warm glow. When the guests arrived, the limits established by the piles actually pushed them closer together. This turned out to be— along with the fresh summer cocktails—a social lubricant.

A stunning buffet of curries was laid out on the table over a second thick linen cloth. Many small dishes of toppings were set in a line. The plates themselves were delicate and so beautiful that people hesitated to serve themselves. It was an exotic choice, making Mrs. Barnes look like an intriguing woman.

On one of our many walking jaunts to a neighboring town, Belinda and I had bought matching shirts. Belinda's mother thought it would be cute if we wore them to the party as a kind of service uniform. We would be her waitresses. Belinda's siblings had been shipped off to one of the grandmothers' houses for the night, so we felt honored to be in attendance, no matter our role.

I practiced various ways to present the finger food to each group I approached. "Would you like an appetizer?" "Would you like something to eat?" "Would you like one of these?" "Hello! Would you like one?" It became a game to me.

Still, working at a grown-ups' party got old pretty fast. After what seemed like hours, Belinda came over to me empty-handed. The party was in full swing.

"Put your tray down on the coffee table and let's go outside."

She didn't have to ask me twice.

The party spilled out the back door and onto a flagstone patio. A charcoal grill was smoking, and on it were meats on wooden sticks I would later come to know as bamboo skewers. Choking a bit on the acrid fumes, we scrambled across the backyard and climbed a huge weeping willow tree. We were perhaps twenty feet off the ground, but close enough to hear every word spoken. Belinda's father was schmoozing below us.

The man had few physical boundaries. I noticed, and not for the first time, that his arms wound up around every woman at some point in the evening. He was overweight and in terrible physical condition. The flesh at his jawline jiggled when he inhaled on his cigarette or exhaled. His eyes were bloated from drink, and his protruding belly sagged under his short-sleeved shirt. I had once overheard my mother say he looked like a heart attack waiting to happen; yet he projected a smugness regarding his allure. On constant display was his conviction that he was irresistible to the opposite sex.

Even at my tender age, I found such men and their neediness pathetic. I was, even then, repulsed as I watched Belinda's father work his way through the women in the crowd. I vowed to never again allow myself to be taken in by his charm. He'd once told me he wanted a hug hello. I pointed my head over his shoulder as he pulled me close, but he was stronger. Within moments, he'd maneuvered his slimy, grown-man lips over mine. I was still a child! I wrestled myself free and made a point of avoiding him from then on.

Studying Belinda's father from my perch up in the tree made my skin crawl. He would first test how close he could stand to a woman and then how often he could touch her. Most of the women would become uncomfortable and walk away from him. We watched as a friend of my mother's upbraided him for his advances, saying, "You're drunk! I just came over to pay my respects to you, not to get mauled!" I wanted to cheer when she stormed away.

I could see Mr. Barnes was getting tired. It was hot. He sat down on an outdoor couch and put his sweating cocktail of juice and hard liquor on the glass table in front of him. He mopped his brow with a paper napkin, which he then stuck under the lowball glass. A petite woman in a sundress arrived and sat next to him. She had his attention. She primly held her knees together, pointing them slightly toward him, and she placed her drink on the table beside his. As they talked, he moved his face in closer and closer to hers, and I watched his chin circle around. He appeared to be hypnotizing the woman with his large eyes that were the exact color of Belinda's. His swirling movements were enough to make the brown curls atop his head bounce a little. He tucked his chin down and looked at her through his lashes, searching her every expression for meaning. When she answered him, his eyes widened as though he were in a state of wonder.

The woman was dressed like a child, although she had not been young for some time. While Belinda's mother was sophisticated, this lady wore the pink satin ribbon of a schoolgirl in her hair. Everything about her was smaller than it should have been, and she did nothing to help correct the disproportion. She wore black Mary Jane shoes, and her hair was far too long for her diminutive size. Although she was pretty, she was no match for Belinda's mom.

Mr. Barnes laughed. He seemed to think everything the woman said was *sidesplitting*. And she trilled back at him in return, just a tiny bird of a woman having the time of her life.

At one point, he went to refresh their drinks and came back with a tray. On it was an ice bucket, a pitcher of something that looked like fruit punch, and a bottle of clear liquor. For a long time, they sat on the couch entranced by each other and the ashtray they had placed between them. They shifted positions only to suck on their cigarettes and flick their ashes into the large glass disk. From time to time, Mr. Barnes would make a ceremony out of refilling their drinks. I noticed when they began to sporadically reach out and tentatively touch each other. The woman swept a finger under Mr. Barnes's eye, as if removing an errant lash. He glowed at her after that.

I knew she was drunk when her face grew slack. Propriety was eroding quickly. Mr. Barnes leaned over repeatedly and whispered in her ear. She pushed back at him with her hand. "Oh, go on!" we could hear her shout and "You are too much."

It was nearly dark by now, but not dark enough to hide what happened next. Mrs. Barnes had been running around all night. She was a great hostess. Not only had she prepared everything that was being served tonight, but she also made sure her guests' plates and glasses were always full. This was a drinking crowd; taking care of everyone had her in constant motion. Her husband was quite the opposite. He sat in the one place and mooned over the girlish middle-aged woman.

Suddenly, Mr. Barnes bent his head down to the petite woman. Their eyes were interlocked. He kissed her briefly on the lips. I could not believe it! Next to me on the tree branch, Belinda let out a harsh involuntary bark. Then her father, not having been rebuked by the woman, made the decision to continue. The two of them exchanged a deep soul kiss, a French kiss, without regard for the crowd that witnessed it. I was so focused on the bulging of their respective tongues inside each other's cheeks that at first that I didn't see Mrs. Barnes approach.

She had a pitcher of beer in one hand as she stood behind her husband. She was clearly shocked, but she recovered quickly. She lifted the pitcher up and poured the contents over his head. When it was empty, he licked his face and gasped, his hand still resting on the naked thigh of the bird lady.

We climbed down out of the tree in a hurry. Belinda called to me as she hung from a low branch, and then dropped off on the far side of her parents' cedar stockade fence, into the neighbor's yard.

"This way!"

I saw the back of Belinda's feet pumping as she flew in the direction of my house. We ran barefoot across the wet grass and warm asphalt. At the back of our home was a three-season sunroom constructed with louvered windows. The door was unlocked. We went inside and lay down on the two cedar-frame couches upholstered in striped yellow plastic. I clicked on a tiny black-and-white television, its volume already turned down low. The show being broadcast revolved around two American spies who kissed foreign women wearing negligees. My mother had forbidden me to watch it, but at this moment, the kissing fascinated me. I sat down on the floor, closer to the flickering screen.

"Your face looks kinda scary with the light flashing on it like that," Belinda said.

The image on the screen began to roll vertically. I felt for a knob on the back of the TV and adjusted it as I answered her: "I thought you were supposed to be married before you kissed like this."

When she replied, I thought she was crying. "Yeah, you're supposed to be."

The show that followed was about cowboys who grew up on a ranch. We woke the next morning to the sound of "The Star-Spangled Banner" announcing the start of the television broadcast day. I was stiff and sweating as I picked myself up off the floor. We hadn't had dinner the night before. Belinda was still sleeping, so I went into the kitchen to find us something to eat.

The Toohey Family

Belinda found it peculiar that my mother spent so much time in bed with the drapes drawn. She had a nickname for my parents' bedroom: *the room of gloom and doom.* "And your father scares me," she said. "I guess I wasn't moving fast enough for him yesterday. He pushed me out of his way!"

I felt embarrassed when Belinda told me this, yet my dad could go much further than pushing. Sometimes his eyes would bug out, and then would come the jingling sound as he unfastened his belt. He'd grab the end and, in one swift and graceful movement, pull it through the loops of his pants, then bring it up high as a whip. For a split second, it would point vertically in the air, like a leather saber. This was for dramatic effect. What I found terrifying was that he was completely in control of himself when he decided to beat us. Cold-blooded. I was old enough to run, but that would mean leaving the babies behind. It was worth it, in my mind, to take the whipping because he might really hurt the little ones. Belinda would sprint right out the door when she heard the belt buckle jingle. I would find her in the woods later, trembling in fear.

Belinda was accustomed to her own father behaving badly, and so it was my mother who she found more fault with. One afternoon, we walked into my house and, as always, headed straight for baby Malachy's room. He was often in his crib with a full diaper when I got home from school. My mother said he took an afternoon nap without fail, but I was apprehensive about how long he had been ignored by the time I got there. Curly, dark hair framed his dark brown eyes. He would be up on his hands and knees, oscillating back and forth because he was bored.

Sometimes he would have managed to move the crib across the wooden floor. He was always so happy to see me, holding up his pudgy little arms and wearing a wide smile on his face.

Changing a baby was hard work. There were two layers of thick cloth diapers to push the metal pins through. It was such an effort for my small hands that I couldn't control where the pin would emerge on the other side. I often stabbed myself, and one horrible afternoon, I pierced my baby brother's side. But if *I* didn't change him, he would have to lie in it until someone else did. He often had terrible diaper rash and periodically had to be taken to the doctor because of the open sores. A metal tube of thick, white paste that contained zinc oxide was prescribed. The ointment bonded with his skin and protected it, but we often ran out. When the pharmacy's delivery service rang the doorbell, the medicine wasn't ever for the baby, but for my mother.

Once the dirty diaper was off and his butt cleaned with toilet paper and a washcloth, I pinned the double layers of fresh diaper. Then he and I worked together to pull his plastic pants up and over his rear end. I did the best I could, but I couldn't get rid of the odor. Sometimes I would make him stand up in the bathtub while I washed him from the waist down. I couldn't do more because we kids were only allowed to take a bath twice a week.

Dealing with the soiled cloth diapers was an ordeal. I tried to dump the solid mess into the toilet and flush it. Then I would put the diaper into the fresher toilet water and swish it around, trying to get more off the white cloth, and flush again. The sopping wet cloth would then go into a bucket that a professional diaper service supplied. I held my breath and opened it with the foot pedal. A reek of ammonia wafted out as I threw the diaper in as quickly as I could. I would wash and wash my hands, although I never seemed to be able to get the smell off me.

This particular afternoon, I went to the baby and lifted him out of his crib and onto my hip. "Hey, Mackey, hey, little buddy, you want to come downstairs with us?" He curled around me like a koala bear. His thumb immediately went to his mouth in contentment. Belinda followed me as we started to walk downstairs.

"Pack?" we heard my mother croak through her closed bedroom door. Malachy lifted his head high because he thought she was talking to him, saying "Mackey," but our mother was calling *me*. Family legend had it that when I was learning to speak I couldn't say "Patty," so instead I called myself Packy. This became my mother's nickname for me.

"Packy!" we heard her call again, this time more insistently. I held on to the baby with one arm and used the other to open her door. Belinda stayed in the hallway, hidden from sight yet still close enough to hear.

I popped my head into the room. "Hi, Mom."

She was in her bed, under the covers, with a wet washcloth on her forehead. The drapes were drawn against the light. "I have a sick headache," she told me as if this day was different from any other. "Take this." She held out her arm toward me, and I could just make out that she had a ten-dollar bill in her hand. "Someone will be stopping by with pills for my head. Give them the money and then bring them up to me. And water, too. And watch the baby. Your brother and sister will be home from school any minute. What am I going to do about dinner?"

She looked panicked. Suddenly, she jumped out of bed and ran into her bathroom. I heard her gag and vomit. I slipped out of the room, almost forgetting that Belinda was there. Her already large light brown eyes expanded into a look of outright disgust.

When the doorbell rang, it was not the delivery service from the pharmacy, as I had expected. Instead, a woman I vaguely recognized handed me a lumpy envelope. I wasn't sure what to do. She rolled her eyes and held out her hand. I fished around in my front pocket for the money. I ran about halfway up the stairs with the envelope before I realized I had forgotten to pour a glass of water. Back to the kitchen I sprinted, then raced up the stairs to my mother.

Dinner was our usual fallback: frozen chicken potpies. I dug into to the refrigerator for something healthier to supplement them with and found ripe Jersey tomatoes, which I sliced thick. Our green salad was always iceberg lettuce; I tossed it and the tomatoes with bottled Italian dressing. I put a block of New York State cheddar cheese on a cutting board with a knife and plopped it right onto the table.

Belinda and I set five places for the kids' dinner. I moved a full load of wash from the washer into the dryer because I needed to take a clean gym uniform to school the next day. My two brothers and younger sister were in the family room watching television, and Belinda called them to the table. We poured a glass of milk for each of us and the two older children, and, as often happened, my brother spilled his. I cleaned it up and got him another.

While we were eating, we heard the front door open and my father call out. We all froze. You just never knew with him. When my mother addressed him in a cheerful tone, we relaxed a bit.

Mom swept into the kitchen carrying a large to-go bag from the steakhouse in town. Dad must have brought it home with him. The restaurant was directly across the square from where my father got off the train. The aroma of the steaks and onion rings made me a little delirious. I so much wanted to ask for just one bite, but I didn't have the courage.

Mom put the bag on the kitchen counter and got a tray of ice out of the freezer. I couldn't help but notice that she was transformed. She must have washed her hair, because it looked shiny and bouncy. She wore lipstick, earrings, and a brand-new outfit I had never seen before. She went back out to the living room with the ice cubes piled into an insulated silver container with a top that also served as a carrying handle. I could hear my father mixing a martini. He used a tall crystal pitcher and a long glass rod that made a clinking sound as he stirred.

Belinda and I cleaned up the kitchen. I asked the younger kids if they had any homework, and then I carefully timed my entrance into the living room. I appeared before my parents, although I did not speak until I was spoken to.

My mother, enjoying her cocktail hour with her husband, looked annoyed. "Be sure you sweep the kitchen floor when you're done."

The sneer she had cast in my direction brightened when she shifted her gaze flirtatiously toward my father. I screwed up my courage and *dared* to make an announcement: "We have to do homework."

My stomach leapt when my mother dismissed the idea. "The baby needs a bath. In fact, they all do." She turned her high-wattage smile on me. "Besides, our favorite shows are on tonight!"

Without warning, Belinda defiantly strode in from the kitchen. I felt dizzy. Her legs were stiff with her false confidence, but her voice was steady: "Mary Patricia, we have to get going."

I looked at my father and decided to brave it. "We have a test and a paper due tomorrow. We want to go to the library. We'll be sure to stick to the streetlights when we walk."

My father was a pushover with anything connected to schoolwork.

Resigned, my mother got in her last dig at me: "Sweep the floor first."

The Summer of Love–1968

By the summer after sixth grade, Belinda had grown six inches and was as tall as a Las Vegas showgirl. Her legs were very long, though a bit gangly. She was well on her way to being buxom, even though her waist was still tiny. Mrs. Barnes had no choice but to buy her daughter women's clothing.

Belinda had also taken to setting her long, honey-blond hair with curlers and then teasing it with a rat-tailed comb so it had more volume at the crown of her head. Even I questioned Mrs. Barnes's decision to allow her to wear eyeliner and mascara. The girl was a distracting presence, to say the least. Men gave her the once-over. Boys would outright stare in a way that was intense and almost hostile. Mrs. Barnes mother advised her daughter to enjoy her new figure now because she would never look this good again.

Belinda and I were still close, but the focus of our friendship had changed. She had emotionally shifted away from me and now directed her attention toward boys. She was boy *crazy*. All she wanted to talk about was whether this or that one liked her. "Liking her" meant ending each rendezvous with a kiss. What she actually said when she told stories of her conquests was "...and then he sealed it with a kiss."

Our alliance had once been a closed circle of trust. Now it was broken every time a boy beckoned and she went running off. Our bike rides out to the railroad trestle or to the swim club occurred only if they led to a kiss from a boy. My feelings were constantly hurt.

One summer day, we were at the town swim club, lying on towels trying to get a tan. While she talked to me, her eyes roamed. She glanced in one direction, then cut her eyes over to

24

another, all the while carefully composing her face into what she must have imagined was an attractive expression. To me, she appeared to be fake and haughty. She turned her body to the side to seem even thinner. She stuck her breasts way out with an exaggerated stretch, clearly enjoying this new superpower of hers. I fought the almost overwhelming desire to slap her.

My own figure was a few years away from developing. Even then, I would remain thin and small-breasted. I had the perfect ballet body, but I didn't know that sitting next to Belinda on our beach towels that humid summer day. I looked like a little girl with my pixie haircut beside a honey-blond bombshell.

An afternoon a few days later, while I was helping my mother make dinner, she ordered me to tell Belinda to stop hanging around with boys who had graduated from eighth grade. Our elementary school was composed of grades kindergarten through eight, which meant we had known the boys for years. I was puzzled.

"Those boys are headed to high school," my mother said. "Tell Belinda they don't care one whit about her."

That was my mother's way. She simply announced what she wanted, knowing that I would carry out her bidding. There were many times when I was tempted to ask her why she didn't do a particular thing herself; after all, she was the grown-up. However, on those rare occasions when I did question her, she would retrieve her yardstick from the broom closet and remind me with a whack who, in fact, was in charge. And so, the very next time I saw Belinda, I felt compelled to tell her what my mother had said.

"If she's talking about Gerry, you can tell your mother he's *in love* with me."

This was articulated in a melodramatic hushed voice. Then she sucked her cheeks into the haughty face she favored lately.

In love?

As young as I was, I knew intuitively that going around kissing an array of different boys was not love. It frightened me a bit. I wished so hard that we could go back to the time when I could tell her privately that what she was doing was not *normal*.

Some of the girls in our class had boyfriends, but only one at a time. The boys would walk them home from school and then go play with their friends. Earlier in the summer, a girl we knew had had a coed birthday party. Two of the invited girls had not been allowed to attend. I hadn't been asked because I wasn't going out with anyone, but my mother was still furious about the event. When it was rumored that the kids who had gone had played Spin the Bottle, she had phoned the mother who'd hosted the party.

"These children are too young for mixed parties!" she said. "They should be playing outside, not worrying about how to kiss. You should be ashamed of yourself! It's immoral. I want you to know that I intend to have a word with Father O'Leary. I'm sure the nuns will speak to the children about it at their next catechism class. May I remind you it is a *mortal* sin?"

A mortal sin would damn you for eternity. There were no exceptions: you committed one and you were doomed. The nuns taught us that we must avoid impure thoughts at all costs. Until that summer, their lectures had fallen on deaf ears—at least in my case—because try as I might, I could not understand what they were referring to. Then a boy began to pursue me, and I became anxious and confused. I had known him since I'd moved to Avalon Park, but he was suddenly everywhere I was. If I went down to the tennis courts, he arrived with an old racket and one tattered tennis ball. If I walked over to the town pool, he appeared with friends.

His name was Nathaniel Hayes, and he was going into the eighth grade. He was only one grade ahead of me in school, yet he seemed much older due to his extraordinary confidence. I would feel like someone was looking at me, turn into the direct line of his blue-green eyes, and flush red up into my hairline. Clearly, this was what he wanted, for he would give me a sweet smile and go back to whatever he was doing—that is, until he wanted to catch my eye again.

There were kids in his class who were much more talented athletes, better-looking, and certainly more popular. He was something of an outlier of the former seventh-grade clique because of his precocious maturity. He was more comfortable chatting with his teachers than with kids his own age. I began to notice that when his family arrived for the evening swim, he would hang out in a lounge chair with his big brother and his parents. Most of the kids I knew would be at the opposite end of the pool from their own family.

My friends started to whisper to me, "He likes you."

I was flattered that an older boy was paying attention to me, but I wasn't sure I wanted to be his girlfriend—or anyone else's, for that matter. At the same time, it was a new and exciting experience. The gaggle of girls from my class were preoccupied with his interest in me. It was something to speculate about as we hung around in the sunshine.

Adults gravitated to Nathaniel. Grown men teased him, knowing he would come right back at them with no fear of being scolded for disrespect. They found this very entertaining. Women reacted the same way I did, flushing at his direct gaze and relaxed conversational style.

He had a helmet of blond hair so curly that he kept it very short. He was tall, and his muscles were rock hard. The color of his eyes, a pale aqua, had a mystical cast to them that drew people in. I heard a much older waitress at the corner diner say to him, "If only I was ten years younger, Nathaniel."

Ten? I thought. *Try thirty!*

In contrast to Nathaniel, I was always doing my best to blend in socially. The photographs of me at this age show me staring down at the floor, hoping not to be noticed. This changed when I was onstage, where I could become someone else. In my mind, the stage acted as a prism that refracted the light from within me. Once I discovered the power of performing, I auditioned for everything. Rehearsal halls were also safe places to do homework. After I had practiced my dance or song, I could crawl into a dusty flat-black corner with my books. My parents approved, for they considered it character building to honor a commitment once a project was started. Apparently, having children with good character reflected well on them.

It was a busy summer. Donald Hampton, Keith Velez, Deb Guianti, and I started a theater group we named Bergen County Youth Theater North. There was another company called the BCYT South, but I had never attended any of their performances. We officially applied for the name, voting each other in as officers and signing the document with a solemnity we thought resembled our Founding Fathers when they put their names on the Declaration of Independence.

The Boy and Girl Scout troops in our small town organized a combined camping trip each year for junior high school–aged students. The kids I knew did not go away to summer camp, except for this one week, which was considered a rite of passage. As a new seventh grader, I was finally eligible to attend.

One of the camp counselors had approached Don and asked if we would consider performing some of the songs from the play we were working on, *Bye Bye Birdie*. They invited us to a planning meeting to discuss it. In addition to group songs, I would be performing my solo, "How Lovely to be a Woman." We were happy about it because it would help us promote the show we would put on later in the season.

It came as a terrible blow when Belinda told me she wouldn't be going with me to the camp because she had accepted an invitation to go to the Jersey Shore the same week. The older boy my mother had been concerned about Belinda seeing, Gerry, had asked her. I was uncertain how I would navigate the week without Belinda by my side.

My mother had collected equipment for my older sister the year before. Sis had been bored at camp and didn't want to go back. I surveyed the pile of stuff and compared it to the list the scout masters handed out.

"Mom, how do you wash a sleeping bag? Mom, where are the eating utensils for this mess kit? Mom! Jeez! This backpack has dog poo on it."

So it went until I was satisfied I was ready for the big sleep away.

I arrived at Camp Ramaquois along with 119 other children. We rode in a school bus with all the windows rolled completely down. My girlfriends and I sat toward the front, singing songs to pass the time. Nathaniel and his buddies were in the seats all the way in the back. When they entered, some of his friends had taunted us with a singsong: "Nathaniel and Patty sitting in a tree. K-I-S-S-I-N-G. First comes love, then comes marriage, then comes Patty with a baby carriage."

My girlfriends were disgusted. "They are *so* immature."

I noticed that Nathaniel was as embarrassed as I was. He sat a few seats ahead of the boys who were furiously waving to the cars driving behind us. They made goofy faces until they tired of it. The heat and the fumes from the engine made me feel a bit carsick.

As it was a Sunday, most of us had attended church before the departure, which meant we didn't pull into the campsite until late afternoon. The center of our outdoor camp was a large fire pit built for communal gatherings. Platforms were constructed in concentric circles moving outward from the pit. Each platform had a greenish canvas tent installed on it; inside the tents were six canvas sling cots. The weather during our week was filled with extremes. We would soon discover that our canvas tents and cloth sleeping bags provided little warmth when it was cool and damp. One long, shivering night, after finally dozing off, I awoke to find that my feet were tingling from the cold.

The next day was hazy, hot, and humid. The three H's of a typical Jersey July. Warm air became trapped inside the tents, which had been baking in the sun all day. Our tent now reeked of mildew. Trying to sleep in a thick flannel sleeping bag left me drenched in sweat, but what could I do? I refused to lie on top of the bag wearing my pajamas, exposed to the entire group! There were boys nearby and adults who were practically strangers. Anyone could look in and see me. I stayed tucked in and awoke with wet hair stuck to my pillow.

The counselors were strict about lights-out and curfew. No one was to leave their tent unless it was an emergency. One night,

I had lain awake for a long time panting from the oppressive heat and humidity. I kept sipping from my canteen of water, and suddenly I had to pee. Girls did *not* urinate outdoors, yet the dark hole in the latrine scared me even in daylight. It was deep enough that I was convinced something lived down there. A rat was what I most feared. The sight of a rodent would make me feel dizzy and nauseated, which remains true to this day.

I had no choice. I had to go. I tiptoed by an adult tent on the way to the outhouses. The sides were raised to let in the night air, and a lamp illuminated the interior. Fans swooshed back and forth in an arc. I heard the telltale clink of ice knocking against a cocktail glass. Peering in, I saw a group of coed counselors sitting on the edges of twin-size beds, laughing. A guy stood in the center, holding a tumbler of brown liquid. Although males and females slept in separate quarters, they obviously socialized together at night. I hurried past, careful not to draw attention to myself.

I felt my way along the path. In the pitch black, I opened the creaky wooden door to the outhouse. *Screeeeech* it announced when I opened it, and *screech-thunk* when it closed. The inside was an even deeper shade of darkness. I stumbled around and felt for the metal hook that locked the door. The only thing worse than having to sit over a rat hole was having someone come in on me by mistake and catch me in the process. I had put on shorts over my pajama bottoms. I carefully pulled the layers of clothes down to my ankles to avoid getting any pee on them. As I blindly worked myself onto the wooden toilet seat, one hand slipped and my arm was thrust down the hole. My shoulder caught me up hard on the seat so that even in total darkness, stars circled around my head, making me feel like a character in an old cartoon. The full length of my arm was extended down into the void. At least I wasn't touching anything. A buzzing noise had started inside my skull that I knew was due to panic. The side of my pajama shirt was damp. I was disgusted, but self-preservation took over. I scrambled up to a sitting position on the old wooden toilet seat and willed my muscles to relax. I had to go so badly that I counted myself lucky not to have urinated in my pants when I fell.

The seat was one of those one-size-fits-none affairs that petite women struggle with their entire lives. My butt kept collapsing into the hole, leaving the backs of my knees to hang on for dear life. I knew there was a shelf behind me about a foot up from the surface of the latrine. I reached back with both hands and balanced myself above the cavity. Eventually my bladder's recalcitrance gave way to a blessed release. I let out a relieved sigh.

Then, I heard it.

A rustle, the sound of movement through dried leaves, and — I was sure about this — a gnawing sound on the wood of the outhouse. The next thing I knew, I was standing at the halfway point on the dirt path between the outhouse and my tent. It was as if I had been beamed up to space and then back down to this exact spot. I could make out the outline of the adults' tents in the moonlight. I looked to see that I had released one ankle from the layers of clothing and pulled them up high at an angle to cover my private parts. It had been too late to stop the pee stream once I had begun, and so my shorts, pajama bottoms, and panties were saturated. As soon as I stopped running, I could smell the urine. The irony wasn't lost on me that I had been too modest to go in the woods, and now here I was, half-naked on a public path.

The only sound was the clamor of the cicadas. I wiped my legs off with the pieces of clothing that were still dry. The moon broke free from a cloud to light my way. A trash barrel was revealed along the path, and I dumped all of my clothing into it. I had a primal sense of color and form: the pale blue on my behind, and the shadowy navy in front, with an edging of soft white creating the demarcation. Feeling covered by the moon's body paint, I boldly stood tall and began to trek down the path as I imagined an Aborigine might do it.

A twig cracked, and I felt a strong sensation that someone was watching me. Instinctively, I placed one arm across my breasts and the other over my genitals and hunched over. No longer standing tall, I scurried along, finally diving through flaps of my tent, where I collapsed with relief.

The girls sleeping on their cots didn't stir. Deb was snoring in the bed next to mine. It is very possible I didn't sleep at all that night, waiting for morning. The second it was light out, I jumped into the lake to bathe myself before the other campers woke. The nuns had taught us that most lies were sins and they left a black mark on your soul. It you had enough black marks, you would go to purgatory, maybe even hell. I agonized over what I would say to my tent mates. "I just felt like a morning swim," I told them as I changed for breakfast. It sounded forced, everyone knew that I was never confident in the water, but no one questioned me. The fear that God would strike me dead for telling the lie passed quickly.

I felt sluggish by afternoon when a group of us were walking back from a hike to the river. Now that the weather was extremely hot, the best thing about Camp Ramaquois was how many swimming holes it had. The trail we were on meandered and then became so narrow that everyone started walking in single file. All but Nathaniel Hayes, who squeezed in next to me.

His shoulders were high and broad enough that I fit like a puzzle piece along his side. We walked in silence until we realized that the other kids had run ahead or fallen behind. The privacy gave him courage, and he blurted out, "I liked the story you wrote."

I blushed. "Mr. McGill made me read it at the assembly. I was worried the other kids would think I was showing off."

He shrugged. "Who cares what they think? You're good at a lot of things, and you're pretty, too. There will always be people who'll be jealous of you."

Jealous of me?

Now, this was a revelation.

And *pretty?* My parents' sole goal for me was to make sure I didn't wind up conceited. I couldn't remember a single time when either of them had given me a sincere compliment. I had once overheard my father bragging to a neighbor because I got all A's in school without even trying. However, this wasn't even true, because I got mostly A's by working very hard.

I was just warming to Nathaniel's offhanded compliments when he pointed his hand across the path and to our left. The late-afternoon sun lit up a cluster of ferns from behind. "I like how the sun shining on the leaves makes the plants seem transparent."

I described to him how he could paint the ferns if he wanted to. "Oil paint gets its colors from natural pigments, and they only have about twenty-five different tubes at the art store," I explained. "For instance, ochre is a yellow, but it's on the brownish side. What's cool is you can mix the paints together to make other colors. For the ferns you pointed out, we could use terre verte with lemon yellow in it. If you took about two-thirds of green and added a dollop of yellow on your palette, the color would match the center of the ferns in the bunch. As they fan out, the hue gets lighter in color and a bit more yellow because the fronds get thinner and the sun shines through them more. If I painted it, I would add a little white and yellow, then even more as I moved toward the outside. By the time I did the edges, it would be almost all white."

A little embarrassed by how animated I had become I peered over at Nathaniel, but he seemed interested in what I had to say.

"See?" he said casually, as if proving a point, "Good at so many things." Then he stopped and, studying my face, said, "You have dirt on the end of your nose."

A pattern was established that summer week in July 1968. Nathaniel would say something complimentary, and then grow serious as he pointed out a flaw of mine. Though it was a form of teasing, some of the comments came dangerously close to insults.

Nathaniel took my arm and gestured toward a steep deer run below the path we were on. We scrambled down, and it opened up to a moss-covered bank next to a rocky stream. We lay back on our elbows, enjoying the coolness emitted by the babbling water and the springy softness of the moss. I told him about my venture to the outhouse the night before because I had broken a rule and I was concerned about possible consequences. I left out the part about winding up naked in the cool night air.

"Please don't tell anyone," I said.

I was presenting him with a challenge. A loyalty test. His ability to keep my secrets would determine the course of our friendship. He pushed me to elaborate further. I told him about passing the adults' tent.

"How do you know the grown-ups were drinking?" he asked.

"One of the guys had a rocks glass—you know, a short little one with just an inch of brown liquid in it and a couple of ice cubes."

"He could have been drinking a soda."

"When it moved and splashed up on the glass, it kind of stuck for a second. It was definitely whiskey."

Nathaniel confided to me that he thought two of the counselors were fooling around. He asked if they were sitting together when I passed and wanted to know if they'd been touching.

Somehow, we ended up by the outhouses, and he inspected the exterior of the one I had used the night before. He turned to me and encircled my waist with his arm. Although I realized he was being protective, I could barely breathe. My body felt wooden with uncertainty. He took my hand and carefully walked all the way around the small building, paying special attention to the base.

"I don't see any animal burrows, but that doesn't really mean anything. These old wooden structures sit abandoned all winter. It could easily have been squirrels or mice nesting in the walls."

The dinner bell sounded, so we walked over to the pavilion together. Once we had passed through the food line with our trays, he went to join the boys, and I sat with my girlfriends at a picnic table.

Evening ended, as usual, when the communal campfire had died back to coals and we watched the sun set. Our Girl Scout master called upon me to sing "Taps" to close out the evening. This was supposed to be a sing-along, but the weight of the final moments of the day fell on my thin shoulders. I was as tired as everyone else, yet a charge of adrenaline gave me a second wind. I stood, slowly inhaled, and began to sing:

"Day is done, gone the sun.
From the lake, from the hills, from the sky;
All is well, safely rest,
God is nigh."

There were five verses to the song. At no point did I believe I was the best singer out of this large group of junior high school students. I speculated that I'd been singled out to sing every night because I could be counted on to pull it off. I could sell a song.

Don, Keith, Deb, and I had sung in a variety of choruses and played music together. The boys were able to join me once I began by creating a passable baritone harmony. Deb added an alto part that changed from one night to the next. The notes they layered on to my melody produced pleasing, if tentative, major chords. Every time we did it, we felt close to each other.

Nathaniel sat with his friends across the fire from me. From time to time, I glanced at him when I sang, and I liked that he glowed with pride. His eyes sent back to me a warmth I had never known before. He made a point of saying good night before he headed to his own tent at lights-out.

I listened to him trade banter with the older male counselors in his laughing, easy way. The adult women actually tried to flirt with him.

"What's shaking?" they'd ask.

"Nothing here."

"If you're lonely, I can come by later for a visit."

"I'm never lonely, but thanks for asking."

He let their pointed double entendres bounce off him. I once saw him, shirtless, reach his long arms up to a tree branch and stretch his body while an adult scout master, a middle-aged woman, watched. Her face became wistful, her eyes somewhat unfocused and dreamy.

When the morning came to pack up and head back home, I heard a knock on the tent frame. Deb lifted up the flap and called, "Patty, Nathaniel wants to see you."

I joined her, peering out to the bright sunshine, where Nathaniel's outline almost filled the triangle formed by the slanting canvas roof.

"Can you step outside for a minute, Mary Patricia?" he asked me. I did, and he grabbed my arm and led me off the platform. When he was sure we wouldn't be overheard, he handed me a large paper bag. I opened it and took in the crisp smell of an industrial dryer. Inside the bag were the clothes I had thrown in the trash can on the night of the outhouse fiasco. They'd been washed and folded.

He held one hand up before I could say a thing. "Don't even ask," he said as he turned on his heel and walked away.

The October of Change–1968

Adults occupied the three public tennis courts in our town. I assumed they were all friends because they volleyed compliments and insults from one court to another. Both men and women were competing against each other. Nathaniel and I held our battered rackets across our laps and commented about the twelve of them as they played doubles.

"Wow! They bicker," I said to Nathaniel, "Her partner must be her husband."

We sat on the littered grass listening to their teasing and trying to decide what to do next. We were down to one tennis ball between us. Even this had been hard to find because my brother had taken it from my room to throw against the back wall of our garage. After a long search around my house, we found it inside an empty box. I asked Nathaniel to carry it because it smelled like gasoline. It was already late afternoon when the adults rotated courts and partners. By the time they were done playing their sets, we would be expected home for dinner.

Reluctantly we stood up and brushed the leaves and dirty bits of paper from our pants. Feeling cheated out of our game, we began to amble in a diagonal line from the tennis courts across the football field toward the elementary school. Football practice had broken up about fifteen minutes before. We had heard the sound of cars pulling up to the curb, horns tooting, and doors opening and then slamming shut.

It was a warm Indian summer day in the Garden State, the late sun slanted at a steep angle toward us through tall trees that bordered the school grounds. The field was empty, but for a pair of shoes and someone's abandoned blue shirt. The trash barrel was

37

swollen and overflowed; a ring of debris had formed around its base. A few papers blew this way and that in the wind.

Avalon Park School sat on a hill above the field. We heard a cheer go up outside the gym, and were curious. Even at a distance, we knew the group gathered there included some of the football players. All the boys, mostly eighth grade students, faced the wall of the gym's back entrance. We continued to move forward. As we drew closer, we saw the double door leading into the gym was shut. Where the structure of the gymnasium's all-purpose room tied into the school's main building a jog formed in the brick creating an alcove. It was not very deep, just enough to break the wind, as I had discovered during the years when Belinda and I would read there.

As Nathaniel and I approached, I realized the cheering boys were watching something going on in the alcove. The corner was in shadow. When we arrived, we found ourselves standing behind a semi-circle of boys three deep. When we saw what was happening, we both made a gut wrenching noise.

Belinda was almost naked from the waist up; although her bra was still fastened at the back, the straps had been pulled down to expose her breasts. The quarterback of the team had her arms pinned down to her sides. I noticed his girlfriend was nowhere in sight, although they were usually inseparable. The boys who stood in front of me were much taller than I was and it was hard for me to see through the crooks of their elbows and armpits. I reached out and tugged one of the kids who lived across the street from me to step aside so I could see. Immediately, I regretted it.

Belinda was crying and repeatedly trying to raise her arms to cover herself. Her body lurched with sobs. Nathaniel and I abruptly knew what we thought were cheers had actually been jeers; sounds that only come from some young men.

In one motion, a member of the semi-circle reached out and tore Belinda from the quarterback's reach. He pinned her arms behind her so she was helpless and her naked breasts stuck out in front of her. He swayed her back and forth, laughing. Her face was anguished.

Another huge jeer went up from the small crowd. My neighbor turned around, jerked his thumb in my direction, and yelled to Nathaniel, "You better get her out of here."

Nathaniel's conflict was palpable. I could tell he would gladly have jumped in and pulled the boy off Belinda, but he would not leave me alone in the crowd for even one second. He made his choice. He wrapped both his arms under my armpits and carried me into the crowd toward Belinda. Then, he held onto me with one powerful arm, and with his other, he grabbed the boy holding Belinda hostage by the scruff of his shirt. The boy started making desperate choking sounds. I struggled free and then hugged Belinda so her nakedness was covered and she had a moment to calm down. She quickly slipped the straps of her bra back up over her shoulders. I had a sweater tied around my waist that I handed to her. In a flash, she slipped it over her head.

Nathaniel must have summoned the strength of Samson because he suddenly tucked each of us under an arm and began to run away. My heart was in my throat, and I knew Belinda's was, too. I was certain the lust-crazed boys would chase us. Just then, perhaps a heartbeat behind, the double back doors of the gym exploded open.

A man, who looked very much like our gym teacher, red-faced with rage, stood gesturing wildly. "What are you DOOOOOING? What are you guys DOOOOOING out here?" he screamed over and over again until his face turned purple.

I assumed he must have caught sight of what was happening from a window. The *doooooooing* part of the question rang in the air as Nathaniel continued toting us across the field with surprising speed. Belinda sat astride his left hip, her arms around his neck. I was smaller and so he carried me like a bag of potatoes under his right arm. Once it became clear the boys weren't following us, I began to wriggle and begged to be put down, because every time Nathaniel's foot hit the ground my head lurched downward, thrashing my neck.

When we reached the picnic tables at the far end of the field, he dropped us on top of one. Feeling numb, I watched with

39

fascination as he leaned over, holding his sides and gasping for air. Dust blew all around us and muddy tears streaked down his face.

In unfeigned innocence, I asked him, "What were they doing to her?"

He buried his head in his arms that were on the table beside me. Now, he really was crying.

"What?" I kept asking him. "What were they doing?"

He regained control and wiped his tears away. It was hard for him to speak. "It's good that Mr. Binagui came out when he did." The statement seemed to exhaust him and he put his head back on his arms.

"I don't understand."

He peered over at me and then away. He was clearly embarrassed. "Don't you know about men and women? What they do together?"

I was exasperated by the question. "If that's how babies are made, I'm never going to have any!"

His face was still covered by his arms as he started to laugh.

Up until this moment Belinda, deathly quiet, appeared as though she were in a state of shock. Now a shriek of laughter erupted from her. It was ripe with relief. "Neither am I!"

Nathaniel doubled over, became helpless with laugher, unable to straighten up, and, perhaps, was a little hysterical. He couldn't talk. By that point I was laughing, too. The intense strain we had been under was broken. We all lay across the top of the picnic table, roaring and holding our stomachs. I rolled from one side to another, hooting until my face actually hurt.

When we saw Mr. Binagui walking toward us, we grew still.

Nathaniel spoke. "Belinda. Patty. What happened back there... it's not supposed to be like that. That's what's so wrong. Boys aren't supposed to make girls do anything they don't want to do."

When Mr. Binagui reached us, he asked Belinda to come with him. It was hard to listen to her beg him not to tell her parents. He said nothing that happened was her fault. He told her he would take her straight home and stay with her as long as she wanted.

"Are the boys in trouble?" she asked.

"Of course they are in trouble. You can't do something like that and expect to get away with it. I called the police. They are inside questioning them."

Belinda bent over at the waist and threw up repeatedly. Mr. Binagui ordered Nathaniel to take me home. We had been raised to obey adults, so we immediately started to walk in the direction of my house and away from the school.

"Do you think your dad will be home from work yet?" Nathaniel asked.

"Sure. Why?"

"I want to talk to him and tell him what happened. I want him to know we didn't do anything wrong that you are... ummm... well... okay."

My mouth went dry and my hands started to shake. Cocktail hour would be over, which meant, my father would be volatile. Feeling how hesitant I was, Nathaniel took my hand. As I stared into his tear-stained blue-green eyes, I heard a roaring sound in my ears, and started to get queasy.

"Let me do this, Patty. It will be better coming from me."

I was nervous the whole way back to my house. My family was seated at the big kitchen trestle table when we walked in the back door. Nathaniel, in the mode of relating to adults as though he were one on them, said to my father, "Sir, I need to talk to you alone."

Daddy led him to the basement door, and they disappeared down the stairs. The rest of the family continued eating as if this sort of thing happened every day.

No one spoke until my father and Nathaniel returned. We all watched Dad escort him to the back door and shake his hand.

"Thank you, son."

Nathaniel shot me a look of concern over his shoulder just before he was ushered out.

My father came back to the table and began to eat, stopping intermittently to sigh and stare off into space. He never spoke to me. In fact, he didn't even *look* in my direction. The family dispersed and I was left to clean up the kitchen as I did every night. Anxiety went through me in waves like rounds of fireworks. I still had a lot of homework and now I was obsessed with the question, "What was my father *thinking*?"

The very next night, my dad surprised us all at the dinner table. "That Nathaniel has to be the bravest, most decent boy I have ever met."

I was not sure how my brothers felt as they sat there absorbing my father's assessment. What I did know was the rules changed overnight. I had never been allowed to have a boy in my house unless my parents were home. Nathaniel now had access at any time. In fact, my parents felt I was safer when he was around.

This was how Nathaniel replaced Belinda, for a while anyway, as my best friend. We were inseparable during my seventh grade and his eighth. It got to be a little challenging the following year while I was still in elementary school and he was a freshman, but after I graduated to high school, we roamed the same hallways. He would be leaning against the doorjamb waiting for me when my class ended. We would walk together to the next one, and he would say, "See you after," as he went off to his own.

Nathaniel worked hard at breaking down the physical barriers that existed between us. One day, I reached up into the top compartment of my locker while he stood behind me watching. I jumped when he put his hand on my arm. We both stood awkwardly together for a few seconds, and I didn't know what he expected me to do next. He dropped his hand and we went on with our day.

After that, he started occasionally bumping the back of his hand against mine, but he acted like it was an accident when I looked down at our dangling arms. Then, one day on the way outside to watch the boys' football practice, he took my hand in his. I could barely take a breath as we went over to say "hello" to our friends holding hands.

At the first dance of the year, he casually kissed me on the lips. It became known that we were "going out" and my parents were obviously pleased. By the time I was a sophomore, we were finding dark corners to make out in. Eventually, I began to feel a fullness and heat down below when we kissed for a long time. It never crossed my mind we would take our lovemaking any further.

The transition from friendship to girlfriend-boyfriend was made easier for me because Nathaniel understood me. And, he got a kick out of me. He wanted others to see me the way he did, and so he helped me to shine among our friends.

"Patty," he would say. "Tell the story of the crazy lady we saw when we went to the Central Park Zoo."

I planted my feet and inhaled and exhaled deeply to prepare.

"There she was sitting on a park bench under a beautiful shade tree. She wore a long brown coat that hung to her ankles. A shapeless black-rimmed hat covered most of her head. What hair we could see was greasy and shot through with wiry gray. All around her were piles of bags. She seemed like a big, fat hen sitting on a nest. Nathaniel and I were oblivious to anyone else. It was a summer day and we were strolling by *arm in arm*."

Our friends groaned as I had expected them to.

"Well it *was* romantic! New York City in June. We were basking in the sun. And in our *looove* for each other."

Again, the crowd moaned. I laughed, and so did everyone else. The line always landed well.

"We were in such a dream state that we broke the unwritten city code never to make eye contact with strangers. We both nodded to the old woman by way of a hello as we shot right past her direct line of sight. It was to our backs that she directed a scream."

I had used my hands to sign a gesture for the *direct line of sight* and then *our backs*. Nathaniel assured me one of the things that made me such a good storyteller were the motions I used for emphasis.

Continuing, I said, "We both froze when we felt her suddenly come up behind us. The bag lady was practically breathing down our necks. We whirled around and she grabbed our outside arms tightly. She gazed deeply and meaningfully into our eyes and spoke with great power and confidence. 'I'll get you! I'll get you.

I'll get *both* of you.'" I impersonated the bag lady as the Wicked Witch of the West from the Wizard of Oz. The imitation was complete with my shirt collar standing in for her cape and spot-on body swaying. "The hair on the back of our necks stood on end. We just froze; Nathaniel with his hands shoved deep into his pockets. The old woman's voice raised a register at the same time her eyes suddenly transformed into glittering insanity. When Nathaniel raised his hands mid-air, he didn't realize he clutched the money that was to be our bus fare. Some of it stuck out from between his index and middle fingers."

I held my hand out to the group to show how the money had bulged.

"Her arm lashed out like a whip. She grabbed the dollars and ran. We were left in a dazed silence. We were also left short of the cash we needed to take the bus from the Port Authority back to Avalon Park."

A pause was required to attain the full effect. I looked from one person to another to buy time. "And Nathaniel's knee jerk response? He wanted to reduce our station in life to that of *beggars in the street.*"

I fell against him laughing, knowing he would take over the storytelling for the next few minutes.

He said, "I simply and reasonably told Patty we should stop a well-dressed man about our fathers' age and tell him what happened."

"And ask him for money," I chimed in.

"And ask him for a few bucks. But, Mary Patricia wouldn't allow it."

"No I would not. I still had my *pride.*" I said this with self-effacing sarcasm. "So, I decided we could walk all the way back to West 178th Street and across the bridge. I figured the bus fare would be cheaper on the other side because it would be closer to home." By the bridge, I meant the George Washington Bridge.

Nathaniel continued his role in our little performance. "I calmly pointed out to her it must be a ten-mile walk," he said. "Even when we reached the other side, I didn't know where to

Fading Past

pick up the bus. But, she had her mind made up that it was the right thing to do. You all know you can't get between Mary Patricia and the right thing."

Intuitively, I understood it was my turn to run the narrative.

"Six hours later, we limped through the front door of my house. My parents were in the living room having an *after*-dinner drink."

My mother and father's reputation being what it was, I knew our group would understand my meaning. I waved my hands open and back again like the conductor of an orchestra. They nearly sang their response. "Uhhhhhhhhhh ohhhhhhhhhhh."

"I announced to them...."

However, I couldn't continue. I collapsed with laughter and buried my head in Nathaniel's chest. Each of my hands was clasped onto a part of his T-shirt. He put his arms around me and hunched over laughing, too. The fingers on his right hand encircled the wrist of my left trying to get me to loosen my grip a bit as I convulsed.

In stereo, we gasped out a squeal not unlike hyenas. "Hey, hey, heeeeyyy, heeeyyyyyyyyy."

Neither of us could draw a full breath in as we struggled to regain some restraint. We incited the little crowd watching us. They also became hysterical. For them, it was the contagion of humor and intense anticipation. Deb wiped tears from her eyes. Keith was holding onto the back of a chair for support. Don had his face in his hands and his shoulders shook uncontrollably. Finally, I pulled away from Nathaniel knowing my audience was waiting. He continued to encircle my waist from behind.

I said, "I was so anxious that I mutinied on Nathaniel. I *announced* I had to go upstairs and lay down. And I did. Leaving Nathaniel to face my father *alone*."

Our friends were now a Greek chorus. "Oooooooooooooooo."

"Apparently, he told my dad the whole story and my father asked him a single question," I said, holding up my index finger and making everyone wait while another wave of laughter washed over me. "Why didn't you call, son?"

Nathaniel had answered him man-to-man, "Calling from a pay phone would have used up more of the only money we had."

I mimicked my father's most serious face and the voice he used when he thought someone had uttered something profound. "That's very, very good thinking, son. I am proud of you."

I pointed at Nathaniel. "So. This one here was proclaimed a genius and I was grounded for a week."

The Year of the Tomato–1972

The year he turned sixteen, when he was in his junior year of high school, Nathaniel's parents gave him a brand new convertible Volkswagen Beetle. We nicknamed it the Tomato because of its vivid red color, and he and I drove out often to the reservoir to meet up with our friends. A wide bank of sand surrounded the water that was solid enough for the drivers to park their cars in a circle and shine their headlights on those of us who were dancing. Full-length albums playing on eight-track tapes would be blasting as we approached. In retrospect, it strikes me as primitive that the boys would stand back near their cars and watch the girls dance. Not unlike a fertility ritual.

An album then consisted of music with mixed tempos; not every song was danceable. Yet, the fashion of the day was to allow the entire piece to play through. So, the girls would converge onto the sand-bottomed dance floor when a fast song played and retreat when the music slowed to a ballad. We would then join our boyfriends for a pull on a beer or a drag from a cigarette. The boys carefully spread blankets across the hoods of their cars so we could use the windshields as reclining love seats. When the tempo speeded up, the girls would be gone like a shot. The dance floor was where I reigned supreme. I am, if nothing else, a great dancer.

The drinking age at the time was eighteen. It was easy to get beer, though I preferred wine, and not the sweet strawberry Boone's Farm teens gravitated to. I loved the chianti the Italian delicatessen kept in stock. Like many of my generation, Nathaniel enjoyed smoking pot, but I quickly learned it was too much for me. My head fell forward after a few hits and I felt like I was losing control of my neck muscles. More importantly, my parents equated it to shooting up heroin. My father had been a jazz fan in the heyday of bebop and knew the unique odor of marijuana. If I had come home smelling of it, he would have beaten me to a bloody pulp.

No one gave a thought to drinking and driving, and teenage parties were considered a part of growing up. One night, the town fire truck was parked on the side of the road. The boy who was my across-the-street neighbor rammed into it head-on with his car. The volunteers in the department said he was lucky he hadn't made a bigger dent and sent him on his way. They knew he was drunk, but shrugged it off. No one even bothered to tell his parents.

Whenever we pulled Nathaniel's Tomato in through the open chain link gates of the reservoir property, Belinda was already there. She had not returned to Avalon Park Graded School after the attack by the football players. It had caused a scandal, and after a week at home recovering from her humiliation, her parents registered her at Saint Teresa's, an all-girl Catholic School in Englewood. Her commute on the bus was over an hour each way.

The mothers in town blamed Belinda for the assault. "Look at the way she runs around," they'd said.

The fathers were more forgiving, "With a dad like hers, what do you expect?"

All of the adults were relieved when her parents put distance between her and the rest of us. My mother forbade me to be friends with Belinda. I was coached to be cordial if I saw her on the street, but then I was told to turn and walk away.

This "shunning" lasted through seventh grade. The following year, though she still went to the Catholic school, we would run into each other around town. Nathaniel was busy until dinnertime at the high school. When I had time to go out and play, which was not often, I longed for the company of my old friend, Belinda. My parents' censure began to ease. Belinda and I qualified for the same ballet class, so it made sense we would walk home together. Then, my mother gave her permission for us to play a game of tennis. Eventually, I was allowed to socialize with Belinda in groups of friends. Over time, the barriers disappeared.

When we graduated up to high school, she joined us because it only made sense for her to come back to public school. She wasn't a *Catholic* and didn't belong at St. Teresa's. However, her sullied reputation remained intact, as did her behavior that continued to justify it.

When I started my freshman year, Nathaniel and I spent much of our time together. We were both honor students and had a lot of homework we did together in study halls and in the evenings at the town library. We were both in band with him on the bassoon and me on the clarinet. While he was a baritone in the chorus, I stood below him on the risers as a soprano. I was in all the plays and he was on the wrestling team. We had French club together and I had an after-school job five days a week.

The great disparity between us, and it was a very sharp divide, was he was the adored youngest child from a wealthy family. I had many more responsibilities as a caretaker for my siblings. I bought all my own clothes and earned any spending money I needed. Once I was employed, my father stopped giving me a lunch allowance. There were many days I skipped the meal because it was coming out of my paltry earnings.

No matter when I arrived home, day or night, I would usually find my mother in bed. She would call down orders to me. "Patty, change the baby! Dinner is started. Get it finished and feed the kids! Oh, and they need a bath tonight!"

Our family dinners around the table occurred less frequently. Mom would still rally to come downstairs to have cocktails when my father came home from work. He made a gin martini with an olive for himself and mixed a Manhattan with sweet Vermouth and a Bing cherry for my mother.

Despite my obligations, at least one night a week, Nathaniel and I went out to the reservoir. Sometimes I would already have gone to bed when he would throw a pebble at my bedroom window to wake me up. The first time it happened, I pretended to be asleep, horrified to think what my parents' reaction might be. But, to my absolute shock, my mother came to my bedroom door and told me to get dressed.

"Nathaniel *wants* you!" she stressed in an annoyed voice.

Stunned, I almost forgot to take my retainer out and wash the Clearasil off my face. A party was in full swing when we got to the reservoir. Deb and Keith were dancing together to Lou Reed's, *Walk on the Wild Side*. Deb had been with the same boyfriend since fifth grade, but he would only dance to the slow songs. Keith had known Deb since kindergarten; as he wasn't dating anyone, he served as her up-tempo dance partner. Don stood on the dance floor rooted in one spot. Nathaniel stayed back by his car and lit up a joint. I said hello to my friends and then went off to find Belinda.

I sniffed out a haze of pot smoke coming from a dark and isolated corner. I didn't consider Belinda a drug dealer, for she didn't make much money from her enterprises, but she was widely known as the girl who brought the "party favors." Procuring drugs in New York City and then distributing them to her friends and acquaintances made her the center of attention. She could always be found with a circle of people around her and passing a joint or a pipe stuffed with hashish. She often told wild stories about her forays into Manhattan seeking out the products.

I could hear her telling about another adventure. "So, he asked me what I wanted. I said, '*Whatever you got, honey.*'"

Sometimes she scored a drug more dangerous and illegal than cannabis, but she wouldn't dare bring it out to the reservoir. On those nights, Belinda hosted a smaller gathering. To this event, she would invite other adventurous drug seekers. She asked me only once to come over and drop acid, but I declined. She took my response as a rejection, and never invited me again.

I was standing outside her circle of pot clients as they passed a joint around. I knew she could hear me when I called to her. "Belinda! Let's dance!"

She took a last hit and stubbed out the embers against the sole of her sandal. Many of the other kids saw me lead her in and they gathered around to watch our dance routines. I took her by the hand to the very middle of our makeshift dance floor. Keith colluded in our unspoken plan by playing *Brown Sugar* by the

Rolling Stones. Once we got going, the others whooped. My bare feet stomping in the dampened sand to the simple bass line of Rock 'n Roll gave me the feeling of pure joy. The music slowed down and Nathaniel brought me some wine in a paper cup. Belinda returned to her circle and finished her joint. When Stevie Wonder's *Superstition* came on, she and I reunited and danced with total abandon. It was all about the hips back then - the hips and letting them go.

The harsh realities of my life were far away. I could smell the river water and feel the balmy breeze rush across my skin. Golden beacons from the headlights illuminated us, displaying a constant flutter of tiny wings that lifted my heart. Nathaniel came to get me when *Maggie Mae* was over. He picked me up in his arms and kissed me passionately. Then, we went to rest awhile on the hood of his car.

As a musician, Keith was enthralled with new and classic recordings. He kept his car, with all the doors wide open, pulled the closest to the sand dance floor acting as the disc jockey. He was constantly changing out his stereo system and buying the latest records. He had only one brother. One of the few students in our school of Puerto Rican descent, he told me following Fidel Castro's revolution in Cuba; his parents immigrated to New York City. Unlike most people I knew, both his parents worked and I assumed they had good jobs as his mother wore a business suit to her job.

It surprised me when Don started venturing out to the reservoir. He considered himself hopelessly un-cool and was almost proud of it. He didn't drink and had no interest in pot. Like me, he was involved in any theater production that would have him, which was how we became close friends.

I had been fortunate enough to have leads from the start and eventually earned the position of student assistant director. Don was on technical crew and in the singing and dancing choruses. He threw himself into the parts and this led to larger roles. He was cast as my boyfriend in the comedy *Arsenic and Old Lace*. When I suggested we practice our kissing scene, I thought he might pass out. He still tells the story of how out-of-his league he thought I was, at gatherings of our friends. I found him to be intelligent without acting superior. He chatted with everyone at the reservoir and enjoyed himself, but I never saw him shaking it. Instead of dancing, he "bopped." He would stand in the one place and react to the music with his head, arms, and upper body. Sometimes he would even raise his arms above his head or throw a punch high into the air.

As it grew late on those summers nights, Belinda's dance style would begin to change. Whichever boy arrived with her, she rarely felt beholden to him. Instead, she adopted a sort of soul music stance and would shimmy, shimmy, shimmy up to the boys who circled around us. Many of the girls would grow defensive and tell her to back off. One shoved her with both hands and shouted, "Find your own boyfriend!"

When she approached my Nathaniel in her seductive manner, he held up both his hands and said the same thing every time, "Okay, that's it!"

And that *was* it. The party broke up and we went home. Often, her date of the evening drove her back to her parents' house, but sometimes we were forced to jam her into the storage space behind our seats. Nathaniel would caution her repeatedly to "watch the rag top and don't bend the frame" the whole way.

The "swinging sixties" had peaked and passed. Hugh Hefner had convinced America pornography was part of being an intellectual. Drugs, sex, and Rock 'n Roll gave way to deaths by overdose and wasted lives. Still, it was many years before I realized Belinda was both promiscuous and an addict. Nathaniel and I simply thought she was taking the new freedoms of our generation too far. We were still hopeful she would learn to reign herself in.

Summer was exceptionally long and sultry that year, finally fading to an extended Indian summer. Then, in rapid succession came the tailgate parties, Christmas, and the New Year. Out of the slumber of winter burst the startling glory of a New Jersey spring.

Mom and Dad continued to let me go out as long as I was with Nathaniel. When we were parked and kissing, he began to caress my body and I trembled in a new way. Whenever I saw him, my heart leapt and I enjoyed an almost perpetual sense of well-being. Unlike what the nuns had told me, it didn't seem like what was happening was wrong; in fact, it felt very right to me. My brothers and sisters teased me about being in such a good mood all the time. In quiet moments, I replayed the best parts of our lovemaking over and over again in my mind because the memories inflamed all my senses. I secretly believed that no one in the world had ever felt the same kind of love.

And so it was, a year after Nathaniel was given his Volkswagen we became something more. Again.

The Sky is Falling—1972

My Nathaniel left for college in Maine on August 25th. It felt like an emotional slash-and-burn. Not having him as part of my daily life, I actually feared for my sanity. I hadn't even begun to figure out how life would be without him when my parents announced we were moving to Wisconsin.

Wisconsin? Eight-hundred and ninety-one miles from home.

My father had taken a position as Director of Operations for the Schlitz Brewing Company. A *beer* company.

Dad had lost his most recent job in Manhattan. There had been obvious signs of financial struggle at home. Mom didn't make the standing rib roast every Sunday anymore. And, it had been unsettling to see Dad out scraping one side of the house himself to prepare it for painting. In the end, he hired one of my school friends to finish it, but the fact was he had started the project out in the blazing New Jersey sun. My mother was not shopping as much as usual. Twice my father asked her if an outfit she was wearing was new. She lied to him and told him no, but I could tell she felt guilty about the purchases.

My father had been fired before, but we lived in the Tri-state area of Manhattan. He commuted to New York City every day where millions of people worked. The employment possibilities in the City seemed infinite. Why couldn't he find a job in New Jersey? Philadelphia was within driving distance. He could even get to Connecticut by train every day if worse came to worst. My anxiety was unstoppable. This was my senior year of high school. I would miss everything: the senior play, the spring musical, yearbook, senior prom, and graduation. I would not walk with my class or receive the honors for which I had worked so hard.

My father was not an easy man. All five of his children lived in fear of his brutality. I watched the way he bullied the man at the hardware store and the teenager at the supermarket. Since moving to Avalon Park when I was ten, he had had five different jobs in New York. He was a bright man with a good resume and he interviewed well, but he could *not* work well with others. As improbable as it seemed, he had apparently burned every bridge in the New York Metropolitan Area.

I was furious when, despite my objections, my parents quickly put our house on the market. For the first time in my life, I talked back to them. How was I going to see Nathaniel? Where would I go to school? My parents were embarrassed to witness how upset I was. I thought if I could just make them understand how deeply I felt about this, they would surely change their minds. Instead, they built a defense.

The case they made was against my *generation*. My father admonished, "All these hippies and yippies preaching love. What they really are doing is smoking pot. Everything is drugs, sex, and rock and roll! Well, we are going to move to the Midwest where people have wholesome values."

He further argued that he hadn't enlisted at seventeen to fight in the Pacific Theater and then come home and have America's founding principles eroded by a bunch of drug addicts. Next came the rant about the Communists and their conspiracy to destroy the United States. At some point, usually after my mom had imbibed a couple of Manhattans, she would start chiming in about virginity. I supposed this was in response to the sexual revolution unfolding across the country.

She declared dramatically, "The greatest gift you can give your husband is to be a virgin when you get married."

My mother had been engaged to be married three times before she met my father, which had made me wonder more than once about her sexual activity when she was young. I never understood her insistence that I accompany Nathaniel on our midnight jaunts down to the reservoir. Nothing wholesome happens after midnight, surely she knew this when she called to me the first night Nathaniel was waiting. I was utterly confused by her.

Once when she had just started with the virginity speech, I forced myself to look at my father. He was clearly embarrassed. He wouldn't meet my eyes and somehow I knew he disagreed with my mother on this very important *Catholic* issue. Perhaps virginity, I thought, was not the greatest gift she ever gave to *him.*

In the end, we moved to Milwaukee in the middle of the first semester of my senior year where I entered a high school that might as well have been on Mars. When my mother took me to the school to register, a teacher approached us in the office.

"I heard you are a theater bug. We are just casting *The Crucible* by Arthur Miller. You should come try out," she said.

I lit up. An audition! I was ready to grasp at straws.

My mother chimed in, "Oh *no.* Patty was in *The Crucible* last year. I'm not going to sit through that again." My face flushed a bright red and my upper lip started to sweat.

The teacher challenged her, "It would be an excellent way for Mary Patricia to make friends."

My mother had a defiant smirk on her face, "I heard you don't have late busses for extracurricular activities. I have other children and my husband will be traveling a lot with his new job. I will only allow the kids to do activities they can walk to."

"Surely she can drive herself home from rehearsal?" offered the teacher when she saw the tears flooding my eyes.

My mother's response was a slap in the face that rang down the hallway, "I am *not* buying another car so my daughter can be in a play!"

My options were limited. I went to school on the bus and came home at three o'clock. I had plenty of time to study and I did, but I actually *failed* the semester tests including the same courses I'd taken at my old high school. French, for example, was not taught the same way or sequence. My grade point average suffered. I had always been a good student, but now with failing grades on my report card, my self-confidence, always fragile, vanished.

Just before Christmas break, I went to the guidance department to discuss my predicament. "The program back in New Jersey was completely different. With only one semester to go, I don't think I can catch up. My transcript will be a mess."

After careful deliberation, the guidance counselor said, "You have more than enough high school credits for graduation. Why don't you sign up for some classes at the University of Wisconsin at Milwaukee to finish the year out? Who moves their child in the middle of senior year?" and then, catching the judgment in her voice, added, "If you start at UWM, you can skip the rest of the high school year. Assuming you pass your courses, we will issue you a diploma in June. You don't have to apply to be admitted. It's a new program. You would have to pay in-state tuition, though. Then, you can transfer to the college of your choice."

But could I pass college courses?

I would have to find a way to pay for my clothes, personal expenses, and now the cost of commuting on the bus from the suburb of Whitefish Bay into the actual city of Milwaukee. I went to the university alone to ask about registering. Many businesses surrounded the college, so, I went from door to door filling out job applications. I received the promise of a position at the lunch counter at Woolworths. The uniform I was required to wear would cost my entire first paycheck, but they were willing to work a part-time schedule around my classes. Another benefit was I would be able get a free meal with every shift.

That afternoon, I arrived at home feeling hopeful for the first time since we had left New Jersey. Dad was gone for the week and Mom had started her cocktails early. She was belligerent by the time dinner was served. By early evening, she made a show of picking up her hardcover book and clasping it to her chest.

"I'm going to bed to read."

We all knew she would be passed out within minutes and were glad to be rid of her. The new house had an expansive family room with an entire wall of fieldstone. The fireplace built into it had a gas jet. We just stacked the logs, turned the dial to ignite the gas flame, waited long enough for the wood to catch fire, and then turned the gas off. Boom. Instant roaring fire. My brothers, sisters, and I would watch television with a fire every day and night. It was comforting. Of course, Dad exploded when he came home and saw how many cords of wood we had gone through. He had hand-selected apple, maple, and cherry lengths. He spent several Saturdays cutting and splitting the pieces himself. While he was on the business trip, the fire crackled, popped, and warmed our homesick hearts.

Winter's Laboring Pain–1973

The climate of Wisconsin was horrendous. The warm months were hotter and more humid than any I had ever experienced, and the winters, I was soon to learn, were brutally cold. The wind coming off Lake Michigan was frightening in its power. Ropes were strung around the city to hold on to as people walked. A few times I was lifted off my feet and held on for dear life. On the long walk from my parents' house to the bus stop, I had only a pair of mittens my grandmother had knitted for me long ago, and a cloth coat for protection. Any money I made working at the lunch counter went to buy books, supplies, and food. There was no time for fun or outside interests. I had no friends. I was a lump of unhappiness. What sustained me during this first year were the letters from my friends--Deb, Keith, Don, Belinda, and Nathaniel.

My father was fired five months after starting his new position. Both my parents were drinking heavily when my mother had a nervous breakdown. My younger brothers and sister were huddled outside her bedroom door when I got home that day.

"What's going on, guys?"

"Something's wrong with Mom."

"What do you mean wrong?"

"She went crazy."

"You kids wait out here."

My mother was standing in front of her bedroom window with her back turned to me when I walked in and closed the door.

She said, "Jesus is coming! I see him!"

I moved closer to her so I could see her face. Placing an arm around her shoulders, I spoke to her. "Where?" I followed her gaze, as she continued staring out the window. All I saw was the garage sitting behind the house. My mother held her face in her hands, astonished by what lay before her. She was a study in rapture.

"Why, He is right there, Mary Patricia. He's standing in the driveway. He has come to take me home! Jesus! Jeeeessssus!" she called to him.

A disturbing feeling seized my gut, yet I also fought an urge to burst into nervous laughter.

I told my mother, "I'll be back soon." I opened the door and told the kids to come with me. My mother was unhinged and I wasn't sure what she was capable of doing. I wanted my siblings close to me. We went into the kitchen and I called my father's emergency number at the temporary job he had taken at a manufacturing plant.

"Hello. This is Mr. Toohey's daughter, Patty, calling. Bill Toohey. This is an emergency. May I speak to him?"

The man who replied had to shout over the factory noise. There was so much clanging and banging I held the receiver a foot away from my ear as I waited for my father to come to the phone.

"Hello?"

"Dad, it's Patty."

"What's up?" he asked me in a brusque voice.

"Dad, Mom needs to go to the doctor. She isn't making any sense."

"How do you mean?"

"She thinks she sees Jesus in the driveway."

"So?"

"Dad, it's pretty hard to describe. Just trust me... it's bad."

"Well, I can't leave work. Call Dr. Burns. His number is in the address book by the phone. I have to go."

Click.

I held the phone against my ear until the dead silence became a dial tone. The other children were circled around me and hanging on. When I was very young my grandfather told me when I was in trouble I should look for an officer in uniform. I dialed zero for the operator.

"Can you connect me with the police, please?"

My mother was carried out on an ambulance stretcher and taken to a mental hospital. Until the day he died, my father blamed me for creating a scene that day. In the oral tradition of Irish-Americans, the story was retold many times at holiday meals. Facts were altered and embellished. The family myth became that I was the one who was hysterical and misunderstood what my mother was telling me. Although she wound up in a psychiatric ward many times afterward, it remained important to my parents that I had been wrong to involve the police.

Shortly after that event, my father announced at dinner that they were moving to Chicago, but he wanted me to stay in Wisconsin.

"In *Milwaukee?*" I asked incredulously, "Can't I apply to schools back East?"

Dad said he didn't have the money for that, but if I wanted to apply, good luck. He added one more thing for good measure. "I make too much money for you to get any financial aid."

They loaded up the moving van and were gone. At age seventeen, I was utterly and completely on my own. My friends back home were still in high school. We rarely spoke on the phone because long-distance calls were expensive. I wrote to them frequently and treasured every response. Nathaniel wrote on a postcard from Lighthouse Point on Tuckernuck Island:

This is where we are staying, but you can't actually see our house. My parents are going to buy the cottage next door for a second summer home. You better like bluefish because I caught you one the other night, but my parents will probably eat it before we leave anyway. (I hated bluefish.)

The weather has been really strange. It's clear and sunny during the day and just before sunset, the fog rolls in off the ocean, so that when you look in one direction you see the sunset and in the other the fog. Please say hello to Belinda when you write to her. I don't know her address.

Belinda wrote often to tell me about dating Keith, how they going very slowly in an attempt to have a real relationship, and that he was good to her. Deb told me about cheerleading practice and the schools she was going to apply to for the following year. Keith's car was giving him trouble and he had bought tickets to see Eric Clapton at the Fillmore East over the past weekend. Apparently, the band was wasted and took over an hour to tune their guitars. He had cut class the next day because they got home late and he wanted to sleep in.

In juxtaposition, I was living in a depressing apartment one floor below a prostitute. I knew this was her profession because I could see her front door when looking up from mine. One day, it was wide open, and I thought I saw a swing suspended from the ceiling. Curiosity got the better of me, so I crept up the stairs to have a closer look. The only thing in the room was a red-seated velvet swing positioned over a filthy mattress on the floor. That explained the men coming and going, as well as the strange noises at all hours of the night.

Nathaniel's description of the beach had made me once again believe in fresh air. When I walked outside in Milwaukee, I smelled the yeasty pollution of the brewing company mixed with a sickening sweet smoke coming from the Ambrosia Chocolate Factory. On a particularly bad day, the wind would bring in the distinct smell of the paper mills. It was the stink of sauerkraut farts. Anyone who has ever experienced it would not disagree.

In less than another year, my parents and youngest brother and sister had moved again from Chicago to Delaware. My older sister was disowned when she ran away to live with her boyfriend. The eldest of my brothers signed on as a roughneck with an oil drilling company off the coast of Texas. Dad continued working for the same huge conglomerate of businesses, but at a different company. Two years later, he took an important position, a vice-presidency, in Alaska. While the title sounded good, he made it clear that he couldn't contribute to my living expenses or tuition. I had called him because I couldn't find the money to buy books.

"I'm proud of you and I'm sure you will figure it out," he said before hanging up. I began skipping meals to make ends meet, near the end of the month I went three entire days without food. Although she was heavily medicated, my mother returned to Milwaukee to get some of her things out of storage. When we met for lunch, she looked me up and down. "Well I see that you are painfully thin. Is this some new diet? Being too skinny gives you a pinched look."

"After I pay my rent, tuition, heat, utilities and bus fare to school there isn't much left over to buy food Mom."

She dismissed me with a wave of her hand. "You should date more. Make it clear you want dinner when you go out."

"Men always expect something after they take you on a date alone."

She shrugged and said, "I'm sure you can work around it."

Just before her visit, I had taken a new job that paid more money. It was in a private key club called The Hideout. It would become a popular spy-theme restaurant, but in 1975 it was a nightclub. *The Hideout* was secreted behind *Extraordinary and Exotic Imports Ltd.* on Front Street in Milwaukee. Nowhere could you find a sign advertising *Hideout.* I walked down an alley and entered through a utilitarian metal exterior door. Someone sat at a large wooden desk in front of shelving filled with old books, where I could smell the dust on the hardbound cloth covers.

If you fumbled at all, perhaps saying you'd heard there was a nightclub here, you were asked to leave immediately. A button was located discreetly under the desk in case someone refused to go when asked. A muscular bouncer would appear seemingly out of nowhere. To actually gain access to the club, you had to know a password, which was changed weekly. Members paid a substantial fee for the information; it was the key to get inside. When they said the magic word, a lever was pulled. Part of the bookcase swung away revealing a jet-black tunnel that twisted and turned. A set of double doors snapped open automatically and the blackness burst into a speakeasy with a spy theme. It was decorated with James Bond memorabilia; even the waitresses dressed like Bond girls.

I was recruited for the job on my college campus. I had been walking down a brick path from the science lab to my literature course when I heard someone speak.

"Psst. Over here."

I turned in his direction.

"Hey, you want a part-time job?"

"*No* thank you!"

"No. No. No. It's not like that. We need real waitresses. It's hard to find pretty girls who aren't working some kind of angle. We just want you to wait on people and be accurate with the cash."

"You can't put an advertisement in the newspaper like everyone else?"

"I need to find a girl fast. And, I gotta see what they look like. I figured you coming from the science building, you would be smart."

We were out in the open, so I wasn't afraid. I walked toward him.

"Geez, this is like a bad movie with you trying to lure me over here."

He laughed. "It pays great."

"Yeah?" I hesitated because I was now making a minimum wage of one dollar and sixty-five cents an hour at Woolworth's and lunch counters weren't known for great tips. I was still seventeen. My age, I knew, was an obstacle to better employment.

"How great? What will I make?"

"You'll easily clear seven dollars an hour. Listen, I can understand why this seems shady. Do you have any time this afternoon? I'll show you around the place and you can meet my boss."

That very afternoon, I was introduced to Sal. Meeting him flooded me with relief, for he was a temporary cure for my profound homesickness because was obviously from North Jersey. He was Italian.

I lifted my chin at him in challenge. "You? Hoboken?"

He stopped short and seriously pondered the question. "Yeah. And you? Let me guess… Englewood."

"My grandfather was a cop forty years in Englewood. My dad moved us further out."

I immediately knew him and he knew and understood me.

He teased me and I gave it right back. We waged a little war, Jersey accent to accent. He looked me over appreciatively in the way men were allowed to do back in the years before sexual harassment was defined, and outlawed. His head was bobbing in a slow exaggerated yes.

"How old are you?"

I wasn't a good liar so I swallowed hard. "Eighteen."

"You got ID?"

I handed him my college photo identification and my Social Security card. Neither had my birth date on it.

"You don't got a license?"

"I don't drive. I can't afford a car."

He made aggressive eye contact with me for several seconds. I held my breath. Then, he put a finger up to the side of his nose and smiled. Again, he nodded the approving "yes" slowly and winked.

"I guess you have to be eighteen to be in college. When can you start?"

I was on the floor as a cocktail waitress the next night. We all had to wear similar attire, although allowances were made for variety and body type. The girls able to get away with deep décolletage wore the low-cut version. I was assigned a turtleneck black leotard that was high cut in the legs. The rest of the ensemble was comprised of fishnet stockings, stiletto heels, and a gun belt with a hard leather bullet pouch.

The pouch contained our "cash drawer," which was fifty dollars in a variety of bills. Every day I came in at 4:15 p.m. and I was given fifty dollars. At the end of the night, which was 4:15 a.m., I paid back the fifty. What was left over I got to keep for myself. That was the deal, but so was keeping my mouth shut.

It turned out a nationwide gambling service was being run out of Sal's office. Long after I left Milwaukee, he would be named as an unindicted co-conspirator in a major gaming case that sent many people to jail. Details of the case are scarce now, but given the era and the scope of the investigation, it's certain Sal was working with the Chicago mob and they owned the club.

There were a few tense months during my tenure at The Hideout after he was arrested in front of all his employees and put in handcuffs. As the result of a plea bargain agreement, he agreed to testify against another gambling ring in town. He was promptly released from jail and returned to work. Sal's wife, who had a Nancy Sinatra hairdo, was sent out every night at closing time to his car. It had been dusted with powder the moment he arrived. Her job was to check for fingerprints that would be a sign someone had tried to open the hood. Husband and wife assumed he could be the victim of a car bomb at any time that would ignite when he started the ignition.

Sal talked about it honestly. "It'd be a pretty efficient way to kill me," he said. "It would get attention and send a strong message to all the wannabes."

The girls who waited tables were not allowed in Sal's office. I still believe it was as much for our own protection as for his. All of us thought him a kind and generous man although it was clear he had a serious problem with both drink and betting on horses.

The club had two levels and each had a bar. A Saturday night could find nine people behind each one, including bartenders, bar back-ups, and bus boys. The man who managed this part of the business had the title of head bartender. His name was Dennis Weslick. In addition to his duties at the club, he was a professional bowler. When he first told me about his sports credential, I burst out laughing. When I realized he wasn't kidding, I blushed.

"You don't bowl?" he asked me, his expression serious. He was suddenly interested in me and in the differences in our backgrounds.

Knowing he was sincere, I blurted out, "No! And nobody I know does either." He was listening to me carefully, so I continued. "I've never met people of Polish descent before or seen anyone put red wine into a refrigerator."

Sal knew I was underage, and I assumed he had told Dennis whose eyes grew a little sad at my disclosures. He told me later he wasn't sure if I was truly out of my element, or was being condescending to him. "Yeah, well bowling is kind of a big deal out here. See this ring? It's a real diamond. I won the championship last year. I have five of them."

He had come to work for Sal as a teenager in the 1950s, drilling bowling balls and setting up the Brunswick pool tables Sal was selling for top dollar in a shop on Front Street. Dennis was still working there in 1969 when a pack of federal agents descended.

"It was really scary," he told me. "Probably eight FBI agents in the store with their suits open so we could see their guns. They raided the place, went downstairs, and there were ticker-tape machines down there where Sal was getting all the results from the tracks."

When Sal wanted me for something, he took to bellowing, "You! You with the legs up to here," and he would hold one hand flat under his chin. *Legs* became my nickname.

Many nights, we would finish cleaning up and punch out by four thirty, but nobody was ready to go home. If I had a lab class in the morning, it was always scheduled for eight, so on those nights, I went home and studied and then went to school without any sleep. However, when I didn't have a class, we would all hang around and drink. I discovered cocktails since there was no wine worth having, which was strange to me, because Sal was, after all, an Italian-American.

Some of the big spenders from the clientele would join us after-hours. Their need to show off for each other meant more money was spent openly, freely, and often recklessly. "Let's go out to breakfast," someone would say. "Who's in? Legs, you wanna go?"

A diner we frequented stayed open all night. On special occasions, some fancy restaurants exclusively served us. Then, there was our mainstay restaurant, *Beyond the Sea*, a direct reference to the revered singer Bobby Darin. The kitchen at *Beyond the Sea* was open until five in the morning. The first few times I went with the group, I didn't order anything because I couldn't afford to, but I quickly realized one of my bosses or customers would pick up the check.

They liked to pat my hand. "Legs don't worry about it," they would say. "You are a starving student. It's just nice to have your pretty face around. You're funny, too, you know that?"

After we were finished eating, the night would culminate with a presentation of the tip. Exorbitant tipping was an art form with these high rollers. One guy liked to stand up and lead the waiter away, but kept him within sight of the table. As the waiter opened up the leather folder containing the money for the check and also his tip, his legs would almost give way at the amount. The big spender reflexively grabbed his elbows to hold him upright. Then they shook hands, the waiter hanging on to the customer's right hand with both of his, saying thank you over and over. It made for late nights, but when I was dropped off at home, stuffed with cocktails and comfort food, I would sleep like a baby.

If the DJ at The Hideout played *Mack the Knife*, all the older men stopped what they were doing and sang along. Years later, I understood their obsession with Darin and Frank Sinatra better, but at the time, I thought of them as old fuddy-duddies. A disco song usually followed and our younger customers poured out onto the dance floor to do The Hustle. Sometimes, one of them would drag me out to show them how.

There were also nights when business was dead. I would go into our locker room, change into street clothes, and prepare to walk the 2.2 miles from The Hideout to my apartment. The first part of the walk wasn't terrible because it was in the business area of the city. Sometimes bodies curled up in the deep stoops of the doorways, but I soon discovered the homeless drunks were only interested in staying warm. Still, I would hurry past them, headed north on Front Street along the lake. As I made my way toward my apartment, the atmosphere became sketchy on Prospect Street. Men in cars would screech by me, so close I could feel the air rush at my side. Hairs on the back of my neck would stand on end and my sixth sense would go into overdrive. By the time I was opening my door on Summit Avenue, my heart was in my throat. Men visiting the prostitute upstairs were constantly entering and leaving the building. I excused myself and scooted by them, not letting out a full exhale until I locked my deadbolt with a *thunk*.

When I lay down, I would think about the number of hours I had to study tomorrow. If I got all my schoolwork completed, I would treat myself and write to my friends at home in New Jersey. They would be graduating in three months and I wanted them to send me all the news. Worry kept me awake. I thought about the oil bill that needed to be paid. Heat was my top priority, especially when the temperature kept dipping down to twenty and thirty below zero. If I had the time, I decided I would walk all the way down to the Salvation Army thrift store to see if I could find a pair of pants that fit me. It took a long while for the adrenaline that had built up in my system from the walk home to give way to a few hours of sleep. I knew I slept, though, because a few hours later, I woke up from a terrible nightmare, drenched in sweat.

Brew Town–1973

I discovered the reason the wait staff was ordered not to enter into the kitchen of The Hideout. Though some bar menus were scattered around I was already aware that no one ever ordered food. However, a cantankerous man in my section repeatedly asked me if we had anything to eat at the club. He wanted to know why we put the menus out if the kitchen wasn't serving. It was a quiet night with only the front bar open, and I longed to escape from the barrage of my customer's complaints. Dennis was busy serving important regulars, so I walked through the swinging steel doors into the back to investigate.

Four men, two sitting on stools and two standing, were clustered around the butcher-block workstation. Each of them had an arm tied off with rubber surgical tubing and a syringe. They were shooting up. As I entered, one of the men to my left pierced his vein. A stream of blood spurted out and hit me below the eye. In an incredibly graceful motion, I turned a hundred and eighty degrees on my stilettos and flew back out the swinging doors.

Dennis was there when I walked back into the club. He took one look at me and started wiping the blood off with cocktail napkins. He had to keep dipping them into water from the bar sink, because it didn't come off easily. Once I was cleaned to his satisfaction, he held me in a tender embrace for several minutes. He wore so much cologne that it made me cough. "I'm going to make you a drink, Mary Patricia. You want a Gin Gimlet?"

Over his shoulder, he called to the man I had been serving. "The kitchen is closed. Last call."

The customer pointed to his watch and shouted back, "It's only midnight!"

But Dennis went over to my table and settled up with the guy himself. As I drank my Gimlet, I watched Dennis lock up the entryway and front doors. He came back in and made himself a Manhattan, and then he took a seat on the barstool next to me. He lit two cigarettes, handing one of them to me. We sat quietly for what seemed like a long time.

His eyes were the pale blue of a hot August sky, and he knew how to use them to his advantage. "You remember Linda? She was here when you first came?"

"Uh-huh." I grunted because I really couldn't speak yet.

"Well, she got into it." He motioned with his eyes and head toward the kitchen. "I had to fire her." Sipping my Gimlet, I pretended to understand, but didn't yet. "And Karen. She thought waitressing was too much work." I suddenly knew what he was trying to tell me. Karen had been pulled off the schedule, yet she still hung around The Hideout for a while. She seemed to be involved with Sal, then Dennis, and after him, another bartender. She would come in and sit alone at a table waiting for men to approach her. Suddenly, no one was allowed to serve her if she came in. Karen disappeared and I never saw her again, although I heard she worked the special parties, something I had never been asked to do.

Dennis was blunt. "She's a hooker now."

A sudden dread turned my stomach. Could I one day sink so low?

He stared at a red telephone booth at the end of the bar, and I followed his gaze. It was an enlarged model of a typical British phone kiosk, minus the gold crown emblem. He took my arm and walked me over to it. "Dial any numbers that equal 18." With a swoosh, I dialed a six to the finger stop on the rotary phone, then waited to hear the *click-click-click* as it returned counter-clockwise to its starting position. I dialed two more sixes, and the back wall of the booth slid open. Dirty cement stairs led down to a dank hole.

"Go on down. I'll be right behind you," Dennis told me. He carried a powerful flashlight. On my right at the bottom of the stairs was an old wooden door with many layers of peeling paint. Dennis knocked on it quickly three times, as if for luck.

"*You* don't ever go in *there*." He gently pushed me forward down a tunnel. At the end was a door with a push bar on it. "Go ahead" he said. I shoved it open and stepped out into a small area that was a cross path for several brick alleyways. He whispered into my ear from behind. "So what do you think that this is for?" When I didn't answer he laughed. "For nothing good, I'll tell you that much for free. Come on, let's go back in."

He held the door from the tunnel open with his foot. We walked back through and up the stairs. It was too dark for me to see how he got the back of the phone booth to slide open again. After leading me to the bar stool, he mixed us both another drink before he started to work his magic.

Dennis was suave and handsome in a Las Vegas-y kind of way. He dressed carefully, in the style of a 1970s mobster. I would find myself wondering where these guys shopped. Where could you find socks like his if you wanted them? They were closer to being stockings due to the way the tubes of silk were woven together with a fine, almost transparent mesh. All the men wore pastel leisure suits tailored to have a slightly western fit. Their hairstyles involved hairspray and teasing, but Dennis was younger than Sal and so his hair was longer. They had thick mustaches and wore musky cologne. On special nights, there was a quick changeover to tuxedos. They each owned more than one and took pride in their quality. You could almost count the dollars that went into making those garments. The fabrics cried out to be touched and sometimes I did just that.

I was seventeen and Dennis was thirty-five. He was funny and smooth. Tonight he had a little smile on his face, and I noticed his eyes crinkled, which was the case when he was at his most charming.

"You understand what I'm telling you about this place, Patty?"

After a few seconds, I nodded a definitive yes.

"And about what happens to some of the girls?"

72

Again I nodded.

"That is not going to happen to *you."*

I agreed with him wholeheartedly.

"What you are doing," he lectured me, "working your way through school and all, it must be really hard. Try to make peace with being broke and don't let the money tempt you. Someday you will graduate. The hard times won't last forever. You just keep your head down and do your job. Stay out of the rest of it."

My eyes met his and again I responded affirmatively.

"Good. I am going to talk to Sal about giving you a raise. You want to learn to cash out the main bar on your nights, Mary Patricia? You're good with numbers. I'll start training you on Wednesday."

As young as I was, I served as a kind of mascot at the club. I was good at banter and a quick retort and that was disarming. On this night, however, I remained almost silent. The gin numbed my ability to feel the shock of what I had witnessed. It was quarter to three, and even then, the particular irony of my situation matched against the famous Frank Sinatra song lyrics of *One for my Baby* was not lost on me. Dennis announced we were going home. He carried me from his car up to his apartment. It was the first bachelor pad I had ever seen.

I didn't know what to make of the white leather couches or all the bowling plaques hung on the walls. Hundreds of trophies filled glass display cases lining an entire wall of the apartment. I barely had time to look at the awards as he ushered me past them into his bedroom. He had a giant mirror mounted on the ceiling framed with gilded gold.

He spread his arms wide to indicate his bedroom and asked, "What do you think?" I bent over and laughed into my hands. "What?" he asked with a little frown on his face. I sat down on the bed. It was made with actual white satin sheets so slippery they couldn't stay tucked in. Sex was the last thing on my mind as the only thing I longed for was a good night sleep.

Apparently this was a big turn-on for Dennis. His advances were passionate. I was tired and didn't want to argue with him.

The intercourse was abrupt. Before I relaxed into the rhythm of it, he announced he was going to come. I don't think I felt anything at all.

Dennis took me home in the morning. We never slept together again, but he had, in his own mind, I supposed, made a kind of commitment to me. After that night, he always made sure I had a ride home and someone to walk me to my front door. When he had an important engagement, he would take me shopping for a new dress and I went as his date. He never let me wear the same outfit twice. I owned one pair of jeans and a small closet filled with gowns and high-heeled shoes. Late at night, he would often phone and interrupt my precious sleep to discuss his business plans and personal dreams. No one at The Hideout thought of us as a couple. It was all just part of my new job.

Summer Wind–1974

Nathaniel and I exchanged passionate letters.

"I fell in love with you the first time I met you," he wrote. "I never want you to doubt how I feel." He was in a good private college in New England. His family was disappointed he hadn't gotten into an Ivy League school, or even one of the baby Ivies. They had the advantage of a legacy at one of the illustrious institutions and certainly connections at many others, yet Nathaniel was not admitted. The one that finally accepted him did so on the condition he joined their wrestling team.

Athletic and pre-medical programs absorbed Nathaniel. He wanted to be a doctor, a very rich one. Altruism did not factor into his decision. I was absorbed, too, and rarely slept a full night in my desperate struggle to feed myself, pay for classes, and study. We spoke often on the phone, though Nathaniel was insistent *I* call *him* as his parents would get upset if he had a big phone bill. It never occurred to me that he could get a job as well to help us out. While I lived paycheck to paycheck, his way was paid by an educational trust fund and a wrestling scholarship. I accepted the cost for our calls as part of the heavy burden I carried.

Nathaniel's life of college parties, drinking, hash oil, pot, and what sounded like occasional studying seemed a world apart. How he reconciled all this as a competitive athlete I still don't know.

I was surrounded by much older people at my job, and didn't have time to socialize with the younger kids I met at school. I didn't dare to question whether Nathaniel was dating anyone else, as I was lonely and our letters and conversations were the one thing that made me feel grounded. In them, I felt hope for something better than the drudgery I was slogging through. And, I clung to the hope he would want me to move closer to him where I would be known and understood.

Nathaniel felt like home to me.

I often fantasized about going back to New Jersey even though most of my classmates were now in college. My own family was long gone and so I wouldn't have a place to stay while I got my feet on the ground. Besides, I could barely pay my bills and eat where I was, let alone save the money to make a trek across the country.

During Thanksgiving week, Nathaniel drove the Tomato all the way out to Wisconsin to visit me. I was so happy to see him that the reunion was filled with extremes, both emotionally and sexually. I could tell he was shocked to see the squalid neighborhood where I lived. It was all I could afford and I refused to be embarrassed. By the time he rolled down my street and parked in front of my apartment, he didn't have a cent left in his pocket. He had spent all he had on gas. He told me he received an allowance from his parents, but didn't realize how much he would need to budget for this trip.

I paid for all our meals and had also planned a night out. Sal had given me permission to bring Nathaniel into The Hideout for a drink. He got a kick out of the secret entryway, as I knew he would, but he found my instructions to him to be a bit strange. "Try not to, uh, well, you don't want to… uh… tell them too much about yourself."

Nathaniel blinked. "What do you mean?"

"For example, you can say you are at a college in New England, but I wouldn't say which one."

"Why not?"

"Just don't give out any more information than you have to. That's all I'm saying."

Sal saw us walk in and came over to greet me. "Legs! So this is the boyfriend, huh? It's good to see our girl has friends her own age. Legs, order him up one of our special cocktails, on the house." He turned to Nathaniel and put his hand on his shoulder. "Fair warning. They got all kinds of booze in them. That's why they get served with a sparkler for the garnish. Have some fun tonight. This one here, she works too hard."

Sal shooed us toward the main bar. I chose two stools in front of Dennis' station since I figured he would want to meet Nathaniel, too. He came out from around the bar to shake his hand. In one hostile sweeping glance, Dennis took in Nathaniel's feathered haircut parted in the middle, Izod sports shirt, khaki pants, and Dockside loafers worn without socks. Nathaniel seemed unaware of the antagonism in Dennis' gaze.

Dennis didn't look at him again; instead he spoke to me directly. "What you drinkin', Legs?"

"Sal said to order one of the specials, on the house."

I had never had one of these fancy drinks and I was pleased as a child on Christmas morning when the tall frosty glass was placed in front of me. We waited while the sparklers burned all the way down. I took a sip. It tasted like herbs and slightly bitter. Delicious.

Dennis made a motion toward my glass. "Easy on that, Legs."

I had planned that after we finished our cocktails, Nathaniel and I would head around the corner to a relatively inexpensive restaurant. Then, I was going to splurge and spend twenty dollars apiece to see a Rolling Stones cover band at a hot new dance spot that had just opened up. It was housed in a converted warehouse within walking distance from The Hideout and my apartment.

Dennis caught my eye and winked. "You going to see *Gimme Shelter* tonight?"

When I nodded enthusiastically, he pulled two tickets out of his shirt pocket, held them in the air, did a little dance, and then laid them slowly on the bar in front of me with a smile.

I practically squealed. "Oh, Dennis! How did you get these?"

It was a stupid question. Dennis could get anything in the city of Milwaukee good or bad. He shrugged his shoulders and cocked his head a little to one side. I burst out laughing and ran around to the back of the bar to give him a hug. This was a game change for the rest of my month's budget. All I had to pay for that night was dinner and a few drinks.

When Nathaniel and I stood up to get ready to leave, Dennis came out from behind the bar to say his goodbyes. He really did have perfect manners. Yet, he only looked directly into *my* eyes. "You kids have a good time tonight. She deserves to have some fun for a change."

I thanked him again for the tickets, and when I gave him another hug, he whispered into my ear, "He looks like a fag." I pulled away quickly and was halfway across the room when I heard him call out.

"See you Friday, Legs." He had left his mark on me like a territorial alpha dog.

In the coat room, Nathaniel started to interrogate me, but I put my finger to my lips. He held his hands out and shrugged as if to ask, "Why?" I reached up to a heating grate and pointed. Seeing his puzzled expression, I gently pulled the grate out a little bit to reveal a microphone on a chord.

Nathaniel was startled. He spoke with an uncharacteristically thick North Jersey accent. "What? Are you kidding me?"

"No. Nathaniel, I am not."

I knew he was shaken up by my underground life, but by the time we reached the venue where the band *Gimme Shelter* was playing, we discovered not only had Dennis paid the price of our admission, he had also bought us seats in the VIP section of the club. In a flash, Nathaniel's mood flipped from judgmental to elated. We were led to a table on the perimeter of the dance floor with a perfect view of the stage. As soon as we were seated, one of my customers, who was also seated at a VIP table, recognized me.

"Legs!" He came over with his date and introduced her and us. "Let me buy you young people a drink. Waiter!"

I quickly discovered the bartender serving our section was a friend of mine who filled in at The Hideout when he wasn't needed here. "Another round, Legs?" he asked me several times that night.

Nathaniel started teasing me about being a celebrity. Other than ordering a couple of glasses of water and tipping generously for the service, I didn't pay for a cocktail all night.

The band opened with *Honky Tonk Woman*. Nathaniel and I practically leapt onto the packed dance floor. By the time they played *It's Only Rock and Roll* the crowd had transformed into one giant living organism. We all knew every lyric and sang along. Our hips and shoulders were in sync to each drum hit. Lost in the music, Nathaniel and I shared a brain, a heart, and a soul.

I felt a little wild and after the last set of music ended, I was thrilled to be headed home. We had made love many times in his car or in haste when his college roommate was out for a while, but in my apartment we enjoyed total privacy for as long as we wished. I had gone to Planned Parenthood and started taking the pill to prepare for his arrival in Milwaukee. I lit some candles and put a record on the phonograph. The needle jumped and projected the slightly scratchy big band jazz records I had bought at the thrift store for a quarter. Since we had danced so hard and long, we decided to shower as soon as we got home

Working at The Hideout had given me a confidence in my appearance I had never enjoyed before. I boldly stripped down and we climbed into the claw-foot tub together. I lifted my arms straight up as the water pummeled me. Nathaniel began to apply soap to me, gently massaging every part of my body. I got out and wrapped myself in a towel, and then picked up another larger one I had warming on the radiator. When Nathaniel stepped down onto the bath mat, I covered him.

He took me in his arms. "This may be the best night of my life, Patty."

It lasted until the morning light, filled with pleasure and repeated declarations of love.

Nathaniel stayed a week. For the first time in my life, I was at peace. We were a committed couple and optimism took hold of me. Before he drove away from the curb outside my apartment, Nathaniel swore to me he would find a way for us to be together. The morning of his departure, after many tearful kisses, I stood and watched his red Volkswagen Beetle drive two blocks down to the traffic light and turn right. Just as it was about to vanish from sight, something deep inside me shattered, and with primal shrieks escaping from me, I started to run after him. By the time I turned the same corner, he was gone. I had run so hard my stomach started to cramp and I bent over.

A single thunderclap exploded above me.

It began to pour rain.

A Brutal Truth–1974

Nathaniel didn't make good on his promise; in fact, we only saw each other sporadically. I had to take extra shifts and squirrel away money to fly out to see him compete in a regional wrestling match in Maine. He was injured and spent the entire long weekend sulking like a child. I had not only spent all of my savings to see him, I lost days of work during which I could have been making money. His behavior was discouraging; while I was there, he introduced me to one coed after another who wore a carefree expression and clothes I could only dream about. It dawned on me that he wasn't yet capable of a full commitment. With his innate sense of entitlement, it would take many years for him to mature into a man.

Belinda was home in New Jersey working full time. She rented a room in Avalon Park from a senior who needed the extra money. Her plan was to save up for an apartment of her own. She called one day to tell me she had scraped together enough for a plane ticket and that she was coming to visit. I was both excited and grateful.

Her debut at The Hideout was what I predicted it would be. The bartenders loved her and asked her to go out with them after the shift was over. I explained to her that I had a morning class and couldn't go.

"When will you be home from school tomorrow?" Belinda asked.

I knew she wanted to accept their invitation, "About four, but I don't know if you realize the guys you want to go out with were recruited when they were released from jail."

Belinda was cocky. "We went to high school with the Gigante and Givanosso boys. I'm pretty sure I can handle these two."

"Belinda, we didn't date those boys. We didn't even socialize with them."

She grabbed my hand, "Speak for yourself. I have your address and your spare key. I know your phone number by heart. When you get home tomorrow, I will be at your apartment making dinner."

True to her word, she was in the kitchen frying onions and chopping vegetables when I unlocked my door the next day. She was in a wonderful mood, singing and dancing around the apartment as she handed me a glass of red wine.

"Where did you get this?" I asked holding the glass up to the light to inspect the color of the obviously expensive wine.

She shrugged. Belinda knew I wouldn't approve of her fabulous night out with the bad boys. I would later hear from the bartenders' stories about an escapade involving group sex. They also told me they had all ended up in the kitchen of The Hideout. I felt embarrassed by what she had done because I felt it reflected badly on me at my workplace. I was sitting in my kitchen stewing about it when she gazed down at me from her workstation. The expression on her face was so sweet that I instantly forgave her transgression. The bulb over the kitchen sink lit her from behind, creating a halo effect around her head. Always animated, her expression transitioned to concern.

"Mary Pat, I'm curious. What did Nathaniel say when he came here and saw where you are living and working?"

If I had learned one thing in my young life, it was how to carry on. I stuffed down inside whatever hope I had of ending up with Nathaniel. I didn't want to make a fool of myself; it was hard enough to allow myself the vulnerability of love. I couldn't afford to have my heart broken. I wouldn't allow it. My voice was devoid of emotion when I answered her. "He doesn't want to be responsible for me, Belinda. Sometimes I get mad and tell him, 'Don't do my any favors.' I could tell he was shocked by my circumstances, but I didn't give him a chance to say much about it. I don't need him judging me when I am already stretched to the breaking point. I know he called my parents. Mom phoned me the next day and told me to get out of this 'dumb' apartment. When I asked her how I could afford to do that she hung up on me."

Belinda left a pan simmering and joined me at my tiny kitchen table. She took my hand, "It must hurt that he doesn't step up in some way, especially after your parents have discarded you. But *I* am going to state the obvious. I want you to get out of Milwaukee, Patty."

"How? I don't have any money to move. Where would I go? Besides, I want to finish my degree."

"I wish I could tell you to come home and live with me. I really do. I am staying in an old lady's house at the moment. Someday you could come back east and we could live together, but not right now. It's not like this University of Wisconsin Milwaukee is the best school. It's certainly not the only school. You can transfer. This whole situation is a dead end." She sipped her wine. "And the job at The Hideout? How long will it be before you see and know too much and there is *no getting out*? Just find a way to leave town and keep going, and then call me."

With that, she stood up to finish cooking our meal. A few days later, I was ending a shift when Belinda showed up at the front bar.

"How did you get in here?" I asked her.

"I told them I was here to see Legs."

"The bouncer didn't stop you?"

Belinda gave me a lascivious look. "No, he did not."

Dennis saw her standing next to me. "The friend, right?"

She extended her hand across the bar and said, "Belinda."

He took her hand in his and lowered his head to kiss it. Intimately.

"Well, *hey* you." Belinda preened.

"Uggghhh!" I threw my hands up in the air, disgusted, and set about counting money and cashing out the register. They went on canoodling. I strode over to the locker room to change my clothes.

When I came out, the two younger bartenders had joined Dennis, all of them clustered around Belinda. Her melodious voice rose and fell, punctuated by the roar of their coarse laughter. She still had the showgirl body that made men make fools out of themselves. On this night, she was dressed in a plunging stretchy jumpsuit that glittered with rhinestones and hugged every curve. Her hair was now a mass of crazy curls due to a new permanent wave and expensive hair products. Her lips were lined and glossed in a strawberry red she kept pulling out of her purse and applying slowly in front of the men. However, it was her cleavage that drew the eye of men and women alike. The guys tended to lean forward a little as if they wanted to bury their faces in her breasts. This was the moment when her eyes would widen as though she had no idea what was going on. I thought she was breathtaking. And, she was stealing my thunder. All of it.

"Mary Pat," she called over to me. "The boys want to take us out. You don't have class in the morning. Let's go."

"Where are we going?" I was testing the waters. There was no way I was going to an illegal venue, nor was I going to be totally left out of the fun.

"Don't be such a killjoy, Mary Patricia."

I eyeballed Dennis for a split second and he quickly decreed the course of the evening. "No *drugs*! No *dice*!"

The two bartenders let out noises of disappointment. "It's a Thursday. What else are we going to do?"

Dennis snapped his fingers and called to a boy that was his runner. "Charlie!"

He took a hundred-dollar bill out of his pocket, folded it, and placed it between his pointer and middle fingers. He stretched out the two fingers with the money. His thumb, ring finger, and pinky were clasped together as he backhanded his arm to hand the cash off to the boy. Dennis' large diamond ring flashed in the gesture.

"That New Jersey band Patty likes played in town tonight. I hear some of the high rollers flew in to see it. There will be an after-party. Charlie, go get us some passes."

The boy disappeared silently through the blackened back door of the red phone booth. We waited for half an hour, sipping cocktails the younger bartenders made for us. I noticed Charlie re-enter the bar through the folding glass door.

Dennis addressed us as a group, "Give me a minute to lock up. I'll go with."

We wound up playing dice after all. When we entered the opulent hotel suite of the Karl Ratzse Hotel, Bruce Springsteen and his band were down on the floor shooting craps up against a wall. The lead guitar player, wearing the same gypsy scarf he wore on their recent album cover, rose up from one knee when he saw me. He pointed to the circle.

"You play, kid?"

"Sure, but I only have ten dollars."

"Keep it, I'll stake you. Maybe you'll bring me luck."

Dennis had found himself a drink and leaned against the catering bar on one elbow. Belinda set to talking with a well-dressed man. I last saw her going into the bathroom with him, but lost track of her once I started a winning streak.

The lead guitarist told me to let him blow on the dice before I threw them. My first shoot was a five and a six. Eleven! A cheer went up from the group.

"Bring her a drink," he said, "Get comfortable, honey, and let's try again."

My next toss was a three and a four. Seven!

The guy serving as the stickman picked the dice up and retired them to an end table. He next presented me with five new dice and asked me to pick two of them. As long as I rolled a seven or an eleven I could continue winning. It happened every time I rolled and the cheers grew louder. We took breaks to get more drinks and change the dice out. It was just one of those nights. I couldn't lose. Dennis never came near me as I played, yet I could tell he was aroused. When I glanced over at him, he was always both smiling and smoldering.

At some point, I thought to ask a question of my partner in crime. "How much is my cut?"

"Right now?"

"Yeah, right now."

He shuffled the money around in his hands counting. "Uh... three hundred."

Dennis was suddenly at his side. "I counted nine naturals," he said.

"Oh, sorry. *Five* hundred."

"Can I have it, please?" I asked him sweetly, projecting my youth and relative innocence onto him.

"Now? We're on a roll."

"I'm just a girl working my way through college, not a rock star. I have a lot to do in the morning."

By the time he handed me my cash, Dennis had already found our coats. He took me home and walked me up to my door. For the first time since I had spent the night at his place, he gave me a real kiss. It was deep, and so intense that my knees grew weak. He pulled away and stroked my cheek. Our eyes were locked and we stood absolutely still until our breathing naturally synchronized. A slow inhale, then exhale, tenderly searching the windows to our souls. I am still haunted by the memory of his August-pale blue eyes when he finally spoke to me.

"Bye Legs."

Alone Again

Putting Belinda on a plane back to New Jersey was brutal.

"You can stay." I said, "We'll figure out our next move together. You hate your job and the place you are living in. Stay. At least we will have each other."

"Mary Patricia. The only thing worse than you being stuck here is both of us being stuck."

My tears flowed so freely that I stopped trying to wipe my eyes. We hugged. We rocked. I moaned with grief and panic. When they called her flight for the third time, she reached up and loosened my grip on her. Holding onto my arms, she said, "All I want you to do is get out of this city, Mary Patricia. We will figure the rest out in time. First things first."

That night, I reflected on what she had said about the Milwaukee scene. Her words rang true, and it was unnerving. I had $500.00 in cash taped to the bottom of the drawer of my bedside table. A young couple I had met at school, Paul and Christine, had asked me to move with them out to the West Coast after final exams. The deal was I would split the gas money and the rent on a two-bedroom apartment they had already secured. I could stay with them until they were on their feet financially and I found my own place to live.

I didn't tell anyone at The Hideout that I was going. I didn't leave a forwarding address or pick up my last paycheck. I packed the little I had into the trunk of the couple's white 1965 Datsun, leaving the evening gowns Dennis bought me hanging in my closet. We left after sundown on a Friday and I fell asleep as soon as we pulled onto I-80 West. When I awoke, we were already in Kansas.

California Girl–1975

Arriving in San Diego was like waking from a deep sleep. The sun was always shining. Mexico was just across the border and that cultural influence permeated all aspects of the city, from architecture to food. I could go anywhere in a T-shirt and shorts. Shoes were optional most of the time, which meant I didn't stand out as being poor. Pedestrians could walk down the street and pick fruit off the trees. I joined two different food cooperatives where produce, grains, and meats were dirt-cheap. For the first time in my life, I felt nourished. It was hard to be in a bad mood when I had a full stomach and the weather was perfect every single day.

During my volunteer hours at one of the co-ops, I worked alongside a young man named Peter. I thought him beautiful, not a common adjective for a man. His dark brown hair fell halfway down his back and his black eyes glowed with youth. And vigor. He told me he had grown up in Oregon. It made me feel good when he laughed heartily at all of my jokes. He displayed unmasked appreciation, and many times he would say, "You are just delightful!"

I was a healthy young woman, and after knowing him for a few weeks, I fantasized about running my hands across his sculpted muscles, but I kept it to myself. When he eventually asked me out, despite my attraction to him, I felt uneasy about the date. What exactly did he expect from me?

Peter picked me up and we drove into the mountains northeast of San Diego. Our destination was a cowboy bar in the small ranching town of Pauma Valley. It was easy to find as it was the biggest building on the small main street. A six-piece band played country swing music to a crowd that had grown up dancing to it. I had never seen anything like the scene unfolding in front of us. Most of the patrons were dressed in boldly colored satin shirts and pointy-toed cowboy boots. Peter and I drank a couple of beers as we watched the elaborate dance steps with fascination. Neither of us suggested going out on the floor as long as the regulars were swirling around. I was worried we might get run over as we fumbled along in our attempts to match their footwork. When the music slowed to a two-step, I told Peter I was sure we could do this one.

"It's just slow, slow, quick, quick. What do you think? Can you dance at all?"

He held out his hand to me. "Watch and learn, little lady."

We glided around the wood floor as if we were born to it. The dancing made us thirsty, so we kept drinking beer. One of the local cowboys insisted on buying us a shot of tequila. He said he had known every other patron in the bar for his entire life and it was fun to talk to somebody different. He had us suck on a lime and lick salt before we downed the liquor. We enjoyed the little ceremony so much, that a Spanish-speaking cowboy, clearly Mexican, stepped in to buy us another. It became a competition between them. Peter and I were lucky the bar had a small motel attached to it.

When I awoke the next morning, it was with tentative regret. I was grateful he had used a condom. Peter was a generous lover, yet he came across as practiced and even a bit jaded. I had to acknowledge to myself that this night had been of my choosing, so there was the looming matter of mortal sin weighing on me. When we returned to San Diego, Peter introduced me to his circle of friends. I assumed we were now dating and made every effort to get to know him better.

Nathaniel had started calling again, and leaving messages with my roommates. When my phone rang at three o'clock in the morning, I ran to pick it up before it woke Christine and Paul. I stubbed my toe and tore the nail in the mad scramble. Nathaniel was drunk. "I made a terrible mistake letting you go Patty. Losing you is destroying me."

"Please call me back in the morning after you sober up. I'd like to know if I am still irresistible to you then."

"I mean it this time. Wait and see. "

After that, he called regularly to talk about medical school. He was also checking up on me. It was our old pattern. The more detached I was, the harder he tried to convince me that he loved me. I had invited Peter over for dinner and to play Crazy Eights at our house. The four of us had a great night and so Christine made a judgmental face whenever Nathaniel was mentioned.

The West Coast culture was the reverse of the Irish Catholic mores of my youth. When Peter took me to a huge party one night, I joked that it seemed like Ken Kesey's Merry Pranksters had procreated here at an exponential rate. The host had laced the drink he offered me with LSD and I narrowly avoided drinking it. I was angry when I figured out the ploy and asked Peter to take me home. He shrugged his shoulders and ignored me.

As the night wore on, many girls shed their clothing, and then danced for the men and each other. Several televisions were on with the sound muted. I found it remarkable to witness how the movement on the television screens attracted more attention than the naked women.

My face must have given away how I felt about it all because one middle-aged hippie turned to me and said, "Don't be so uptight. It's all cool, man."

He actually called me man.

An intoxicated older couple openly copulated on top of the dining room table as the music blared. When I looked for Peter, he had disappeared and I begged a ride home from strangers. I didn't go back to the food cooperative where I had met him.

While San Diego was a better fit for me than Wisconsin, it still wasn't home. I didn't share any of these details with Nathaniel when we talked; as far as he was concerned, I was having the time of my life. And suddenly he was including me in his plans, assuming I would want to join him once he was accepted into medical school.

His most recent letter to me declared his intentions:

I can come and help you to move back East. I truly hope you will consider it. It has been so long since your last visit. Your departure hit me hard. For weeks, I would wake up thinking you were in bed beside me. It wasn't fun when I realized it was a dream. All my friends say "hello." A couple of them have told me they wished they could find a girl like you. You really are something else! Maybe I am just starting to realize how special. I told the guys I was going to marry you, and they believe me.

In the end, though, not a single American medical school offered him a spot. He figured it was because his college grades could have been much better. He stopped talking about us moving in together and began to apply abroad. A school in Europe accepted him—and anyone else who could come up with tuition. Most of the students were from wealthy families from Africa and the Middle East.

When Nathaniel called to tell me he had been accepted, he said, "I can't promise you anything, Patty. I am going to be away for a long time. It's my dream to be a doctor. You need to go on with your own life."

What he failed to comprehend was I already *had* moved on.

Fly With Me–1976

While I was in Southern California, I bought the paper every day and scanned the want ads. Rent in San Diego was relatively cheap, but jobs were hard to come by. The best one I could find was the late-night shift as a waitress at a truck stop. I knew I was smart, and I felt driven to better myself. I talked to recruiters at various branches of the military and learned they were happy to offer me a paid education. However, when I called my parents to discuss enlisting, they were furious; they threatened to cut me off if I signed the final papers. They hadn't spoken to my older sister in years and I didn't understand how she lived with their censure. In the hope of earning their approval, I tried to find another way to earn my college degree. I realized what I really wanted was to return to the East Coast, so I obeyed my parents and I kept looking.

One day, I saw an advertisement for Trans World Airlines airhosts. I was surprised because becoming a stewardess was considered a glamorous career with great travel benefits. Within ten days, I had completed a series of interviews and was hired. I was off on my own grand adventure.

The airline flew me to Kansas City and Breech Airline Academy. TWA had opened the school in 1969 on a twenty-five-acre parcel of land. Three large brick buildings housed the candidates who were training to become stewardesses and air hostesses. The dormitories were divided into 'pods,' with themes such as 'Africa' and 'Asia' attached to them. In the African pod, there were leopard skins, wooden bows, and other artifacts on the walls. Ten dorm-style bedrooms circled a sunken living room, which was where we socialized in the evenings. The entire school was air-conditioned, which was necessary, but it also felt like a luxury to me.

It was exciting to be in such a state-of-the-art facility; even the other airlines sent their employees here to train. Simulation classes in actual sections of 747 and L-1011 aircrafts were offered daily. Two of the lecture rooms were decorated in the contemporary style of white walls offset with oval furniture that could have come from a science fiction movie. We attended an emergency medical class in a clinic few hospitals could rival.

Competition for customers among airlines during the 1970s was fierce. Quality of service and opulence of food and beverages were significant factors when potential passengers bought tickets. First-class cabins were meant to rival the best restaurants in the country, and a great deal of our training focused on service. Our instructors routinely assessed our performance by giving us high-pressure practical exams.

We were also subjected to weekly physical inspections that included weigh-ins. Until I moved to California, I had spent much of my life hungry. There was never enough food when I lived with my family, and once on my own I often couldn't afford to eat well. Breech Academy had a cheerful cafeteria with attractive buffets where the meals were free. For the first time, I could have as much as I wanted to eat. Within weeks, I had gained seven pounds and was grateful I had started out so thin.

I arrived in Kansas City having always been told I was pretty, but among the trainees at the academy, I might have been considered average looking. The high humidity in Missouri made my skin break out and my grooming instructor advised me to buy expensive skin care products as a countermeasure. At the time, I had thirty-seven dollars in my bank account. The other girls had beautiful clothing, and most of them owned their own cars. They were from every area of the country and represented every race, each presenting a version of hip style. Precision haircuts, highlights, and hair extensions crowned their heads. I felt ugly and fat by comparison. When I probed, it was clear the girls were temporarily bankrolled either by their parents or a boyfriend back home. My innate insecurity was amplified to a fever pitch.

There was a push to hire men as well as women. That year, a more professional term, *Flight Attendant,* replaced the moniker "stewardess," but it would take years for the public at large to accept the change. Many of the men in my classes were gay. Still, the new coed enrollment produced a frisson that electrified the air as the women vied for their attention.

After six weeks, parents and visitors arrived to watch us receive our wings. The auditorium was packed, which surprised me. The families of my peers seemed thrilled by their children's accomplishment while my parents never considered taking the trip. I called to tell them about the ceremony and they laughed and said, "It's not as if it's a college graduation." When my name was called, I was relieved to know I would be reporting to work in New York City.

My roommate at Breech Academy, Vicky Fraizer, was also assigned to fly out of New York. Financially, she was in the same boat as me. All trainees were given the opportunity to buddy-bid for the city where they wanted to live. This meant two friends would be assigned to the same major airline hub. After graduation, we were given three days to find a place to live.

As I was packing my suitcase for departure, someone brought a message to my room. I was to call Belinda immediately. I started apologizing profusely for the collect call, but she shushed me and said she had a chance to rent an apartment on East 87th Street east of York. Did Vicky and I want to move in with her? She explained it was a two-bedroom, five-floor walk-up.

"But, we can afford it," she said. "It's on a really nice block. The ceilings are high and the exterior walls are exposed brick."

Belinda was hired as one of the first women to make service calls for a major Manhattan gas company. She had already been promoted and ran her own crew of men. Other friends had written to me that she could display a decidedly masculine side. At work, she dressed like any other blue-collar guy. She had been commuting into the city every day from New Jersey.

"I've got some money saved," she said. "You can pay me back for the first and last month's rent and the security deposit. Vicky can have one bedroom all to herself if she's willing to pay a little more on rent. "

"You don't mind sharing a room with me?"

"You'll be traveling constantly. Besides, it will be fun. Like the sleepovers we used to have."

Vicky was fine with the arrangement. We were all happy when we saw the street and that the building had black cast iron railings, window guards, and garden fencing. The façade was rich red brick with layers of white moldings where we entered through tall oak double doors.

The day Vicky and I arrived, we stood huddled together with our suitcases on the mosaic flooring of the first story. We admired the long flight of dark mahogany and marble stairs that climbed to a landing and wound up to the second floor. We couldn't see as far as the fifth. We laughed and told each other the climb would keep us in good shape.

In our apartment, the windows facing the street were bowed. Someone had propped a piece of wood in one to make it stay up and the air coming through it was refreshing. We sat on the floor for a minute to peruse our new home, then went to a corner dime store and bought blankets to sleep on. It would take us months to save enough money to start buying actual furniture.

A few days later, I was flying out of JFK and LaGuardia airports in New York and Newark Airport in New Jersey. When a senior flight attendant called in sick, I was ordered to come. I rarely had enough time to get back to the apartment on East 87th Street and wash my uniform before the phone would ring again. I was often transported by helicopter on my dashes to Newark.

One hot July day, the pilot reminded me to strap in, and I realized the helicopter didn't have any doors. The view was breathtaking as the aircraft hovered, pivoted, swirled around, and headed to New Jersey. I could see the East River below. All five bridges from the Whitestone in the Bronx to the Brooklyn Bridge shimmered in the low-angled light. The windows of the Chrysler

Building, Rockefeller Center, and to the left, the Empire State Building, cast off a harsh gold reflection. The loud *swoop swoop swoop* of the blades made talk impossible.

Looking down, I thought I should be more afraid than I was. I would soon be celebrating my twentieth birthday.

The New Yorker

In 1976 you could still live in Manhattan without hemorrhaging money. You had to be crafty and careful, but it could be done.

Belinda stopped to talk to everyone. Shop owners, folks sitting on their front stoops, children, and the elderly greeted her when she passed by. She soon had our neighbors taking an interest in the three young women trying to make a go of it in the big city. One day she dashed into the apartment and woke me up. I had come home late after working the red-eye from Los Angeles to New York. Coming out of a dead sleep, I could barely move from sleeping on the hard floor.

"What?" I barked at her.

"Mr. Chang over on Second Avenue!" she said. I waited. "His mother was in the hospital and she died last night." She was so excited that her nostrils flared.

"And?"

"He said he would sell us her furniture really cheap, but we have to move it fast, otherwise he's going to donate it to the Salvation Army. He wants it cleared out so he can rent her apartment on the first of the month."

The news shot me upright. I pulled on some jeans and a jacket and we ran over. There were two bedrooms, each containing a double bedroom set from the 1940s. The living room couch had clear plastic slipcovers and looked brand new. Belinda and I moved the couch ourselves five blocks and up the five flights of stairs. We were spent by the effort.

"There has to be a better way," I said.

I had a brainstorm. We frequented an Irish pub on the corner owned by the O'Connor family. Mrs. O'Connor, Fiona was her name, asked after our every move. She openly worried about how we were getting on. I knew they had a truck out back they used to haul in food and liquor. We ran down the street and entered in through the kitchen. We were lucky to find Mr. and Mrs. O'Connor standing there. It was Monday and they were closed, so I told them the whole story.

They blinked at us in astonishment. "You moved a couch five blocks by yourself? And up five flights of stairs?"

I begged them, "Can we borrow your truck for a few hours? We will pay you! I promise we won't let anything happen to it."

It wasn't lost on me that the O'Connors were of *Irish* descent. They took charge of the situation. Mrs. O'Connor loaded us up with empty boxes, and then sent her husband off to find their sons. She walked with us back to Mrs. Chang's apartment, took a look around, and announced, "This woman was immaculate. God rest her soul." She advised us to not get carried away and take too much. "It would be like absorbing her entire life into your own," she said. We settled on the couch, armchair, and the bedroom sets.

Two of the O'Connors' sons came with their dad and a friend. They made quick work of moving the furniture out and loading it in the truck. We filled up the boxes with pots and pans, an Electrolux vacuum cleaner, and some tools. After everything had been hauled up to our apartment, the guys went to the pub for a beer and we started arranging our home.

My eyes were filled with tears as I hugged Mrs. O'Connor good-bye. "So much for your day off," I quipped. "Once we all recover, we will have to think of some way to thank you."

Fiona grew flustered by my emotion. "Seeing you girls off the floor is thanks enough."

Why Didn't Somebody Tell Me?

Like many women, I didn't comprehend that I was beautiful. I wish now that an older woman had stopped me on the street and said, "Darling! You are gorgeous! Set your standards very high. Expect the best life has to offer."

I was fit and thin. I could shop in thrift stores and still look like a million bucks. And my hair! It was shiny auburn, thick as a horse's mane, and long. In uniform, I simply twisted it up and secured it with a large barrette costing less than a dollar. I had no need for a hair stylist. Since I was a substitute for other more senior flight attendants who were out sick, I worked constantly. A day's work meant a per diem payment in addition to my salary. I could feed myself and make a little profit.

My childhood friends, Deb and Keith, were also in Manhattan at that time. Deb attended Hunter College, which was on the East Side within walking distance of my apartment. Keith was in New York trying to make it in the music business. He played out almost every night of the week, so when I felt like dancing, I went to see him. On my free nights, and I didn't have them often, I had old friends to spend time with. With Deb's encouragement, I signed up for a few classes to continue pursuing my much-dreamed-of Bachelor's degree. In the seventies, Hunter College had an open admissions policy that took into account my standardized tests scores and didn't penalize me for the poor grades I received the fall semester of my senior year of high school. I met with a panel of five for my interview and they asked me how I had made it through my classes at University of Wisconsin. To my surprise, they applauded when I told them.

I started at Hunter College by taking one course, Human Physiology. After my first lab, Deb and I met on campus for coffee. She tried to talk me into going on a blind date with someone she and her boyfriend, Jeff, knew.

"If he's so great, why don't *you* go out with him?"

"Because he's perfect for *you*. He's about to graduate with an accounting degree and sit for his CPA. A huge firm in Boston has already offered him a job, but he's going home to run the family business because his father is sick. It's like the old movie, he's Jimmy Stewart in *It's a Wonderful Life*! He's from a small town in Vermont. I think he wants to meet a girl before he goes back."

His name was Rich Maddin. He was quiet at first, but the three of us drew him out. It was obvious he was intelligent. He told us all about growing up in the small town of Greenfield. "I lived with my parents above the store and my grandparents, who started the business, had a house on the other side of the covered bridge. I used to play with my toy trucks right on Route 100 back then. It was rare for a car to drive by. Everyone in town knows me and still calls me Richey. Two years after my father built the new store in Village Square, my parents built a new house for us up on the hill. I started working at the store when I was nine years old. They had me sorting eggs and cutting up the wheels of cheese."

The four of us had fun. He asked me out for a second date before he left to move back to Vermont, but my work schedule didn't allow it. We stayed in touch by writing cards once in a while.

My dear friend, Don, called to tell me when he graduated from the University of Virginia he was going to apply to every law school in New York City. I was elated. We talked about all the plays we wanted to see together. In 1976, you could buy "standing room" tickets at Broadway theatres for five dollars. Don arrived on schedule, and for years we were Sunday brunch pals. After our meal, we spent the afternoons at museums or a matinee.

At the end of a long flight, we female flight attendants were beseeched by passengers to attend various events. The New York Yankees had a home game and a restaurant owner hosting a party for them wanted pretty girls around. Would we be willing to attend if all the food and drink were on them? Sure! There were so many offers that I only chose what intrigued me. A party for a famous actor. An event for an iconic boxing champion. What was so great about 1976 was no one expected you to *do* anything. Did they hope for sex? Of course, but saying no didn't prevent us from being invited out again. Not if you were pretty, funny, and charming. During that Bicentennial summer, with an abundance of galas organized, I discovered I was all of those things. Entertainment expense was not part of my monthly budget.

My roommate, Vicky, a statuesque African-American woman, came from Detroit. She happened to grow up with two famous basketball players for the Detroit Pistons and they stopped by when they were in town. There were many nights that we made them a home cooked meal and played cards together. The guys would invite us to games and parties, providing entrée to other famous people. One night, Vicky called me and asked me to a dinner party at the historic Sylvia's Restaurant in Harlem. She met me at the subway entrance near our apartment and we rode over together. When we walked in, she waved to our hosts who were already seated. At the table sat one of the most famous stand-up comedians of my lifetime, Bill Cosby. Vicky had a huge smile on her face as she waited for my reaction. Seated next to Mr. Cosby was... I blinked. Was it really him?

Let's be discreet here. I don't know who might have been married at the time. I shall refer to the man sitting there as Movie Star. Vicky was cracking up waiting for me to lose my composure, but I took it very much in stride, at least on the surface. The food was fantastic. Conversation was topical and light. Vicky left with the movie star. Mr. Cosby (I addressed him this way during the entire evening) had a limo on call; he insisted that he drop me at home. "It's too late for you to be riding on the subway alone," he said. "I have daughters of my own."

He was lovely to me. I kissed him on the cheek and hugged him when we said goodbye.

On July 4th, Vicky and I were invited to the World Trade Center to watch the tall ships regatta followed by fireworks. An attorney whose firm was on the 23rd floor of the South Tower had invited us. It was the usual—men wanting pretty, classy women around to entertain much older influential male clients. I came to think of myself as wallpaper at these events, where my job was to dress well and make interesting conversation. For this July Fourth event, I would sip the finest champagne, eat exquisite food, and get a great view of the regatta. I asked Belinda to come with us because it was such an important holiday in New York.

I cautioned her, though. "We are not going there to meet a boyfriend. Most of the men will be long and happily married. And, we are certainly not going to score drugs. One hint of that and we will be thrown out on our keisters."

I brought my new 35 mm camera with me and shot color slides of the event. The term "tall ship" is a generic term used to describe large sailing ships. For this regatta, historical vessels had been sent from fifteen other countries to celebrate. The United States of America was two hundred years old! The upstart nation, an experiment in democracy, had not only survived two centuries, but had prospered. It was impossible not to get caught up in the spirit of the day.

At the height of the parade, I was swiveling back and forth 180 degrees to shoot incoming, passing, and departing ships, my eyes tearing up because I was overlooking the two icons that most represented our country: the Statue of Liberty and Ellis Island. I thought about my grandparents and all they had sacrificed to get our family to this great country of ours. I had to stop and blink several times in order to compose my photographs. In some instances, I thought I could identify the ships from their flags once I studied the photographs, but just in case I kept a program. The Goodyear blimp made passes overhead. A fleet of fireboats "saluted," shooting six enormous jet streams of water upward for each tall ship that passed.

The caterer mimicked the food of old-fashioned covered dish picnics from various regions across the United States, but this was New York City, and the room was filled with wealthy clients. I had never eaten ham of the quality carved that afternoon, or tasted crayfish étouffée flown in from New Orleans that morning. None of my girlfriends could identify the vegetables and herbs in a dish resembling coleslaw, yet it had a much more distinctive taste. If anyone wanted a break from alcohol, fresh lemons were squeezed before our eyes and mixed into lemonade. It was the Big Apple version of a Fourth of July feast.

Belinda, Vicky, and I stood together in front of the room-sized plate-glass windows facing southwest to watch the fireworks. When it was clear it was the finale, we instinctively reached out to put our arms around each other. We didn't want the night to end. We savored the explosive celebration until all that remained were the dying embers at the feet of Lady Liberty.

Belinda was the first to speak, "We are going to walk the whole way home. All of New York is one big party tonight."

Vicky snorted, "That must be eight miles."

"More like five," Belinda said. "It's doable. There's no timetable. We'll stop and have a drink when we get tired. Let's do this! Each of us will have to talk to one person along the way who we wouldn't normally speak to. The other two will be the judges of whether a real conversation occurred. In fact, the twosome will choose the person who will be the target. We'll call it *Barrier Breakdown* and the goal of the game is bona fide conversation. Mary Patricia will take a picture of us when we complete the task. Come on… it will be fun. We won't be able to get on the subway now anyway."

Vicky and I made Belinda go first. She would talk to anyone, so it was hard finding a challenge for her. We came across a well-dressed man who we would learn was an attorney and a weight lifter. Gorgeous. I challenged her, "You must actually talk to the man. You can't flirt. You have to make a connection and find out one important thing about him." We clapped her on the back when she got him to explain why he decided to go to law school. Before we moved on, he asked for her phone number. We were surprised that she was frazzled by his attention.

Vicky had a pleasant conversation with a homeless man and found out he was from North Dakota. He told her about his childhood growing up there. When it was my turn, they targeted a Vietnamese woman who was the owner of a produce shop. She described a long voyage that eventually ended when she reached New York City. I took a snapshot of Belinda with her muscular lawyer who bulged out of his suit. Vicky tried not to cringe when the homeless man, who had been lying on the ground when we introduced ourselves, put his arm around her for the picture. Belinda took my camera when I was allowed behind the store counter with Mrs. Phan, just before the flash exploded white light.

It was three o'clock in the morning when we reached *O'Connor's*. The place was jammed. It had a special mood because most of the patrons were first-generation Americans whose parents had come to Ellis Island. Some were immigrants themselves. Many had served in the Second World War and so, overall, the crowd was extremely patriotic.

Mr. O'Connor waved me toward the bar when he saw me. Knowing I wasn't a beer drinker, he poured us both a healthy Irish whiskey in short glasses. Neat. There were tears in his eyes when he raised his glass to me. In the Dublin accent of his parents, he said, "Only in America, Mary Patricia Toohey."

In return, I summoned the voices of the elders of my youth, as I clinked the rim of my glass with his. "Only in America, Seamus Aloysius O'Connor!" We drank deeply.

Meeting at Thirty Rock

Late that summer, and out of the clear blue sky, Nathaniel called to tell me he was leaving for medical school in Budapest that day. I hadn't spoken to him in almost five months. I later learned he had called my brother to ask for my new phone number. He wanted me to meet him in front of Rockefeller Center. The oppressive heat and humidity of the past week had finally lifted, and Manhattan was in a rare pristine state.

I approached him wearing my TWA uniform, rolling my suitcase behind me. Nathaniel kissed me hello, and when he pulled back he seemed elated to see me. We were barely aware of the pedestrians swarming around. The spray of the fountain misted over us and sunlight diffracted a million rainbows. The atmosphere was electrifying.

"I wish you had given me more notice," I said. "It's a miracle you caught me when you phoned. I'm supposed to be in Los Angeles."

I was shocked to glance up and see tears in his eyes. The confusion I felt made me suddenly furious at the man I had wanted to marry a year ago. Part of me wanted to throw my arms around him and kiss his face until he started to laugh. I longed for him to tell me it had all been a terrible mistake and he was ready to start our life together now. Instead, terrified of embarrassing myself, I suppressed any genuine feelings and began to prattle on as though I were speaking to an acquaintance.

"August is your family's month to be together on Tuckernuck Island. Are you coming from North Jersey? Have you been there for the summer? So much has been happening in Manhattan with the Bicentennial. You could have come and watched the Regatta that came up the East River. You love sailboats. We could have had dinner."

Tourists snapped pictures and milled around. "Do you want to get something to eat now?" he asked. "Do you even have time for a cup of coffee?" He clung to both my hands as though he were hanging on for dear life.

"I have a flight out of La Guardia and you didn't answer my questions," I said.

"Yes, I was home. I had to shop and pack for my trip. I'm going to be in Europe for four years."

"Where is your luggage now?"

"In a locker at JFK airport."

My voice sounded unfamiliar to me, almost indifferent. "I'm sorry I can't stay long, but I have to get to the airport and complete my safety check of the airplane. It's a pretty big responsibility. There are people counting on me to do a thorough job." I glanced around at the crowds of tourists thrilled to be here. I felt like we were on the set of a high budget romantic film. Nathaniel had a lovesick expression when I turned back to him. It all felt preposterous.

If he had been in Bergen County, New Jersey all summer, I thought, why had he waited until the last second to call me? When we were teens, we had once driven from his house to the George Washington Bridge in *thirteen minutes.*

He must have been reading my mind. "I couldn't bear to leave without seeing you," he said. "I'm really nervous about going to a foreign country. My classes will be in *French.* And, I'll have to learn some Hungarian just to navigate the city."

I couldn't keep the sarcasm out of voice when I responded. "Nathaniel, it's a private school, a fall back medical school. You will be well taken care of."

"You don't understand…"

"I don't understand? I'm pretty sure I know that life can get difficult. I was abandoned in the middle of a Wisconsin winter. I was seventeen years old, working full-time and completing my coursework for college. Then, I had to take a second job to pay for oil so I wouldn't freeze to death. *That* was demanding. You're worried you might not do well in your classes and your parents will be angry with you."

He stared at his feet. "When you put it like that." It was the old social divide, I realized. This was his most difficult challenge so far.

No matter what, I still loved him. With that simple acknowledgment, the floodgates opened. We sat down on a cement wall and I listened as he told me all his concerns. He was even anxious about flying in a plane for eight hours. When he arrived in Europe, he would have been up all night and probably suffering from jet lag. He would have to exchange money at the airport. Travel was my business, so I was in a position to advise him.

"You are flying on Pan Am, our main competitors. They really go all out. They will start by serving champagne. You will probably have a choice between filet mignon and lobster tail for dinner. And, there will be a full-length feature film. Limit yourself to two drinks. Just enough to make you sleepy, but not dehydrated. After your two drinks keep asking for water. My advice is to skip the movie." I stopped and pulled a Benadryl from my handbag. "Take this and it will help you sleep."

I knew I was avoiding intimate conversation, but Nathaniel wasn't. "Mary Pat, I haven't called you because I seriously thought it was better to try and make a clean break from you. I am going to be away a very long time. I couldn't just leave you without saying good-bye. I just couldn't."

Yes, I heard him. Even a short time ago, I would have clung to his words for any nuance that would indicate his true love for me. However, the cold fact was he had waited until the last possible minute to ask to see me. He was leaving in a few hours, with no plans for the near future. I knew he was frightened and I was the best friend he had ever had. He wanted to talk to me about his trip, which did not mean he wanted me to wait for him.

I forced myself to remain detached. I looked at my watch. I had to go. It occurred to me I had lived an entire lifetime since I had last seen Nathaniel. I casually kissed him farewell. I may have actually said, "Au revoir," as I crossed the street to the subway. With a backward wave, I rolled my suitcase down Sixth Avenue.

Nathaniel's flight hadn't landed on European soil when he started to write me letters in rapid succession.

8/27/1976

I have a layover in Keflavik, Iceland, and thought I would start a letter to you. I am sorry I have never been good at telling you how I feel about you. It's hard for me to find the right words. I am so glad we talked yesterday. The way you looked standing by the fountain is going to stay with me a lifetime. No matter what the future brings, I now realize we will always have a special relationship. I want to keep it. I know I have no right to ask this of you, but I must. Can you see a future with me? Despite the fact I am going to be living abroad for years? That I will then have to find a residency somewhere in the United States?

Let's face it, I will not be any hospital's first choice. I am going to have to take a position anywhere I can get it. Could you still love me if I made you move back to Milwaukee? I know you can only do your own course work as your work schedule demands. Today I am dreaming you will focus on getting your degree finished while I concentrate on medical school. We will still be young when I graduate! Do you think we can do it?

8/28/1976

I spent the first night in Luxemburg and today I'm in Brussels. Tomorrow I'll start the train travel to Budapest. Then, I'll be completely on my own and the fun will really start. My French has really improved in just two days because no one speaks English.

Please remember I think of you always. It makes me very sad to think it will take a long time to get a letter back from you.

Toujours mon amour,
Nathaniel

Belinda is in Fashion

Studio 54 opened on April 26, 1977. Everything Belinda had been criticized for in the past was suddenly in vogue. If she was loud, well, one had to shout to be heard inside the famous club. If she acted a bit crude, she was considered a hoot. She was free to use cocaine and sometimes even heroin with impunity. She drank heavily, but that was considered the norm. Belinda dressed outrageously and crossed genders at whim; bisexuality was revered within the walls of the club. Regulars looked forward to seeing what she would wear and following her commentaries on a variety of subjects.

One evening ten of us were in the back room sitting around a big table. A male celebrity's name was mentioned.

"I've had him," Belinda said. "He's hung like a mouse."

The laughter that greeted her remark alarmed me because I knew we would be seeing the man again soon. Sure enough, a few weeks later, he showed up with his entourage in tow. He marched right over to the bar where I was standing beside Belinda. "I heard you said I have a small dick," he said to her.

Belinda stared at him, obviously amused, sucked on her cigarette, and rolled her eyes. "So?"

I was mystified when he pulled her into a corner of the back room and spent hours kissing her neck and whispering in her ear. At one point, they ducked into a bathroom. After they returned, they were grinding against each other on the dance floor, despite the many onlookers. This guy was famous and the word was out she had insulted him. Apparently, this made her all the more alluring.

I stood alone with my "goody-goody" Catholic school values, feeling awkward when a member of the entourage asked me to dance. I loosened up. Dancing I could do. I threw my hands up in the air and let the flecks of light from the disco ball shower over me. I wanted to whirl and rock on forever, but he stopped and bought me a drink so he could catch his breath. During a rare quiet moment between songs, he whispered to me, "It's going to *snow* in the back room." He turned and walked away. When he disappeared into the shadows, I gathered my things up and left the building.

Steve Rubell was the owner of the club. He was a born and bred New Yorker who guarded the entrance to his business as though his life depended on it. He would only let in patrons who were famous or those he thought were glamorous. Whenever he saw Belinda approach the velvet ropes outside the club, he motioned to the bouncer to wave her through. One night I overheard him say to her, "The key to a good party is filling the room with guests who are interesting. My darling, Belinda, no one is more interesting than *you*."

In contrast, I felt invisible. Steve let me in the door because I was with her. He never even glanced in my direction.

Vicky had married and moved out of the East 87th Street apartment. Belinda and I could now afford our own bedroom with the heavy 1940s mahogany furniture. When I came home from traveling, I never knew if a man or woman would emerge from her bedroom asking for coffee. Most of them had the same androgynous haircut. There was also the matter of various drug paraphernalia left on the coffee table, along with the disarray that met me after my long cross-country trips and flights around the world. Belinda started sleeping until three in the afternoon.

Studio 54 stayed open only thirty-three months. By the time it closed down, Belinda was a full-blown drug addict. Keith had wearied of the club scene and left New York to try out as a session player in Nashville. Don was hired away by a law firm in Washington D.C., and Deb was already upstate working on her master's degree. That left me alone in the big city with my fading dream of a college degree. I walked around my neighborhood and realized that every building had a memory attached to it about my friends who were gone. I sat down and wrote a long letter to Nathaniel. In it, I wrote, "I need a big change."

Tuckernuck Island–1977

Nathaniel came home for summer break in August of 1977. We had been corresponding regularly and he asked me to fly to Tuckernuck Island for a two-week visit. The idea of getting out of the oven Manhattan turns into in summer was enticing.

The old propeller jet took off in thick fog from a parking lot at JFK; I knew enough about flying to be nervous. Then the turbulence started. The one flight attendant was strapped into her jump seat. A man stood up, presumably to use the bathroom, and was thrown against the ceiling of the cabin. The back of his neck hit so hard we were all amazed he hadn't broken it.

The flight was short, but terrifying, as the air currents tossed the plane around like a toy. Bolts of lightning streaked across the sky. It was a hard landing. The plane bounced three times before it began to slow down. Every passenger gratefully hugged the pilot as we exited the aircraft. I noticed two people were actually crying.

Nathaniel stood outside the gate entrance dressed in scrubs. He had come directly from the hospital where he was putting in some clinic hours as a volunteer. The sight of him took my breath away. He scooped me up off the ground in a huge bear hug. My body pressed up against the muscular wall of his chest. I was home. He picked up my bag and placed his hand on the small of my back. "This way, Mademoiselle Mary Patricia Toohey."

Once we were settled in the Tomato, which was a little worse for wear, he asked, "So, do you want the good news or the bad news first?"

"Bad news first... always."

"I failed my first year of med school."

"Nathaniel!" He hadn't said a word about it and I had assumed that he was doing well. My pulse quickened. It was an effort to get out the words, "I am so sorry. What did your parents say?"

"They said it was pretty brave of me to go to another country and try to take the classes in a different language. I had four years of high school French, but it wasn't enough. I am going to take some time to figure out what I want to do. It's really good you are here, Patty."

We embraced and I knew he was trying not to cry in front of me.

"Good news?" I asked.

"My dad got us a room at the Balefire Inn tonight. He said it would give us a chance to talk."

We both let out a hearty laugh. Talking was not the only thing that was going to happen.

"Nathaniel! How nice of your father. Please let me pick up the dinner check, and I will cook for your parents a few times while I am here. They used to enjoy that. I brought them a little gift, too."

"You know how much they like you," he said, smiling at me. "I have a good bottle of wine in my bag."

Nathaniel pulled out of the parking lot and headed northeast toward Balefire Road. The inn, and his parents' summer place, were on a secluded point of the island. It was an easy stroll to the private beaches or the harbor; generations of privileged families had access to the best real estate on earth. He had spent a lot of summers here with other young barefoot kids. The lifestyle was so casual that his family never knew who was going to walk in their back door.

The storm had split the sky wide open. There were still thunderclouds toward the east, but a wedge of blue was moving in from the west and it was growing larger as we drove. The rain had stopped, so we rolled the windows down. We didn't say a word for the ten minutes it took for us to get to the inn. We held hands. Each time Nathaniel had to shift gears he would let go, but then would immediately pick my hand up again. We shared a goal for this vacation. We were going to make the most of our time together.

The Balefire Inn was a perfect balance of place and proportion. Grey-shingled and white-trimmed, the building was a rambling hybrid of Cape Cod and Colonial. It had opened in 1875 as one of the island's first hotels, and in the early 1900s a second floor had been added. The current owners had maintained the almost shabby elegance loved by families with old money.

A great lawn, strewn with white deck chairs, overlooked Tuckernuck Island Bay. A wooden walkway led to the water, where brightly colored sailboats awaited. Wild rugosa bushes were trimmed into walls, creating secret gardens. Tucked inside were discrete groupings of wicker furniture and riotous blooms of flowers. I told myself there would be plenty of time to explore the grounds. I had already started taking photographs in order to remember every detail of this vacation.

We went up to the front desk where the lobby's furnishings were a collection of classics from the last hundred years. Some I knew the names of, others I only recognized from magazines and history books, all effortlessly arranged. The large open space was suitable for lounging with a good book, or hosting a black-tie event.

Our room overlooked the water. Crystal wine glasses sat on a tray. Nathaniel opened the bottle of wine he had brought with him. Unable to resist, I jumped up onto the plump mattress on the tall antique bed. The man I loved stood in front of the windows.

"Get over here, you."

For the first time, we had sex. We had made love many times, even experimented with pleasure, but this was different. We were adults who already knew every inch of each other's bodies. We engaged in a furious release of lust. Mortal sin didn't cross my mind. At that moment, there was nothing I didn't like about Nathaniel. When we finished, we sipped the wine and then I went to shower.

I called to him from under the water's spray. "I want to enjoy this place. Let's have a cocktail on the porch. Then dinner. Order anything you want. I've been saving up. After dinner we can watch the sunset out on the lawn. Then, we can go upstairs for a little while. *You* know. Afterward, we can read in the library. When we finally retire, I am going to keep you busy deep into the night. In the morning, if there is time, we'll have breakfast on the covered patio."

When I stepped back into the bedroom, I could plainly see how he adored me. His eyes glowed when he answered, "It's a plan."

When we went downstairs for the drink, and I leaned quietly over to the bartender. "Please open a tab for the evening," I said.

I had learned a thing or two from my years at The Hideout. After dinner, I handed our waitress a big tip just as the high rollers in Milwaukee had done, and I smiled as her eyes widened in the familiar way. By the end of the evening, the extent of my appreciation for excellent service was widely known. Later in the week, when Nathaniel's parents took us to dine again at The Balefire, they were thrilled over the dinner.

Nathaniel's father added, "Patty certainly made quite the impression. The innkeepers rave about her."

After that first night, we stayed with Nathaniel's parents in one of the two cottages they owned adjacent to each other. They gave us a wide berth. One night, we made love on the beach and slept there. The morning light woke us and we stumbled back home. We sailed, we played tennis like we used to, and we body-surfed in the ocean like two little kids.

Saying good-bye to him was, as usual, heartbreaking. We talked about medical school and he begged me to be patient with him, as he wanted to go back to Budapest and try again. This time he did ask me to wait for him.

"It's only four years, Patty. You work for Trans World Airlines. You can visit me several times a year and I'll be back next August. Don't make me choose between you and becoming a doctor. I want both."

"Nathaniel," I said. "I want to go to school, too. Living in Manhattan has become impossible. I don't make enough as a flight attendant to save much money. I need my job and it eats up most of my time. I'm not even halfway through my bachelor's degree. You could stay here, and we could move in together. There are plenty of other jobs in medicine."

He went quiet and I read his mind. His putting his ambition before me was infuriating. "Nathaniel, money isn't everything."

"Patty! I will not apologize for wanting to make money."

In the end, he had his way and I returned to Manhattan with a resolve to make it work.

Nathaniel never failed to write and tell me how often he thought of me. He described all the things he missed about me. Yet, once he returned to Europe, he never again mentioned marriage or tried to make specific plans. I felt then, and still hold the opinion, that he was waiting to see if he would find someone better.

When he returned the following August, I insisted he would have to come into the city. I was busy packing up. A school in Vermont had agreed to take all the college credits I had accrued. My financial aid paperwork was completed and funding was in place. As a Resident Advisor, I would have my own room in one of the dorms and they had even provided me with a meal plan. I had calculated I could complete my degree in four semesters and a summer. All that was left to do was figure out what to put in the one suitcase I would take with me to Penn Station.

Nathaniel hit the roof when I told him. "You're going to be a college RA? Don't you think that's a little demeaning at your age?"

I put my hands on my hips and looked at him defiantly. The blood rushed to my face. "I'm twenty-three. That's not exactly old."

"Most kids graduate at twenty-two. I don't understand why you can't go to college in the city."

"I want to earn a degree sooner rather than later. My job takes me all over the world at a moment's notice. TWA has been great to me, but this isn't the career I had hoped for. I've missed too many classes. And living in New York is expensive. After I pay my bills, there is very little left over at the end of the month."

He took a deep breath and sat back in his chair. He wore a snicker on his face. "What do you think you're going to do with this degree?"

"I want to be a math and science teacher."

"You are giving up all our travel benefits for *that?* As George Bernard Shaw famously said, 'Those who can, do; those who can't, teach.'"

"I'm sure that's the only line of Shaw you *can* quote. Or any other writer for that matter."

I didn't speak to him again, but my thoughts were intruding. *Who does he think that he is? I have made it this far alone, he has no right to tell me what to do. Vermont is the next chapter in my life.*

Trinity College in Burlington, Vermont–1978

The train north was called the Montrealer because it originated in Washington, D.C. and went all the way to Montreal, Quebec. It dropped me along the way in the small town of Waterbury, Vermont, which was close to several of the larger ski resorts. I had asked the secretary who answered the phone at Trinity College about public transportation from the Waterbury depot to Burlington. The response I got was laughter. It was an extra charge on the phone bill to call information, but I did it anyway. I asked the operator for the number of Maddin's Supermarket in Greenfield, Vermont. I only meant to ask Rich Maddin for advice, but he insisted he would be happy pick me up and drive me to Burlington.

Once I was settled in, Rich pursued me like a fairy tale knight in shining armor. He was crazy about me. Our children can't believe he ever wrote me love letters, but he did. Recently, I showed them the stack of envelopes I treasure. They are held together with a gold elastic ribbon. He wrote them in a careful script.

"You are beautiful. You are creative. You are smart. You are exciting. You are the best thing that ever happened to me. I will love you forever."

It was refreshing after the years Nathaniel had pulled me closer, only to push me away further.

Rich and I had not become intimate yet, and he understood I was waiting for a special night. He took me to Boston to the ballet.

The hotel in the Back Bay was magnificent with a sweeping view of Boston Common. He chilled a bottle of expensive champagne. I used the marble bathroom where there was both a phone and a television. When I came out, a long dress was laid out on the bed and a matching pair of shoes on the floor in front of it. They both fit me like a glove. How did he know my size?

"I peeked when you weren't looking," he told me shyly.

Our bond was hot crazy desire meets deep respectful love and we had a blast for a very long time.

I graduated with a degree in science and teaching licenses for both math and science. My father was terribly disappointed as he had fantasized I would become a doctor. Getting into medical school was more competitive than ever and my school advisor told me that since I had a ragtag transcript from three different colleges which eliminated the possibility for me. The truth was being a doctor was my father's goal for me; I didn't want medicine as a career.

The day of my graduation, Rich Maddin was there to cheer for me. When he took me out to dinner that night, he proposed and I said yes. The junior high school in Greenfield was advertising for a science/math teacher. It all seemed too good to be true when I interviewed and they offered me the job.

At twenty-five, I had finally come home, to a bucolic and historic small Vermont town. It had two white church steeples and one of everything else. There was a yellow brick library; a three-story white structure built in 1864 housed the middle school and high school; storefronts turned the corner from Main Street to Bridge Street and the Masons had a red brick lodge across the street with a white front porch. I stayed with the Larrow family on Main Street until Rich and I got married. Then I moved with him into his cabin while we planned the house we built on land he had inherited from his grandfather.

Teaching gave me a sense of purpose and enormous gratification. I was *the* seventh grade math and science teacher. If you grew up in our community you had me as an instructor. I had been right about myself, and when I sent Nathaniel my annual

Christmas card, I let him know how fulfilling my career was.

Rich and I traveled, built a house, and went out to concerts and community fund-raising events. I used to tell him he was the most fun I had ever had. It was true. He also made sure I felt safe. There was not a person in our town who would cross him, not that he was a hothead, but Rich was an alpha male. He was successful and was respected for the time he had always devoted to the community. He told me he was proud to be with me and I knew I was proud to go anywhere with him.

My parents came for the wedding, although they didn't contribute to the cost of the event. They were impressed with our new timber-framed house, Rich's business, and all the well-wishers stopping us around town to chat. Friends of ours hosted a rehearsal dinner decorated with nearly one hundred hand carved jack-o'-lanterns brought by the guests. Rich closed the store down for the next day so all his long-time employees could attend the ceremony and reception. We had the best band in the region and I danced to every song.

For the first six years we were together, I was on a honeymoon.

Our oldest son, Richard, was born on May 11, 1983. Since everyone in town had known my husband when he was a child, he was known as Rich or Richey. To differentiate between the two, we used the baby's full name of Richard. Naming the first son after his father was part of the Irish naming patterns, so once the doctor announced we had a boy I never considered anything else. The name of Richard sounded grown up to our friends and Rich would joke, "My baby gets all the respect."

Two years later, our now toddler Richard asked us for a doll. His father was a little nervous about it. I read up on the subject and the experts said boys like babies, too. I bought him a small baby doll with a realistic face, hands, and feet. Its body was stuffed and soft. Richard would suck his thumb with the doll tucked under his arm. He was an early talker, already stringing sentences together at the age of two. He started to repeat a story he made up. "My doll's named Nate. I gonna have a brosser Nate."

"A brother? You want a brother, honey?"

"No. I having one. He Nate."

The third or fourth time he told me this story, I stopped having a glass of wine when I made dinner. When I missed my menstrual period, I went to the doctor right away. He took some blood and called the next day to tell me I was pregnant. We weren't even trying. The whole idea of another child was a bit of an adjustment. Richard continued to refer to the baby as Nate whenever he mentioned it. Then, his father Rich and I starting doing it too, laughing at the nickname for the growing fetus.

Toward the end of the pregnancy, Richard overheard one of my phone conversations. Belinda had called to ask me to remind her how far along I was. I told her about eight months and we continued chatting. Richard was sitting in his high chair in the kitchen having a snack of dry Cheerios. As usual, his little baby doll was under his arm. After I hung up, I noticed he was singing a song as he made the doll dance along the top of the chair's tray.

"Nate, he great, he just turned eight. Nate, he great, he just turned eight."

"Honey, I'm worried you will be disappointed if the baby turns out to be a girl."

For a moment, Richard looked up at me with the confident gaze of someone ten times his age. "He not."

My mouth dropped open. I knew his words were true. He picked up a Cheerio and popped it into his mouth with a chubby hand. "You see my mind, Mom?"

It gave me a chill and I tried to minimize the clairvoyance. "Well, I hope you are right. We haven't picked out a girl's name."

The baby was born on my ex-boyfriend Nathaniel's birthday. I'll be honest that it felt a little spooky. My husband, Rich, assured me he was fine with the name.

"Richard will have a fit if we don't name the kid Nathaniel. Besides, we both like the name. It's a little different without being weird. The Maddins have a Nathaniel on the family tree. Nathaniel Christian." So, the name was chosen. Nathaniel Christian Maddin.

Four years later, when my son, Richard, was seven, he

announced to me God was sending him a birthday present.

I asked him, "What do you mean, honey?"

"Another brother. He's going to be born on my birthday."

I knew better than to argue with him. The next day at work, I walked through the cafeteria on my way to my classroom. The sight of a bowl of mayonnaise sent me sprinting toward the nearest bathroom where I vomited violently. I called my doctor and begged him to do the blood test. He thought it might be too early to show a positive result. It wasn't. Rich was delighted by the news; I don't think I have ever seen him happier, although I was in a bit of a panic. I was already in over my head with a four-year-old and a seven-year-old and a full time job. The pregnancy was difficult.

I kept trying to explain to Richard that my due date wasn't close to his birthday.

"Honey, if the baby is born on your birthday, it will be two-and-a half weeks late. The doctors will never let that happen."

He would shrug and look up at me with his hazel brown eyes. "He's my present," he insisted.

Imagine our surprise when my due date came and went. The doctors did an ultrasound and said maybe they were wrong. Everything was progressing perfectly and they saw no reason to induce the baby. I finally went into labor the day before Richard's eighth birthday. I never even asked the doctor if the baby was a boy or a girl. We already assumed. Our youngest son, John, was born on the same day at the *same time* Richard had been born. Rich, Belinda, and Arlene, my mother-in-law, went and had Richard's birthday party without me. We invited all ten children in his second-grade class. He told them about his big present.

Rich and I were overwhelmed after the birth of our third son. John was born on May 11, and I was on maternity leave until the end of the summer. Rich began to talk to me about resigning from my job. "Look, in order for you to teach full-time, we will have to have full-time help. Financially it doesn't make sense. I know you want to stay home with the boys. Just do it. We'll make it work somehow."

It was the right decision for the boys and for me, but it put more pressure on Rich. When a big box grocery store moved in across the road from Maddin's Supermarket, his business dropped by a third, he worked longer hours to cut down on costs. When he came home at night, he was consistently worried and grouchy. To make matters worse, my good health did not return after the birth of my third son. I had one serious infection after another, a recurring fever, and night sweats, so I wasn't the easiest person to deal with either. When Rich made a comment about me being a hypochondriac, I was furious with him. The crushing weight of the everyday sent our marriage spiraling out of control.

Rich began to spend more time away from home volunteering and traveling with his friends to golf competitions. I was exhausted, but I would rise to the occasion when we were asked to go out. My mother-in-law, Arlene, was happy to help, and the young people at our local school took a class in babysitting that included CPR. I left my children with a clear conscious and savored those nights because it was a break in my monotonous routine.

At one fundraiser, I met a regional legend in the music business. He had a ten-piece country swing band that toured from Canada to Rhode Island. He had been watching me dance with my friends and, although I didn't know him, he spoke to me when I approached the bar for a glass of water.

"Will you marry me?"

I answered him tartly, "I get a lot of that."

He let out a deep-throated chuckle, "I bet you do." He held out his hand to me, and said, "I'm Eddie Cross."

"What are you doing here, Eddie? Are you a supporter of our Community Fund?"

"In a way. I'm a musician. I'm going to play the next set. Let me ask you a question, do you sing? You're a great dancer, I was wondering if you can sing, too."

Rich didn't take the matter seriously when I told him I was driving to Burlington to audition for the band, "Eddie and the Eldorados." I hadn't had the opportunity to perform in years. When Eddie offered me the chance to join the band as the "girl singer," I was delighted. Rich was angry.

"You're tired all the time. How are you going to go out and sing?"

"You have your activities! You are out three nights a week. You golf, ski, work out at the gym, and are on the Community Fund, the Chamber of Commerce, and Rotary. And you and your friends are leaving for a week to go to Orlando."

Rich decreed he didn't want me in a band, but I didn't consider the matter closed. He was busy packing for Florida where he and his golf buddies had rented two condos and cars. They were going to see how many golf courses they could play in seven days. Arlene had told me she would pitch in with the kids, but I was still anxious about being alone with the three of them and the house to take care of in the dead of winter. We heated our house with two Vermont Castings woodstoves and that alone was a big job. I had three children under the age of eight. How could I go out and shovel the walkways when it was hard to find a few minutes to take a shower?

While the guys were off on vacation, one of the other wives called me.

"Did you know they went to a strip club last night?" she asked. "Apparently, they were hammered."

My mind was made up on the spot. I told Eddie I would love to join the Eldorados and he sent me a tape of their music, which I immediately memorized. I went out the next day and bought myself a nice guitar. The practice schedule I put myself on was a whirling dervish of vocal exercises and musical scales on my instrument. I disciplined myself to learn the chord progression to one new song every single day while the baby napped. My perfect housekeeping relaxed and my dinners were sometimes more about convenience than culinary skills. It was fun, and the better I got, the more consumed I became.

Part of the Fifty-Two Percent–
1998

I rationalized my new obsession by saying, "If Rich could go out in the world and play, I can too." Beneath my resentment was the thought that maybe doing something I loved would make me feel better.

My band mates liked me, and although I was the only woman in the group, I quickly became one of the guys. It seemed to me that they laughed at everything I said. My boss, Eddie, said when I started playing with the Eldorados, I took off like a rocket. They encouraged me to write music and record. We worked three or four weekends a month during the spring and summer, and I looked forward to those Friday-to-Sunday trips. The band traveled together in a vintage mint green camper from the 1950s and we sang as we drove along.

Eddie and The Eldorados played at state fairs and conventions, never at a bar, although we did wind up in a few after our gigs were over. I loved it. Rich, on the other hand, made his disapproval known by not coming out to see any of the shows. When Eddie offered me the opportunity to co-write and record three tracks on his new album, my hobby became a commitment. If I accepted the deal, I was promising to continue the weekend touring to support the record. I had pages of lyrics and melodies ready to show him. I knew Rich was looking forward to the end of our touring season in November and he would be livid when he knew I had signed a contract for the following year.

We are both stubborn, my husband and I. I was thirty-nine years old at this point. That big 4-0 was closing in fast. I wanted this chance to perform before I was past my prime, and the opportunity to see how far I could take it. My fans were complimentary to the point that I felt embarrassed. There was always someone waiting to help me down off the stage.

"You are a goddess," a stranger would say. Or... "Where's your husband? If you were my wife I'd be here every night."

But the over-the-top comments happened even when I had a terrible night.

I quickly realized many people are tone-deaf. They don't hear the nuances that make great songs. Every member of the Eldorados was a much better musician than I was because they had played in bands since their teens. Even our drummer was a better guitar player than me. Still, I was having the time of my life, and they were happy I was with them. Those were heady times and I wouldn't have missed it for the world.

On our fifteenth anniversary, I wrote a card to Rich. I thanked him for the chance to get out and play music. His reply to me was stiff and carefully worded:

"I know you are really happy with the way things are, but I would be lying if I told you I feel the same way. It is something we are going to have to work out. When I try to talk to you about it, you say I am distracted with other things and other people, too. But really, I am doing it for the sake of our family."

I wondered just how Rich's golf trips were helping our family.

Two years later I was further annoyed that he couldn't put his feelings aside to celebrate our seventeenth anniversary. I had pictured us reminiscing about all our blessings over that time. Richard was fourteen, Nathaniel eleven, and John six. It became more important for us to be right than to find a reasonable compromise. We spent hours trying to convince each other about our respective points of view and more hours fuming.

I wanted to go to marriage counseling, but Rich, being a man of his time and place, wouldn't even consider it. I began to confide in my friends, many of who were amused by or interested in my music career. They advised me not to back down. The Eldorados provided male companionship, and, needing that, I allowed Rich and me to drift apart.

I begged him to come to a big show that was being televised, and, to my surprise, he did. When I walked off-stage, elated by my performance, he told me he didn't like my singing voice and drove away in his car. He may as well have punched me in the face.

Selected memories of the first Nathaniel, the boy who I grew up with, began to pollute my mind. He had always enjoyed my performances; in fact, he said they made him look good because he was dating someone as talented as me. His shortcomings were forgotten. What I chose to remember was that when we were young, we had always been able to talk things over. I also focused on the fact that we had the same sense of humor and enjoyed the fine details of a story. I could remember him saying, "Oh Patty, tell everybody what happened yesterday." His eyes blazed with pride as I recounted the facts, and he would seamlessly jump in when he wanted to add his own thoughts. We were a comedy team.

When Rich announced he was going on another guys-only trip to Orlando, all the heat of our marriage got turned around. The flame which had once burned white-hot shrunk into embers and it touched off a wildfire that raged out of control. We blamed each other for the discord in our home so, metaphorically, we burnt the place down.

We separated.

The divorce was contentious.

We fought about money and custody. We barely spoke in the years that immediately followed except for what was necessary to co-parent the children. Rich and I had joined the fifty-two percent of our generation whose families were casualties of divorce.

Have Yourself a Merry Little Christmas–2000

I opened a Christmas card from my ex-husband and a letter fell out and onto the floor.

December 10, 2000

Dear Patty,

I hope you and the boys have a wonderful Christmas. As usual, I will pick them up about eleven on Christmas to spend the rest of the day at my house. My mother is coming over that afternoon.

I was telling friends of mine recently that I had never been able to really move on since our divorce. Apparently, I say this often and they advised me to consider telling you. In hindsight, I think all of our problems could have been ironed out if we had just been willing to listen to each other. It seems like we fell into a classic midlife crisis, which is embarrassing to me now. I hate to think I failed at the most important relationship in my life- you.

Looking back, I don't know how we did it! Having three kids under the age of eight took over our lives for a long time.

Since I was out making all the money when the kids were little, I felt I deserved recreation, but I can see I took things too far. Now that the boys are nine, fourteen, and seventeen, it is so much easier to be with them and traveling together is a blast.

Believe me, I have dated a lot of women since we broke up, but the truth is no one else is as much fun as you are. You are the most beautiful woman I've ever known (to me, for my type). And you have a heart as big as the whole outdoors.

No matter what you do with this information, I want you to know you were a wonderful wife and I am grateful for the years we had together. And thank you for my sons and all you do to make them the young men they are.

Have yourself a merry little Christmas (I know that's your favorite Christmas song)!

Love,
Rich

I stood in my kitchen crying and then wrote back to him immediately.

December 10, 2000

Dear Rich,

Divorce seemed like a last chance to find myself. I realize now I was trying to make up for the childhood I never had. When I took the freedom to play music on the road, I felt like a rebellious teenager. Most of my life, making a living had been the most important thing. Working just for the paycheck can get pretty grueling. I sometimes wondered what I could have done with my life if my circumstances had been different. I had a wonderful time with the band, but I can also see I took it too far.

Since we spent so much time apart, I thought I might as well be divorced. It was so naïve. Once we broke up, I never had a free minute. My alarm was set for four-thirty in the morning and I didn't rest until after Richard came in and went to bed. Working a full-time teaching job wasn't making ends meet, so I started graduate school. I knew if I finished my Master's Degree I would get a big pay raise. There went my little music career out the window. There was no time for singing with three boys to raise and a thesis to write.

I, too, think we were hasty in ending our marriage. I am sorry for my part in the divorce.

Merry Christmas,
Patty

When Rich came to pick up the boys Christmas morning, he picked me up off the ground in a big bear hug. Later that night, he called me and asked what I wanted to do. We agreed we didn't want pressure on us as we explored the possibilities of seeing each other. And, we certainly didn't want to get the boys hopes up.

So, we started with clandestine lunches out of town progressing to dinner. Rich had purchased a weekend away at a silent auction to benefit one of his charities. We drove in separate cars to the Norwich Inn in southern Vermont. The secrecy of our time away heightened the fun. We only left our room to eat lunch and dinner. The feel of his skin against mine was a relief, as if I had been away from home for a long time and had finally found my way back.

Three years had passed since we moved into separate homes. Neither one of us had fallen in love with another. As I got to know Rich again, I realized how much he had changed. Why should another woman get the benefit of that?

The very next weekend, we were in an elevator in Burlington. The door opened and a woman got in with us. When the door shut we realized she was Rich's divorce attorney. None of us said a word. We rode three floors down and she strode out the second the doors opened.

Rich said, "Wow, that was weird."

We had been seeing each other for four months when I decided I ought to schedule my annual women's wellness physical. I had skipped doing it for a few years because I wasn't taking birth control and I was so busy.

We debated how to introduce the kids to the idea of us attempting reconciliation. But in the end, a single phone call exploded the lives we had and sent us all flying the same direction.

The Eye of the Storm–2001

"I was told to call on Tuesday for the results of my biopsies."

I had a forty-five minute break between teaching my 7th and 8th grade math classes, and had punched in the number of the doctor's office on a telephone in an office at our middle school.

"Hold on," the physician's assistant said, "I will transfer you."

After a very long wait, another woman got on the line and asked me to hold yet again while she transferred me. Again. It became obvious to me something was terribly wrong. There were numerous clicks as the time dragged on.

Finally, a third voice came on. "I'm sorry... it's *cancer* – in both breasts."

My ears began buzzing. The room tilted a little and my legs started to shake. I couldn't feel my teeth or fingers. It was clear to me I was in shock, and I knew when I hung up I would question whether I had actually heard this news correctly.

"Could you hold on one second?" I said. "I am going to put a friend on the line and I want you to tell her what you just told me."

I stuck my head out the door of the smaller side office into the central one where the main desk was. I called to the office manager, who I knew well. "Can you come in here for just a minute? It's important."

She put the receiver to her ear. Five seconds later she burst into tears.

"Okay. I'm leaving. I am going to the boys' school and tell them the news myself. Please just get someone to cover my classes for me," I said.

I don't remember her answering me as I ran out of the building to get into my car. My two oldest had the same guidance counselor, so I went straight to his office and told him my disturbing news.

"Could you get the boys out of class and let me tell them here?"

Afterward, my son Nathaniel wanted to go to church and Richard wanted to go on to practice and run. He went out to the track and ran hard and fast. I drove Nathaniel to St. Patrick's where he collapsed in the aisle in front of the altar crying and moaning, "Why?!!!!!" His fair skin color heightened to the extent that his ears and the rims of his eyes grew bright red. It was obvious to me that *I* had to be strong for him. I was a divorced mother, and my only option was to take control of this situation. I began to carefully observe the boys in the interest of future damage control.

My eldest son, Richard, was as stoic a boy as his brother was sensitive. He was already successful at long-distance cross-country and track. I had watched him over the years set goals and meet them. When he was twelve, he'd wanted to become a professional free skier, and he made it look easy. At fifteen, he decided to set his sights on a full financial package to an Ivy League school. He was recruited by several. Shortly after he had turned eighteen, he became an All-American athlete. Richard's method of coping with my diagnosis was to continue to excel. His father took him for the interviews and handled the negotiations of a full ride.

It had all begun in earnest the summer before, on July 1st. I was talking to my mother on the phone, and the call waiting started to click. I told Mom I had to take it.

When I answered, the voice said, "Hello, I am the head coach for Princeton University. We want your son."

I sunk down on a kitchen chair and held my chin in one of my hands. "I'm sorry, I don't understand."

"We are allowed to phone potential athletes starting on July 1st before their senior year. We want Richard to come run for Princeton."

I furrowed my brows. "But, we haven't applied yet," I said. "Is it that cut and dry? Can you just give him a place?"

"We know he has the SAT scores and the grades to qualify. They will give me ten spots next year. We want him to come down and check out the school as soon as possible. I plan to make him a written offer. He can sign a contract that day if he wants to."

"Good Lord!"

Something about the process offended me even though our family was going to benefit from it.

The coach knew I was taken aback. "Look," he said. "The better the school, the more money we have to give to students. If Princeton needs a flute player, we will take the best one as long as they qualify academically. *And* we will give them the money they need to come here."

It had taken me seven years to acquire my Bachelor's degree, and my son was being offered a free ride. I knew I should have been thrilled, yet instead I found the coach's certainty distasteful. My son, Richard, quite literally, ran with it.

My two older boys are, of course, completely different. Genetics determine the predisposition of a child. Then birth order has an impact and when a second sibling of the same sex is born, especially if they are only a few years apart, the second child will assess the roads already taken by the oldest and invariably choose a different path. As tough and driven as Richard was, my Nathaniel felt things deeply. "Mom, I feel like the world is crumbling apart around us."

The divorce had been hard on all three boys, but we had managed to create a system that worked for us. I was the center of their lives as I encouraged, cajoled, and acted as cheerleader to their accomplishments. With the frightening diagnosis after my biopsies, Nathaniel started having nightmares about me dying. I would rush into his room in the middle of the night and find him screaming; his pajamas saturated with a cold sweat.

Our youngest, John, was suddenly terrified of everything. His mother's household, which usually ran like clockwork, was suddenly chaotic and it made him insecure. During my cancer treatments, he began to comfort himself with food. I didn't have the energy or the heart to stop him. Our next-door neighbor had an attached barn, similar to most of the houses in the neighborhood. In it, against the wall closest to the house, was an old white chest freezer. Both adults in the household worked for the ice cream company, Ben and Jerry's. Part of the employees' remuneration was ice cream products. John was their son's closest friend. He was told to take home all the ice cream he wanted... which he did. He gained weight almost as dramatically as I lost it.

We didn't have a chance to adjust to the fact I had cancer. The four of us muddled through the first three surgeries after which I started chemotherapy. I was delivered home from each hospital visit a diminished version of my former self, an evanescent shadow of the mother they once knew. Rich was often there with us, but we maintained separate houses since he had a business to run in Greenfield. My women friends took me to treatments and made dinners. There was a strong possibility I wouldn't live five more years. Sex was no longer a factor. The question of formal reconciliation moved far down on the priority list. After each chemo treatment, Rich helped me get to the bathroom in the middle of the night. Between the waves of nausea, he fell asleep on my bed. At first, he slept above the covers so the boys wouldn't misinterpret his intentions; however, as the months dragged on, he just got in next to me. I could tell they felt safer having him around when he could be there and I was grateful for his solid presence.

Rich and I decided to ask for individual counseling for each of our children after ten-year-old John asked us, "You're not going to *die,* are you, Mom?"

I was just becoming aware by this time that I would be going down a long, long road to recovery. Or death. I couldn't begin my journey by lying to him, even if he was only ten years old. I said, "We don't know, honey."

It took such fortitude to force the words from my mouth, especially since my typical response to crises was, "Of course it will all be fine."

But what if it wasn't fine? I thought. His mother would die, leaving him feeling betrayed. Trust me when I say it was between a rock and a hard place, being honest with a ten-year-old.

Although I had sought professional help in the pros and cons of breaking terrifying news to a little boy, no one knew how to advise me. They said there was literature and studies out there about helping cancer patients through their complicated feelings, but nothing had been written for families. I was told all the research money was spent on learning how to keep patients alive. Fair enough.

John lost a year's worth of memories while I was ill. When he was sixteen, he asked to go into therapy to try to recall it, but after a few months, he gave up.

"Maybe you aren't meant to remember," I advised him. "The human brain, and God, has a way of sparing us from some horrible things."

My sons and I were most comfortable when domestic life moved forward mimicking our old day-to-day routine. Although I had no desire to shop and cook, I did it anyway. We were a family who sat down to dinner every evening at our large, round oak table. As much as my nausea allowed for it, we continued the home-cooked meals with fresh fruit as an appetizer, a main course, side dish, and always two vegetables. Nothing in my life had given me a greater sense of satisfaction than putting out steaming bowls of food for my children. As I cleaned up the kitchen, they would start their homework.

Later at night, we sat together on the L-shaped couch in the living room with a large square padded footrest in front of us, ready to watch a movie. These were our most peaceful times. We each had a favorite pillow and we would snuggle up together under a California king-size down comforter. The boys loved my special popcorn, made with a variety of spices, Vermont butter, and Tunisian olive oil. Finally settled down, they would start to argue about which film to select.

On one of those evenings, for obvious reasons, Richard wanted the television film about the famous runner Steve

Prefontaine titled *Without Limits.* We owned three different copies of it. Nathaniel, who would later become a successful director, begged for a science fiction classic. John was thrilled to watch anything remotely grown up. Richard exerted his big brother advantage and won out. I had my arms wrapped around each of the two younger boys during the film. We all knew it by heart because Richard often fought hard to see it again.

He would describe Prefontaine with wonder in his voice. "Now *he* had the mindset of a champion."

The other boys groaned at the comment, yet I noticed they didn't take their eyes off the screen. At age eighteen, Richard crawled in closer to attach himself to us. We were all in this moment safe, under a puffy blanket, contentedly joined at the hip.

September 2001

I was flat on my back having targeted chemicals pumped into my heart when the second plane hit the second tower of the World Trade Center in Manhattan. The hospital had suspended a small TV above the table to help patients pass the endless hours of *drip, drip, drip.* I was adjoined to the device administering the chemotherapy by a port embedded in my chest just below my collarbone. A surgeon had snaked its connecting tube under my skin and up my neck. Another incision was made so it could be crammed down my jugular vein. I lay there helpless, with no choice but to watch every second of the news for six long hours.

When I finally arrived at home late that afternoon, John in tow, we walked into the kitchen door from the side yard. Every hair on my body immediately stood on end. Most of the windows in the house were open to the Indian summer day. As we had stepped into the house, an abrupt gust of wind blew every curtain and shade up so that they were perpendicular to the wall and suspended in midair. What we couldn't wrap our minds around was how this was happening simultaneously from all four directions. All the window coverings remained hovering upended as John and I ran out the door and into the middle of the street. We desperately wanted to feel the presence of another human being. We stood there, holding hands and looking around, our eyes wild with fear.

Our elderly neighbor Norma, who was kneeling in her garden when she saw us, jumped to her feet in alarm. She called to us as she ran closer, "What on earth is going on? You two are half scared to death."

She put her arms around both of us and turned from my face to John's and back again.

I said, "I thi... thi... think someone is in the house." This was the best I could do in describing what had just happened.

Without a second's hesitation, Norma's expression of concern changed to one of fury. "We'll just see about that. This is not going to happen in my neighborhood. Not here in Vermont. I won't have it!" She continued to rave as she marched to my side door.

John and I meekly followed her into the house, still holding hands.

Norma searched every room, yelling the entire time at the invisible invader. I heard her climbing the front stairs "We are not going to live in fear. No sir. If I have to kill you with my bare hands, I will do it. I'm not afraid of you. I'm an old woman. You can try to hurt me and I won't think twice about it. Just try it! I dare you!"

After a few minutes, she came down the old steep back stairs and into the kitchen where John and I stood still huddled together. She stared at me with pity. "Patty, I don't think so, honey. There's no one in here. It's all safe. Look, you have been really sick. You have all been through a lot and..."

Norma was cut off when my kitchen telephone rang. I picked up and my sister Bernadette said our mother had died twenty minutes ago. When I told John and Norma, we exchanged glances.

Norma stated what we all were thinking. "I guess she just came to say goodbye to you."

As soon as it could be arranged, I would have to travel to New York to my mother's funeral and into the eye of the storm of 9/11. Richard could not have his course work and running disrupted. John had already been traumatized by recent events. His father said he would take care of him. It was decided Nathaniel would go with me and we flew to New York City.

I was so weak that Nathaniel had to push me in a wheelchair. For some reason, the security people gave me extra scrutiny. I was hairless and twenty-two percent of my body weight had vaporized with the first surgeries and chemo treatments. I had been a healthy 125 pounds at the start, and was now a walking skeleton at ninety-nine pounds. The chemo port leading to my heart jutted out from under my visible collarbone. Pain was my presenting reality. I sat crumpled in the wheelchair. My limbs involuntarily thrashed this way and that seeking a comfortable position. My hips no longer lay square on a seat; the right one was higher, which caused agony in my back. I clasped my hands in front of me, wringing the spasms out of my fingers. What were the security people looking for? I wondered. The search of my belongings was holding up the already long line into the airport. In the end, they took a set of tweezers from my carry-on, and signaled Nathaniel to roll me through.

Inside the airport, there were more uniformed officials than travelers. They were wearing black clothing with bold white letters indicating which area of law enforcement they represented — F.B.I., C.I.A., F.A.A. Police with search dogs sniffed all around. Everything was chaotic, yet it was probably the safest I have ever been in my life. No crimes would occur here today. Little did I know in that moment, my son, the same boy who pushed my chair and tenderly patted my bald head, carried a packet of marijuana in his shoe. He walked boldly past the TSA bomb-sniffing dogs and found my brother Liam waiting for us. Liam's children would shyly tell me about the pot, not wanting to tattle on their cousin. Nathaniel said he used it to calm his anxiety and night terrors.

My mother's service was a blur. Death in this case meant a lot of turmoil and very little sleep. When I found some pain pills in Mom's medicine cabinet, I gladly took them. They were like a gift from God. Apparently, I sang Ave Maria in Latin at the service, but I have no memory of it. What must I have sounded like? I could barely speak above a whisper.

Clearly, my father was devastated. The story he told was my mother had gotten up in the middle of the night to use the bathroom. Advanced osteoporosis had caused multiple fractures of her ribs and vertebrae and she had been on morphine for years. Although we knew she was suffering, we also realized her lifestyle made the problem worse over time. She spent most of her time in bed although the doctors advised her that exercise might curb the disease.

It was early morning when she came out of the bathroom and it was still dark. The narcotics left her in a perpetual state of confusion; she turned to her right instead of the left, which led back to the bedroom. She may have thought she was heading across the threshold of her door as she stepped off the top step of a flight of stairs. She tumbled down and broke a leg in three places, her pelvis, and both arms. My father doesn't know how long she lay at the bottom on the landing because he was sound asleep and didn't hear anything. When he awakened, it was light outside and he saw her immediately when he went downstairs to make coffee. Although an ambulance was called and she was brought to a trauma center, my mother only lived three more hours.

Daddy wandered around the reception from group to group and told everyone my mother had been his best friend. He said she was the only real friend he ever had. It made me furious because he had been cruel to her. He brutally criticized her on a daily basis, and one-by-one, she gave up trying to do the things she enjoyed. By the end, she was nearly a recluse.

I returned home to my house in Waterbury, exhausted. Nathaniel and I entered the kitchen, and still in my coat, with my handbag on my shoulder, I leaned down and hit play on the answering machine. I moved a pad of paper over in order to write down names and numbers from the messages when Liam's voice came on.

"Dad just died," he managed to get out just before his voice broke.

Instead of feeling grief in that moment, I was panicked about the cost of getting my boys and me down to New Jersey. I was living so close to the edge financially I felt I could never relax. I hadn't worked in months, and had gone through my reserve fund, both financially and health-wise. I lay down on the carpet and shook.

We flew in to Newark and stayed for a week. My four siblings were there, along with their spouses and families. Liam and his wife had a six-bedroom house, and the neighbor across the street offered her home as additional space. She emphasized it was not an inconvenience because she was going out of town, and had a maid who would clean when we were gone. It felt like a stroke of genius that my sister-in-law had made sure we all stayed in close proximity to each other. The cousins played. Various aunts and uncles were constantly preparing meals. My four siblings and I went to the funeral home to be with our father's body. He had died from an aortic aneurism that had ruptured. His face was terribly bloated which I assumed was the result of having bled out into his chest cavity. I couldn't bear to look at his distorted remains.

We hadn't spent extended time together as brothers and sisters in years. All the moving around had geographically separated us and our parents had not fostered familial connection. When we occasionally saw each other, we were a somber reminder of the pain we had suffered as children. At various points, we had each rebelled against and then reunited with our parents. But the timing wasn't ever the same for the five of us, so we remained somewhat alienated.

My father was at once harsh and charming, brilliant and abusive. He was the president of a big company who could also change the oil on the family car. He had a wood shop where he built furniture. He wrote short stories and never missed Mass on Sunday. We were all muddled about our feelings for him, which made our grief more convoluted. Luckily, we had a defense mechanism. The razor wit for which my family was known was out in full force. Humor could cut through our grief just when it became unbearable.

My two brothers had been stand-up comedians in their twenties, yet they were no match for my youngest sister, Bernadette. We planned the funeral with the priest, the musicians, and the grandchildren who would be doing readings. The priest would later declare, as inappropriate as it was to say, he had never had more fun planning a funeral.

My youngest sibling, Malachy, was charged to deliver the eulogy. The same baby brother I had cared for when I was John's age. With the high coloring of the black Irish, Malachy was a born artist and writer. We listened to each new draft. His cheeks would flush a brighter shade of magenta, and he would remove a cloth handkerchief from his pocket, calmly unfold it, wrap it across his eyes, and proceed to burst into tears.

It was painful for me to see. I couldn't ever stand to see my younger siblings suffer. I had always hoped I spared them some of the misery of our childhood, and therefore, some of the wounds. Yet, when I was left in Milwaukee, Mackey was only nine. I was sure I didn't know half of what had happened to the children after they moved.

Our father had been a war hero in the Pacific Theater during World War II. He served on a light cruiser called the *USS Santa Fe*, but like many veterans, my father rarely spoke about it.

"The real heroes didn't make it back," he would say.

We all owned a copy of the book *Lucky Lady*, "an account of life aboard that ship, told from the point of view of the sailors who were defending themselves from kamikaze attacks" and it helped us fill in the facts. Dad had applied to the Marines asking for an assignment as a military journalist, but he wound up on deck as a machine gunner. Apparently, the Marine Corps could not ignore the fact that my father was an award-winning marksman. My grandfather had been a police officer in New Jersey and had taken him to the firing range where he had been become a state champion in target shooting. Family lore had it that my father could have gone on to compete in the Olympics if he'd had the money, but back then, there was little support for amateur sports.

On March 19, 1945, a Japanese bomber dropped two huge bombs on another ship, *The USS Franklin*. Almost three thousand American seamen and aviators were put in serious danger. While the *Franklin* was on fire and nearly capsized, the *USS Santa Fe*, nicknamed the *Lucky Lady*, sailed up alongside. Its crew attempted the most audacious rescue in U.S. naval history.

My father once described to us what it was like to watch a man, his closest friend, fall overboard and be devoured by sharks. His tour of duty had culminated at the decimated city of Nagasaki. In another unguarded moment, he talked about the ground being so hot from the atomic blast that the bottom of his boots melted when he stepped ashore.

Dad returned from the war, attended Syracuse University on the G.I. Bill and graduated with a degree in engineering. With his history as a war hero, J. Edgar Hoover hired him almost immediately as a special agent for the Federal Bureau of Investigation.

We arranged with the Marine Corps to provide an honor guard for Dad's funeral. Malachy had come up with a wonderful eulogy, and I knew he would execute it well. The overwhelming grief continued in waves. Bernadette broke down several times, crying, "Now we are orphans. We are orphans!"

When one of us fell apart, the rest were there to lean on.

Comic relief was our coping mechanism. One of my brothers said, "Do you remember when Mom died and she was being cremated? Daddy was obsessed with her hip replacement. He kept asking us what we thought they would do with the metal hip."

Gales of laughter followed.

"Remember when he had the heart attack?" Malachy asked us. "He was legally dead for seven minutes before they revived him. When we got to see him in intensive care, we commented about how tired he seemed, and he said, in all earnestness, 'I don't know why. I didn't do anything all day.'"

We roared with laughter until the tears started again. People who knew our father often said he was larger than life. My brothers were staggered by the fact that he had not, in fact, been immortal. Dad had always claimed, "I'm too mean to die." Yet, he'd gone at the relatively young age of seventy-six.

Forty years before, when we still lived in the old neighborhood, he built us a treasure chest and filled it with "gold" doubloons, then buried it in our yard and drew a map for us to find it. It was important to him we believed in the authenticity of the map, and Mom said he spent hours staining it with brewed Lipton's tea. But, we were too young to read a map. He had to walk us through the whole process. We weren't strong enough yet to use the shovel required to dig down three feet into the earth. He finally relented, dug the treasure chest out himself, and pulled it to the surface. We were disappointed by the contents. The doubloons weren't coins at all. They were just brassy circles cut out of sheet metal.

I think back on the effort he put into that project and how he made the chest in secret and buried it in the black of night. Yet, he was a man who didn't understand his own children or their capabilities. He wasn't around enough to know. During those years, he worked long hours investigating for the FBI and three nights a week he took graduate courses at Columbia University. Some weekend days, he would fall asleep on the family room floor. In his slumber, he no longer intimidated us, and, in fact, we would crawl on top of him while he snored.

On the day my father died, he had gone for a ten-mile run. He would joke with his five children about the things he wanted to do in his spare time. The thing was, he never left any time to spare. It was true; he had a large presence until the day his light went out. It was the perfect way for him to die, for he never experienced a day being an old man. While my mother had been fragile for years, we fully expected my father to live to be one hundred.

After Mom passed away, Nathaniel and I stayed with my father for a few days. Late one night he told me, "I have many regrets about my life, especially the way I treated you kids. Did you know I went to a therapist a few years back?" I was shocked. "I'm sorry I hit you and I'm sorry you had to work so damn hard just to get by. I'm not going to make excuses. I'm sure I'm the reason you had a hard time in the romance department, too. I know now I was supposed to show you how lovable you are. And you are. Patty, I just hope it's not too late, can you forgive me?" He held my hand and tears were streaming down my face.

It took all my will not to start blubbering because I didn't want this precious moment to end.

"How about I come up to Vermont and help out with the boys until you are done with chemotherapy?

I welcomed the chance to get to know him again as an adult, but I was worried, too. "Dad, you can't hit John, he's only ten. And, Nathaniel's feelings are easily hurt. You will have to watch what you say to him." I held my breath as I waited for him to respond. I appreciated that he wanted to pack up and head north to help me. To get back to my home in Vermont and find out that he died, felt like a crime had been perpetrated on me.

Every night during the week of my father's funeral, the entire extended family pretended to go to bed at a reasonable hour. None of us had been sleeping well even though it was important when you were living with grief. We didn't want to wind up getting sick on top of everything that had happened. Also, my baldness was a constant reminder that due to the kind of chemotherapy the doctors had prescribed for me, damage had been done to my heart. They had instructed me to rest, heal, and avoid stress.

Since my family never accepted that I was divorced from Rich, we didn't have to explain that we were back together. We were given a bedroom on the second story of the house across the street from my brother where streetlights shone into our room. The bed I slept in was next to a window and through it, I could see down into my brother's living room. Rich snored solidly beside me. I was so jealous that he could sleep. I tossed and turned until I saw a movement across the street. I felt around on the floor and found my robe then tiptoed down the stairs and out the front door, closing it quietly behind me. Barefoot, I ran across the cool September pavement. Only one or two stones slowed my stride.

Liam sat on the couch in his living room with a glass in his hand. He pointed to it without saying a word, and I nodded yes. He poured a scotch for me and I settled into an upholstered chair. Before long Malachy showed up and found a spot. Next, Bernadette and Siobhan crept in. This became our nightly routine. While our spouses slept, we would gather. We might tell a story about Mom or Dad and simply cry. Or we told funny stories that had nothing to do with them at all. Sometimes we argued about a memory because, of course, we had perceived the same event differently. During these times, at least one of us would sob.

"They were horrible parents, yet I would give anything for five more minutes with them," Siobhan said.

We sat in a circle throwing out our memories toward the center of it. Bernadette recalled, "For years, I wore my terrible childhood like a badge of honor. I would tell people mine was the worst, but it can't be true. Right now, all I can remember are good times. Or at least hilarious times."

Siobhan added, "Remember when we moved to Wisconsin? We didn't know anyone yet and there was a big snowstorm and we wanted to go sledding? Behind the new house was a private school with a great hill, but we had to climb a high chain link fence. It was pitch dark out and we were all determined to get over it and sled. We knew Mom could never make it, so we held her high over our heads and passed her like she was crowd surfing. I have never heard anyone laugh as hard as she did that night. It might have been the best time we ever had together."

I brought up my most treasured memory although it made my heart ache to say it. "On Sundays they made a standing rib roast. Daddy had a fire in the fireplace. He would only use fruitwood. It had to be from a cherry or an apple tree. Sometimes he would buy maple. It was so fragrant. And, Mom set the most beautiful table. She could have been a designer; her eye for detail was always way ahead of the time. We would play Monopoly and Daddy put on his old jazz records."

We were silent for a few seconds before Liam spoke. "Yeah, it was the only day of the week he was allowed to play music. Mom always said music in the house made her nervous. It's weird because she took us to Broadway, ballet, opera, concerts, and musicals, but she didn't like music in the house."

"Mom was reading a novel years ago. She looked up and asked Dad if he realized how many time zones there were across the USSR. In a flash, he said eleven. Mom was so surprised he knew that, but really, it seemed like he knew everything," Malachy said.

He went on, "When I started kindergarten, the teacher sent a note home with a list of materials we were to bring the next day. I was so embarrassed as the days dragged on because I didn't have what I needed. I was the only kid without the stuff. Finally, I got mad at Mom and she stormed out and left me alone in the house for a long time. I was terrified she had abandoned us and it was my fault. Eventually, she came back and threw all my school supplies at me. I mean, jeez, I was five."

I told them, "Mom was an upwardly mobile member of the cocktail generation. Her ultimate dream was to live in the big city. She didn't advertise the fact she was born in Kansas and raised in farm country. However, every once in a while, she would release her inner twang for comedic effect. I can remember a time when Mom wondered what we were all up to. She called up the stairs. 'Where are you kids? It's so quiet you could hear a rat peeing on cotton.'"

You knew she was going to say something hilarious if she put her hands on her hips and paused. In 1971, we were filled with teenage angst. Nathaniel, Belinda, and I were at the kitchen table discussing philosophy and the possibilities of our purpose here on earth. Mom turned from the stove and said, "Don't take it all so seriously. No matter what you kids think you are going to do, in the end, you won't make it out alive." She removed her hands from her hips and wiped them on a dishtowel masking her contentment over her perfect timing. Mom always knew exactly how to land a joke.

The week with my siblings went by in a flash.

Between my physical pain, fatigue, and the grief, it was hard for me to imagine standing up, let alone organizing my family and driving back home to Vermont. I honestly thought my life was over. I believed in those moments I would forever stay in the comfortable chair because I would never have the will to get out of it.

"So, this is what it feels like," I thought, "to give up entirely."

Belinda had come for the funeral and stayed. She and Rich both were a great help with the fourteen grandchildren who ranged in age from two to twenty. She placed herself squarely in the middle of them and played non-stop. She had a gift with children, no matter the age. She could equally calm the babies or get a sullen teenager to confide in her. They all enjoyed her. Rich cooked pancakes for the kids on the big griddle in my brother's kitchen. He served these on paper plates because "sometimes you just have to use disposable."

I must have dozed off for a few hours in my chair the last day we were there. My brothers and sisters were all passed out around the living room with me. Rich came in and shoved a pancake wrapped in a napkin in my hand. I took a bite. He had rolled it so it looked like an ice cream cone and inside were fresh blueberries and raspberries. He brought with him some Vermont products from his store. I could taste homemade butter and real Vermont maple syrup on the pancake. It may be the most delicious thing I had ever eaten in my entire life.

When we finally went home, we set about resuming something akin to what used to be our lives. My oldest son had chosen Cornell University, but his academic scholarship was contingent on maintaining a "B" average. He had to make up time for training with the cross-country team. None of the professors cut him any slack just because he was a competitive athlete, nor were they overly impressed by the death of a grandparent. His father took him back to college. God love Rich, my ex-husband. It wasn't discussed; he just did it.

10–17–2001 in Vermont

I catch sight of myself in the mirror above my son's dresser. The reflection stops me dead still. I know the woman in the mirror and I am not happy about her. My hand rises to the side of my bald head and I stroke it gently. I have no eyebrows or eyelashes. The skin I caress seems grey and fragile, like dried out parchment. It is smooth though, like the skin of a child. I massage the ridges where my eyebrows used to be, and then move my hand up, over the top of my head. For a moment, I hold on to the back of my neck. A thin sound of anguish escapes me. After a few minutes, I manage to pull myself together.

I had put the bathroom scale away in the attic of the barn. It's best not to weigh myself anymore. I have decided if I live through this, I will never step on a scale again. I try to eat, I really do, but I have become so skinny my family is frightened for me. Rich brought over a case of liquid meals that old people drink for nutrition. He hopes that will put some pounds on me. I resolve to drink one when I go downstairs.

The front of my shirt hangs straight down my torso. There are no mounds except for a plastic disk that was shoved into the two-inch gash in the skin of my chest. It is directly above the spot where my left breast used to be. It's called a Mediport, one of many new "medical-ese" terms I have learned. I secretly refer to the surgeon who inserted it as Dr. Mediport.

There is an almost audible throb from the stitches on either side of it. The pain follows the tube snaked up toward my neck. They left a few stitches on my throat, too, and that is what bothers me the most. I was told about the one-inch long scar on my chest, but no one bothered to mention my throat. You can't cover your

150

throat with clothing and it makes me feel even more conspicuous out in public.

I had a disagreement with Dr. Mediport when he decided to perform this surgery only weeks after the bilateral mastectomies in Boston. The pain overall was still horrible and I couldn't imagine adding more to my suffering. The plan was to have the Mediport surgery in order to start chemotherapy the next day. The *next* day! He was further delighted to inform me I could have this "procedure" without pain medication. A nervous laugh popped out of me because I was certain he was joking.

He appeared to be offended, and then raised his chin, which gave him a superior expression, "Most people do just fine with Tylenol or Advil."

When he left the examining area, I whispered to the nurse, "Would you do this without taking home pain pills?" Afraid of being overheard she remained mute, but held my gaze, bugged her eyes out, and waved her head back and forth in an exaggerated "Nooo. Nooo. Nooo."

The first lesson I had learned about catastrophic illness is some of the nurses will tell you the truth.

Dr. Mediport had a relatively new practice for a relatively new procedure in rural Vermont. I was already discovering that medical folks are in a big business where lots of money is made. They have a product to sell to the patient and to the insurance company, who they hope will pay for many more procedures. They have their sales pitch and their buzzwords.

I was naïve when I was diagnosed. Because narcotics are controversial, pain management requires a lot of overseeing, which takes staff time away from more profitable ventures. Consequently, doctors would rather avoid prescribing pain medication. As a rule, I found that they tend to understate the agony you are about to endure. Most of them have not lived through the experience and can afford to be judgmental.

A middle-aged male surgeon, for example, had a few months earlier tried to convince me a mastectomy didn't really hurt. "You might be sore, but that's about it."

Imagine, if you will, my shock when I awoke in my hospital room.

The surgery to insert a Mediport was presented to me as a fact, not an option. I didn't even know I could have started the chemo in my arms. If the veins can't tolerate it, then you can have the port inserted. As a result, I ultimately ended up with a double set of scars two inches long above my left mastectomy. One incision to insert the port and one to remove it. Yet, they told me *one* scar, one inch long.

As I continued staring into the mirror in Richard's room, I wondered what happened to patients who couldn't tolerate the pain, yet only had Advil or Tylenol on hand. Do they go to the emergency room? Luckily, I still had some synthetic morphine left over from the mastectomies. The pain across my chest and down my right arm had been unbearable from the moment I came to in the recovery room. So much for the doctor's assertion that I might be "sore."

I asked the nurse at Massachusetts General Hospital, "Why does my arm hurt so much?"

She leaned down and whispered, "A lot of people say that."

I whispered back, "How long does it last?"

She shrugged and looked around to make sure no one was listening, but wouldn't answer me.

The morning after the surgery, Belinda occupied the chair beside my bed. I lay under a starchy white sheet and a very thin white blanket. She had moved the green plastic reclining chair as close to my head as she could get it, and sat there entertaining me. Between the chair and the bed was a small steel cabinet table where Belinda had placed a stack of books and magazines. She was reading aloud from *To Kill a Mockingbird*, my favorite book of all time. When she asked me which section I wanted to hear, I had replied, "the part about the rabid dog."

As Belinda recited, I would often interrupt with comments. Progress was slow because we discussed the word choices of the author. The images alone were worth talking about as they reminded us of shared memories from our childhood. Sometimes, the morphine would have me drift away, but I didn't want to sleep all day and then be up all night. Belinda played games to keep me awake. She peeked over the top of the book to get my attention. She would make a face as she slowly lowered the book. Her eyes bulged and then she revealed her lips sucked into a fish face. When she was sure she had my attention, her lips moved up and down to complete the fish-like movement. We were both laughing when the nurse walked in with a syringe. I was told I was being given additional pain medication to prepare me for an exam.

Twenty minutes later, a young male doctor walked in and announced he wanted to inspect my chest. I don't know why Belinda and I felt compelled to comply. In my defense, I need to point out I am a second-generation American, an Irish-Catholic girl from New Jersey. I was born on *St. Patrick's* Day for Christ's sake. Believe me when I say I was raised to do what I was told, to offer my sufferings up to God, and keep quiet about them. I had watched talk shows and read self-help books and had tried to change as the world did between 1955 and 2001, but in vulnerable moments, I am a little girl. I go along and try not to cause any trouble.

Even though Belinda had stayed by my side all night, I didn't want her or anyone else to see my mangled body. I already had a plan for coping with my disfigurement and it was called *denial*. I would wait until the reconstructive surgery was done before I looked too closely at my chest. Make no mistake about it; *denial* has been a key strategy in moving through the most difficult times of my life.

I assumed the young doctor had to remove the bandages because he said so. I laid passively on the bed as he went to work.

He looked intensely into Belinda's eyes and asked her, "Would *you* like to see?"

She nodded.

She said later she didn't want to send the message to me that I was in any way hideously changed by the mastectomies. I think it's because the doctor was as handsome as a Ken doll.

My bed was a high-tech mechanical table that kept my legs in constant motion to prevent blood clots from forming. I still don't understand why breast surgery would cause blood clots in my legs, but I was told it could happen. One leg would bend and then be released in a wave-like motion as the other leg followed. The table emitted a continuous hydraulic hissing sound of raspy inhales and exhales. Right leg bends as Darth Vader inhales, lays out straight as he exhales, left leg inhales, left leg exhales, raspy Darth in, Darth out, on and on all night long. Belinda hadn't slept at all while sitting upright in the chair listening to the rhythm.

I blame her exhaustion for a breach of protection and for allowing Dr. Paul to carry on with his self-important attitude. Typically, she would cut a man like him down to size. It is one of the qualities men love about her; they like to be put in their place.

Dr. Paul wanted us to believe that *he* had performed the surgery, although we knew my surgeon was a woman named Dr. Hall. Perhaps he had assisted her in the operating room? What he made clear now was he wanted to show off his handiwork. *And* he wanted to flirt with Belinda.

Paul, the pretend surgeon, started to snip at the outside layer of gauze wrapped around my chest. In my head, time slowed down and a horror movie musical score began to play.

"No!" I said in a thick and suddenly very drugged voice. "No! I don't want to do this!"

Whatever the nurse had given to me had hit hard. When I tried to stop him from removing the many layers of bandages, I realized I couldn't raise my arms. (I later learned the nerves were damaged.) Women instinctually cross-cover their breasts when they feel threatened. My brain was sending the signal out, but my arms were not responding. I lifted my head and stared down at my delinquent hands.

The bed continued the alternate waving motion, which held me down flat on my back. Dr. Paul continued briskly cutting through the layers of gauze and laying them aside. He never once looked at me, nor did he listen to me, as his attention was on Belinda. He gave her a big, white, healthy-toothed smile. At one point, he actually batted his surprisingly long eyelashes at her. All of this occurred as I desperately worked to get the message to him that to expose me now in my helpless state felt like torture.

I made a final and frantic attempt to keep Belinda from seeing the incisions. In a panic, and confused, I put all my effort into sitting up and rolling away from the doctor's touch. With a final surge of frantic spastic energy, I wound up sitting perfectly tall and straight, so much so that my back was arched. At this exact second, I heard Dr. Paul cut what was left of the gauze with a snap. My chest was thrust up and out as though I were posing for a photograph. I was abruptly and completely naked from the waist up.

I stared at Belinda, my friend who I have always described as dramatically attractive. The camera loves her and people remember her because of it. She inhaled so sharply that her nostrils were sucked in making her nose a perfectly straight line. I was fascinated by the fact she wasn't breathing at all. Her light-brown eyes grew huge as she stared at my chest. I willed her to exhale, but it didn't work. Instead, Belinda fainted forward out of the chair and fell to the floor with a smacking sound.

Paul the *doctor* didn't lift a finger to help the poor woman. He was disgusted with her lack of appreciation for his handiwork, and, I think, *very* disappointed. It was obvious the sight had traumatized her. Did this man not possess any empathy at all? Hadn't he been taught compassion in medical school? *My* feelings about what was happening were irrelevant. I was on a morphine drip, and with the additional dose, was now unable to put an effective sentence together anyway.

A nurse walked in and took in the entire scene in one sweeping glance. She dismissed the doctor with a few harsh words. He gathered up his things and scurried out the door like a schoolboy caught being naughty. The nurse revived Belinda and showed her to a bed in a private room, where she slept for a long time. When she finally woke up, she rode the elevator down to the lobby and had a cigarette. More than one actually.

She disappeared and I didn't see her again for a month.
This experience taught me three important things:

1. The people who loved me would give what they had during this long treatment process; they also needed a break from the intensity.
2. I couldn't predict how anybody would react or act during these dark days.
3. In the medical field, just like the rest of the world, there are many idiots with their own agendas.

Six weeks later and back in Vermont, I sat listening as Dr. Mediport insisted that *most* people could have a Mediport inserted with the local anesthesia used by dentists, which he shoots into your chest and neck. It didn't take me long to conclude that he makes the same amount of money if his patient is wide-awake. However, he can perform more of these operations in his own office where he doesn't have to wait for space in an operating room at the hospital. *Most* people tolerate it. But who are *most* people? That could be fifty-one percent. What happens to the other almost half? Do they embarrass themselves by screaming? Jumping off the table? Spitting in the doctors face?

This is my biggest fear; really, it looms larger than my own death. I am terrified of completely losing my mind and humiliating myself. I became more anxious with each new surgery and procedure. I also started having a recurring nightmare where I am prone below a bright white light while blurred human shapes hovered over me. It reminded me of the alien abduction flashbacks I've read about.

I managed to outwit Dr. Mediport, though. I insisted on some sedation for the operation and I asked for a nurse to hold my hand. He was clearly annoyed with me for demanding anesthesia. He talked to the anesthesiologist throughout the surgery, ignoring me. I had been given a calming drug, but I could still hear everything being said.

Dr. Mediport spent what I thought was an inordinate amount of time describing his new girlfriend's breasts to the other doctor.

"That's interesting," I said. "Because I just lost both of mine."

I felt the room grow tense. Both doctors became quiet. The nurse squeezed my hand and shifted her eyes to the floor to hide her smile. Her entire body, including the hand holding mine, shook as she silently laughed. Despite the drug I had been given, I had a huge satisfied grin on my face.

Recalling that moment in the doctor's office, I started to chuckle. Almost five minutes had passed since I entered my son's room and stood before his mirror. It turned into full laughter. I snorted. I guffawed. I was hysterical. I had to put my hands on the chest of drawers to hold myself up. Tears formed. I tried to stop, but when I straightened up and wiped the tears away, I caught sight of myself again, and then I started to laugh all over again. I was hooting when I heard a voice.

Belinda called up from the bottom of the stairs. "What are you doing up there?"

"Losing my *mind* on top of everything else."

"Join the club. Can I come up?" She entered the room. "Are you packing up Richard's stuff?"

"Richard told John he could sleep in his room now. He says he'll only be home for a few days at a time during school break because he has to train. He's is trying to soften the blow of his leaving, I think."

She nodded in understanding. "Arc the little boys out back?"

"Little boys" referred to John and his friends. When we said big boys, we were referring to Richard and Nathaniel.

I nodded. "They're sitting on the trampoline having a snack."

Belinda gazed directly into my eyes and asked, "How *are* you?"

I gestured at my bald head, my concave chest, and to the empty room. My eyes filled with tears.

"This is just *ridiculous,*" said Belinda, never one to mince words.

"Ridiculous."

"I want to tell God to get his f… ing foot off your back."

"Feel free."

Belinda now stood next to me in front of Richard's dresser and huge mirror. She addressed my image in the reflection of the glass. "Who would believe all of this could happen to one person in a few months' time?"

"Not me, that's for sure. Every night I go to sleep and pray when I wake up it will all have been a bad dream."

"I just have to say… I want to tell you that despite everything…" She fumbled with her thoughts, and then reached deep inside herself to find something good to say. "I always thought you looked great with short hair."

We both started laughing uncontrollably, repeating, "It's ridiculous."

Belinda had been through the whole fiasco with me. Our laughter started to slow down when I got the hiccups. She patted me on the back like I was an infant. It felt great. Eventually, we wiped our faces and straightened up. "I'm making chicken for dinner."

She nodded. "I'll take the little boys to the playground for a while."

It only took an afternoon to pack away Richard's childhood. His eighteen years of life fit into three boxes and two guitar cases. I put the scrapbooks I had made for him in a box, adding to it the many certificates and medals that had hung on the walls. There was the spelling bee, the Geo Bee, chess championships, downhill ski races, mogul ski races, and his professional free skiing awards. Free skiing, with its jumps and dangerous tricks, had been Richard's great passion until he realized he wouldn't get much money for college scholarships from that particular sport at the time. Since I was a public school teacher, and he knew he wanted to go to an Ivy League school, and so made a conscious decision to switch to running. He had articulated this decision well in a journal entry he had made in a notebook he left open on the bathroom floor in front of the toilet. I assumed he wanted me to read it. He thought he might become a pretty good runner if he trained hard enough. The Ivy League gave only academic scholarships, which meant even if he got hurt, he could stay until graduation. See… he was a planner like his mother.

Into a third box, I put the rewards of his decision. There were medals and trophies for cross-country and track, State Championships, New England Championships, and the glory of being an All-American. He had missed his high school graduation to compete in the All-American race. It was *that* important. I was robbed of being there by the endless staging tests to determine how far my cancer had spread. When he called to say he made the All-American Team, I sunk right to the floor with the phone in my hand. It took the wind out of me, but in a really good way.

I carefully put his acceptance letter from Cornell University into the carton, along with the document detailing his financial package. He had set an improbable goal as a high school sophomore and had achieved it.

Into the same box, I entombed his posters of Jimmy Hendrix, Stevie Ray Vaughn, Steve Prefontaine, and photographs of him performing frightening tricks off ski jumps. When he was little, he would say, "No fear, right, Mom?"

His electric and bass guitars fit neatly in their cases under his bed. I looked around the stripped room now ready for his baby brother to move into. What was left of Richard, I packed into the storage closet under the back staircase.

For several days, I felt drawn to open the door and peek inside. It felt like a black hole in the exact shape of Richard's silhouette that sucked me toward it with impressive power. My oldest child was gone. I'm glad I didn't know it would take over a decade for him to really find his way home again.

I stopped to think about the posters now packed away. Two men who changed music forever and a bad-boy runner. These three men must be clues as to who my child would become and yet I didn't see Richard as a rebel at all. If anything, he had achieved his success through conforming within systems. He said he was a Republican. I'd still like to know how that happened. Yet, these men, these outlaws, had hung on his walls for several years.

They were the same later teenage years he stopped confiding in me about every little thing. Richard was quick to remind me it was normal. On an intellectual level, I knew he was right, but it still felt like a fall from grace. Does every parent secretly harbor the notion that the power of his or her love would make their teenager different? That my child would be the first in history to seamlessly move from childhood to adulthood without losing their unconditional love and adoration of me?

My Richard was always so reasonable. "Well, how did you feel about your parents when you were my age?" he would ask me by way of explaining his secrecy about his life and friends.

The thought horrified me.

By the time I was seventeen, I could predict my parents' response to any given question. They were stuck in their political opinions, something they had read in a magazine years ago, or the boozy judgments of their circle of friends. I knew *exactly* what was going to come out of their mouths and I would pray, actually pray, that just this once, they would surprise me. It never happened. I couldn't wait to move out of their house.

I still hoped with each of my children that I might be spared the fall off the same pedestal. I think, and I could be wrong since I have never had a daughter, that the pedestal a son puts his mother on is exceptionally high and the fall especially hard.

I tried to remember Richard had given me a good, long run. When he was sixteen, he called to say he had forgotten something he needed for track practice. When he saw me in the school lobby, even though friends surrounded him, he threw his arms around me and picked me up in a bear hug. He declared, "I love my mom!"

Another mother who was there asked, "He still hugs you? Wow!"

I felt superior and maybe a little full of myself. I remember thinking, but not actually saying, "We're not going to do the whole teenage thing. We've decided to do something else."

He was still so cute, an adorable face with his cap turned askew. One day, he woke up and a critical cruel *changeling* had taken over. Really, it happened just that fast.

For years, it had been my boys and me against the world. We were a well-functioning unit with family meetings and defined goals. Now, at eighteen, my Richard was conquering the world alone. He sometimes still indulged me with the notion that he needed me, but the truth was plain. He had been able to manipulate the big universe out there much better than I ever had.

The bedroom looked fantastic. I had forgotten about the red wallpaper beneath the posters. I glanced around and felt the emptiness, and knew it would be a long while before I would enter Richard's room again. I took the bucket of cleaning materials downstairs. That evening, I told John it was ready for him. He seemed excited, but the next morning I found him curled up in his own bed back in his tiny yellow room. Until I sold my house and moved, Richard's room would remain an empty, hallowed place.

Christmas After the Deluge
12–25–2001

By the time we had all stopped reeling from the catastrophic autumn of 2001, it was time to gear up for Christmas. My household was out of focus and dark, no matter how many lights I turned on. The only bright spot in the dim fog I now inhabited was my ex-husband, Rich.

I went for another chemotherapy treatment on December 22nd and afterward, if anyone in my family ate at all, I don't know who fed them. It must have been Rich.

The entire week after the treatment, he carried me like a sick child to the bathroom. I would protest and tell him to leave the room and close the door. The truth was I didn't have the strength to pull myself up to the height of the toilet to be sick. He held me up with one strong arm and rubbed my back with the other. How he acquired so much experience in the low back pain of sustained vomiting I don't know. But, he knew the exact spot to massage, and I was too grateful to protest any more or be embarrassed.

Rich was a surprise. He was a good man, I am not saying he wasn't, but I always thought he was a little spoiled. Nathaniel the first had been similar in this way. Yet, here Rich was at my side, despite the fact I was at my worst.

He brought a Christmas tree to the house and decorated it with ornaments of his own. I am known for buying my Christmas gifts early, but I don't recall wrapping any that year. My children were ten, fifteen, and eighteen. Rich got us through somehow. It was like we were all in blurry black and white and he was intensely focused and in color.

I would watch him from my wrapped-up nest of covers. How tall he was and so strong! How competent! Had I ever noticed his high chiseled cheekbones before? He was so thoughtful with the children as he pulled this holiday together for us.

He kept singing a silly song, "High Ho, High Ho! We're going back to Normal. Tra La La La Tra La La La. We're back to Nor... hor... mal."

He made us laugh and it was hard for me to remember why we divorced in the first place. As much as I appreciated that he was caring for us, I didn't assume anything. Who knew where we would land after the crisis was over? There was a good chance I could die. I tried hard to manage my expectations.

The preparations for Christmas had always been my thing. I felt guilty, and even a little jealous, that the brunt of creating the holiday was on Rich's shoulders. I did muster up one serious effort to provide presents for my kids. A new electronics Superstore was opening in Vermont, promising unheard of deals if you were present when they unlocked the doors at 6:30 a.m. on Opening Day. I had Nathaniel, who had just received his learner's permit, drive me to Burlington and ask for a wheelchair. He pushed me to the back of the line out in the cold winter wind. I shivered with fever. My eyes watered so it seemed as if I was crying. A security guard saw how fragile and sick I was and asked if I wanted to go into the store ahead of everyone else.

Nathaniel was appalled. He said that would be using my cancer to get preferential treatment. I was living with the fear of losing my house, and maybe worse, not having Christmas gifts from me for my children. I suspected there were limited quantities of each of the advertised items in the store. I was here for the opportunity to purchase some cool gifts cheaply.

"Why, yes, officer, thank you, I would love to go inside." I hissed back at Nathaniel who was reluctantly wheeling me through the double doors, "I actually *have* cancer, Nathaniel. It's not like I'm faking it."

Many years later, Richard told me he and his brothers had shut down by this time. It was too painful to see what was happening to their mother, so they had stopped looking. Nathaniel did not want a reminder that I was too weak to stand in a line. So much had happened to them in a short time.

A New Kind of Normal–2013

More than a decade passed before I felt like I finally had a normal life again. But, it was a new kind of normal. There were many things I had enjoyed in my first life, B.C., (Before Cancer) that I could no longer do. Even coming this far had been a pyrrhic victory.

After chemotherapy, I had many more operations to complete what I call "the patch-up job." I'm not sure of the number because I can't bear to look over my medical records. There were probably fifteen surgeries total, and the resulting pain stuck with me, evolving into a pain *syndrome*. Rebounding from the consequences of cancer treatment was like a steep uphill climb, followed by a relapse, over and over again. It was the big comeback. Across ten years, I gradually and incrementally got much better. By the time I reached this new normal, my sons were grown men.

Rich knew that I missed the kids. "Maybe we should get a pet."

I loved the idea. "Yes, I want a little dog, the kind who could wear a sweater."

In our town, a great group of young women drive vans to Pennsylvania to puppy mill auctions and rescue puppies who don't meet the standards required by commercial pet stores. These leftover dogs are put up for public bidding and if they aren't sold by the end of the day, they are killed. Twice a year two full vans of these animals are brought back to Vermont. I filled out an application on the group's website. The form was specific, and, in fact, I was a bit shocked by the personal nature of the some of the questions. Rich and I were asked to meet with the women who wanted to do a home visit. They had checked all of our references. I worried we wouldn't make the cut, but we were finally approved.

Our friend, Roy, was one of the veterinarians in town. Almost immediately, his office called. The receptionist said, "We heard you got the green light. We have a little girl here we have been fostering for a month. Nobody wanted her because she has a heart murmur. Hang on, Roy wants to talk to you."

He came on the line. "Mary Pat, look, it's no secret her heart has a defect." Roy spoke as directly as a character in a Hemingway novel. "She could live five years or twenty-five, there's just no way to know."

We went to meet her, and well, there was no turning back. She was a pure white cotton ball of a puppy with a pink nose, button eyes, and stick legs; the vet thought she was probably a teacup Pomeranian. He complained about dog owners breeding dogs down in size, which was what had caused her heart defect. I put her in the pocket of my sweatshirt and we brought her home. Her eyes were shaped very much like the late actress Bette Davis, with the same light bristly lashes. My favorite movie of hers was *Jezebel*, so that's what I named my puppy.

My tiny designer dog, Jezebel, at first bewildered Rich. I had a water bottle carrier strapped around my waist and her entire body fit into the padded opening. I would tote her around with just her little white head and front paws peeking out. She would take everything in with her protruding eyes. When she was tired, I wound a big scarf around my neck so she could sleep suspended against my beating heart as I did chores around the house. I sang songs to her bouncing her against my chest like we were dancing. Suddenly, I was in a good mood most of the time and my sons teased me that the puppy was my child replacement system. An unusual feeling was bubbling up inside me. It was *happiness*.

Every day my teaching scheduled allowed, I took her to the supermarket to see Rich. I would open the child seat of the grocery cart and put down a folded towel so her tiny legs didn't slip through the metal. She would ride like royalty around the store. The first stop *had* to be to see her dad. She would make excited little peeping noises until we found him. The love that filled her face when she saw him was a wonder to behold.

It turned out Rich was a genius with small dogs. He told everyone that, at first, he had been embarrassed to be attached to a fluffy little dog that could fit in a purse. He taught her tricks and they played circus games when he came home from work. I liked to watch them romping around together from the kitchen window where I stood washing dishes.

Rich would call to me, "Mary Pat, look at her!" He would laugh his delighted laugh that makes everyone around him feel happy, too. If I stepped out on the back porch, he would have Jez spin, roll over, and flip.

Later in the evening, Jezebel slept on the back of my couch cushion while I watched television. Her slumbering face showed off her careful breeding. While her fur was a fluffy alabaster, the rest of her was pink, particularly her nose and the pads of her paws. Ironically, she had been born on Valentine's Day.

It was a comfort having her near me. Somewhere I had read small breeds live a long time. We had suppressed the vet's warning, and assumed Jez would beat the odds of the heart defect.

She was outside playing with Rich one afternoon when her barking became ominous, reminding me of a seal's. With every breath she let out a noise that was deep, hollow, and raspy. Rich and I jumped into the car and raced her to the vet.

Roy injected her with medications and reminded us, "Dogs do get sick, you know. She's probably got a bug."

Rich walked the floor with her, carrying her with her tiny head against his shoulder all night, as she continued the hoarse barking. We were waiting for Roy in the parking lot early the next morning when he got to work. She was placed in an oxygen tent and the nurse inserted a tiny I.V. line. The office called later in the day to report they saw on the x-ray that she had pneumonia.

Rich and I refused to leave her overnight in a cage in the basement of their clinic. I could tell Roy wasn't keen on her being around the other sick animals either. The private school where I was employed was on break that week and I promised Roy I would bring her in for shots every morning. Rich and I alternated nights of walking with her in our arms. On the third day, Roy said, "It might be that the worst has passed. With her weak heart it's been hard for her to clear her lungs. But you two have got to get some sleep."

Rich asked him, "Are there dog specialists? Can we take her to a cardiologist?"

"Sure, but you'll have to take her to Boston."

I was adamant, "I am not going to put her in the care of strangers in a strange place. It's not like I can explain to her what's going on. The idea of her having heart surgery is intolerable. She only weighs five pounds. If she's going to die, I want her home with us, not on a steel operating table in a sterile room."

Roy looked at the ground, "I'm glad her cough is much better."

However, that night, we put her in bed with us because the "seal bark" started again. Finally, Rich gave up and took Jezebel out to the couch in the living room and cradled her. I fell into a deep sleep, knowing he would need me to relieve him at some point. In the middle of the night, I heard him scream. It was the only time I had ever heard my husband scream in fear.

When I barreled out of my room, I saw her. She was limp in his arms and it was obvious to me she was barely holding on. Her breathing was so shallow that I started to give her mouth-to-mouth resuscitation, pumping her heart after every five breaths. Her eyes begged me to let her go. That was not something I was ready to consider, so I continued in my efforts to keep her alive. Her beautiful movie star face grew more and more haggard. Her eyes continued pleading with me for release. I knew as long as I asked her to try to keep breathing, she would do it. I also knew she was exhausted. Her beseeching eyes bore into mine.

Almost an hour had passed since I started the mouth-to-mouth. I could barely feel her breath when she exhaled. A clear fluid flowed out of her nose and mouth drenching her face and chest. The moment arrived when I had to accept she was dying.

I touched the side of her face. "All right, sweetheart, you can go now."

Just like that, she was gone. It was my turn to wail, and I did.

We wrapped her in an afghan my grandmother had made and left her on the couch. Then, we climbed into our bed and pretended to sleep. The following day, not wanting to have to tell the story over and over again, I posted the following on Facebook:

Our dog, Jezebel, died last night. A Teacup Pomeranian, she was four years and seven months old. At a whopping five pounds, she could climb any mountain we could and swim out into the river to retrieve a stick before other dogs could beat her to it. She was adorable and it was deceptive, because she was also a hunter. Rich called her "Princess Warrior." She was the best dog I have ever had.

Jez was rescued from a puppy mill; her mother had been so inbred that Jez was born with a defective heart. My good girl died of congestive heart failure and pneumonia at one o'clock this morning in our arms. She will be dearly missed.

Please don't ever buy a dog from a pet store supplied by a puppy mill. Final thought: there are rescue organizations for all breeds. If you are thinking about a dog, please consider that option.

Rich and I went through the motions of our day. Every few hours I went to find him at work where we moved into his office and closed the door. We clung to each other and cried. Once home we sat in the rockers on the front porch of our house and told stories about our little Jezebel. It got so I couldn't stand to wake up to the quiet of the house. I couldn't stop anticipating her morning greeting. I would throw on some clothes and let myself into the back of Rich's store. The business wasn't open yet, but I would pour a cup of coffee and go find him and hover around while he did his work.

Each day I would ask him, "How long will I feel this bad?"

He would give the same answer. "I don't know. I liked her more than most of the people I've met in my life. She gave us a pure adoring love. People always talk about unconditional love, but I don't know if we humans are capable of it. But it's what she gave to us, so maybe what we are left with is pure grief."

After four months of mourning, the rescue organizations started calling again. We replaced our grown children with three more dogs. I thought that adopting three was crossing a line and joked about us as the crazy-dog people. We started taking daily hikes with them and naturally had to schedule our lives around theirs. We had learned through Jez that our pets brought us closer together. Together we held hands and led our little pack up wooded trails.

The post about Jezebel on Facebook brought an unexpected consequence. While reading the condolence remarks from friends, I noticed a random message buried among all the others.

May 13, 2013
Nathaniel Hayes

Although your name is Mary Patricia Maddin, I believe you are the Mary Patricia Toohey who once lived in Avalon Park, New Jersey. If this is the case, I still adore you.

Nathaniel! The same confidence, the same assumption, the same intimate tone. Of course, I had wondered over the years about him and how life had turned out for him. I sent a cautious reply.

May 13, 2013
Mary Patricia Maddin

Oh, there you are!

May 14, 2013
Nathaniel Hayes

That's a pretty cavalier response for someone I haven't talked to in fifteen years. So much has happened. You wouldn't have known since you return my Christmas cards every year. I wrote you a letter to tell you everything, but that too was marked Return to Sender. I assume you are trying to tell me something.

In 2010, I had the kind of heart attack people call a Widow Maker. This happens when the main artery down the front of the heart (LAD) is totally blocked. Talk about a wakeup call! I was still smoking back then, and probably drinking too much.

Heart attack increases the risk for other problems, including heart valve damage, and stroke. I had bypass surgery six months later. While I was still under, I suffered a stroke. In 2013, I had another heart attack despite the fact I was doing everything my doctors told me to do. At that point, I had permanent damage. The change in circulation caused all my hair to fall out. I pretty much spent a year in the hospital.

It has been a nightmare.

I think I found your kids on this social network. They are grown men! Contact me if you like.

May 15, 2013
Mary Patricia Maddin

The cards must have been returned because I moved. My address changed when my husband and I separated. It changed again when we reconciled. There were many important things that didn't get forwarded in the mail. One spring, I was stopped for having an expired registration and license on the same day. It was a mess!

When I didn't get your usual Christmas cards, I thought you decided not to be in touch anymore. Let's be honest, this has historical precedent. Isn't it crazy how we can misinterpret each other?

I have a story to tell you, too. It has been a difficult decade for me. But a year in the hospital? I am so sorry that happened to you.

So, you found my boys online? You probably remember Nathaniel was born on your birthday. He just won an award at Cannes for a Best New Director of a Short Film. He is on location in Mexico City right now shooting so he couldn't be in France to get it.

The one thing I did right in my life is my children.

My eldest, Richard, wound up at Cornell, was an All-American runner in high school and college - won many big races- and then surprised me by turning to music full time. His new band is called LOFTS.

The baby, John, takes his MCATs in July. He is already applying to med schools, so please keep your fingers crossed.

My real email is pattym55@gmsvt.net. My IM is mommypatatlarge55.
I would like to know more about your health.

May 15, 2013
<u>Nathaniel Hayes</u>

I didn't really expect you to "friend" me (what a stupid notion), but am glad you did and that I found you. I would not have wanted to go to my Maker without knowing where all of my true friends were. Perhaps that is what I want to say first and foremost. I look back and realize what a good friend you were to me.

I was running on a Sunday and came to in an ICU unit the following Monday morning. They told me my chances of surviving had been five to ten percent. That was four years ago. People tell me I'm still here for a purpose.

I'm glad to see you have a son who is interested in medicine and I wish him luck. Having a director and a musician sounds good, too.

So, tell me about your health scare, (only if you want).

May 16, 2013
<u>Mary Patricia Maddin</u>

It was eleven years ago. It wasn't a scare – they gave me a 50% chance (more than yours, don't think I feel sorry for myself for a minute). I had a different cancer in each breast. I got two opinions, one here in Vermont (where they wanted to take both breasts, my uterus, and ovaries.) Boston said just the breasts. They told me to make out a will and leave my funeral directions. That first operation was on July 3rd. It had spread and there was six months of kick-my-ass chemo (during which both my parents died), then, two years of more drugs that made me sick.

Our family gathers for the 3rd and 4th of July now at our lake house. My brother, Malachy, and his wife, Isabel, come every year, too, and we celebrate. I am back teaching and I hike almost every day. I had to give up downhill skiing and playing guitar. There were many more "patch up" surgeries. I still have neuropathy and a pain syndrome that can be quite disabling.

Did you know I was a professional singer? Yeah, I took that up when John was a baby. I wrote a song called, "Just a Middle-Aged Mother of Three." It was a hoot!

The boys are amazing human beings. I have been fortunate enough to travel and had several careers, and life is pretty darn good.
How is your wife? It sounds like you are still married. Who do you stay in touch with?

Belinda lives in New York State. She joined Alcoholics Anonymous and NA 28 years ago. She is very involved and has helped many others recover too. Although I don't get to see them as often as I would like, Keith, Deb, and Don are still friends. Have you been on the website, "Bergen Youth Theatre North Remembered," on Facebook? Our old theatre group has been trying to get everybody together.

What are your chances now with the heart disease? How serious is this?
I teach now at Three Mountain Valley School in Greenfield. It's a prep school and ski academy. I'm glad you wrote to me.

Tell me more about your volunteer work. I do what I can up here, too. I am working with a woman now who just had a mastectomy.

May 16, 2013
Nathaniel Hayes

I just read your message and am in a state of shock. No kidding. Why didn't you call me?

Who took care of you?

I really don't know where the time went. I remember talking to you at my kitchen table around Christmas. I could hear the music you had playing. You told me you were decorating cookies while we talked. I could hear kids laughing.

I recall the coach from Princeton being interested in your oldest son and you were officially divorced and were homesick for your friends in New Jersey. That was all. We said good-bye and then I lost you. I am so sorry to hear about your illness. You must have suffered terribly and I feel so bad because I had no idea. With a little help from my doctors, wife, and God, I survived. I am grateful you did, too.

Today, I live with half the energy I used to have. I had to close down my practice, but I am not giving up. I go to physical therapy regularly, and I'm looking into a heart strengthening exercise program. But, I have to confess I'm still traumatized by all the medical interventions. Do you have nightmares about it?

May 17, 2013
Mary Patricia Maddin

Every time I see a hospital, the metallic taste of chemotherapy rises to my mouth. I'll drive blocks out of my way to avoid it. Once they said the C-word to me, I just shut down. Belinda came for a week and was left to deal with everything. On the day I had my first appointment, she sat with me in a little windowless room waiting for the surgeon, radiologist, and oncologist. One came in and one went out; they were never in the room at the same time. It was like a revolving door of bad news. Every time the surgeon put both his hands on his own chest, fluttered his fingers, and said, "We are going remove the breasts..." I would swoon.

Finally, Belinda went out into the hallway and corralled the four of them. I could hear her loud and clear. "Listen, you guys need to make some decisions and get your F- ing ACT TOGETHER. You are coming in and out of there contradicting each other! Talk amongst yourselves, as they say where I come from, and then all of you come back in here as a team. Then tell us what the PLAN IS!"

I really think she missed a career opportunity. She should have become a professional patient advocate. She was a Godsend to me.

After the first surgery, Rich kept coming by my house. He would make sure there was food in the refrigerator and the kids had done their homework. My parents died within a week of each other. There he was at the funerals in New Jersey helping out. By the time it was all over, we thought it would be foolish to break up again.

I have been writing about this daily for ten years. I want to write a book. As you know, living beyond catastrophe takes intention, courage, and acceptance. We will never be the same people again, but there is still pleasure to be had and purpose to be fulfilled. Again, I would love to talk and compare thoughts.

Why didn't I call you when I got sick? Part of me wanted to stay strong for my family. There was no time to complain. Every day required everything I had and all my focus. I bargained with God; if he would let me live until John's college graduation, I would do everything the doctors told me to do.

There is also the "old girlfriend" factor. I don't want to intrude on your life or be disrespectful to your wife in any way at all. Mrs. McGeary (who is still alive) was always quick to tell me your mother would tell her, "Nathaniel will never completely get over that Patty." And, of course, deep inside me there is a young girl who feels the same way toward you.

I am so humbled to be alive, as there is no good reason why some of us live and some don't. Lots of people want to believe we have some kind of control over our mortality. They will tell me I lived because I am essentially an optimist. I really want to dispel that myth. In my opinion, graveyards are filled with cancer patients who did their best to remain positive until the end. I'm grateful I believe in God. I figure He has a plan for me.

Then, out of the blue I get a message from Nathaniel—yes, that Nathaniel, and he has lived beyond catastrophic illness, too. It's incredible.

Send me your email. I feel weird communicating through a social networking site.

Let's talk soon on the phone.
Mary Pat

May 17, 2013
Nathaniel Hayes

I am still trying to digest all you have told me. I've read your passages over and over, just like I used to read your letters (good and bad), and I still can't fathom what happened to you and why you had the complications. Nothing is free.

I will call you Monday afternoon, after my physical therapy session.

It's nice to be back in touch, although I am sorry it had to be under these circumstances. Better late than never as I already alluded to.

After all we have been through, I must tell you something. I adore my wife and family, but I need you to know I loved you, too. I don't want either of us passing away without being clear about that. It was long ago, and I was probably a different person, but I still carry around those feelings. And, there are times, especially since I have been sick, when I miss you terribly.

May 20, 2013
Mary Patricia Maddin

Monday should be a good time. Exams are over, my grades are in. How about 2:00 p.m.?

I am having a hard time with the idea of you going through all this. It brings me to tears. Your poor wife - in some ways it's really harder on those who love us. Of course, my greatest fear is what this has done to my children. Each of my sons wrote his college essay on the traumatic memories of my diagnosis and treatment and the way our family pulled through it. It was pivotal; it was life defining. As a family, you could easily fly apart at a time like that. I felt I was holding my family together with my bare hands, but the truth is God blessed us.

Thank you for your kind thoughts. It is nice to know I mattered to you. However, I worked hard to get over missing you in my life and I will not go back to that again. I am actively living for my life as it is right now which includes treasuring my husband and family.

May 20, 2013
Nathaniel Hayes

It's good we are in touch again. I really don't have many close friends who share my experience. Of course, that will change the older we get. I look forward to talking to you.

I appreciate what you wrote about family. But, I'm sorry to tell you, Mary Pat, you can't ever completely get over your first love. It may be bittersweet, but it's too late to fire me now.

The Epiphany–2013

Rich bestowed upon me a great luxury. As I recovered from my long medical ordeal, I decided to return to work, but Rich encouraged me to only do it part-time. We fell into a peaceful rhythm. While I was able to sleep in every day, Rich still got up to the shriek of an alarm. He took the dogs out at 5:00 a.m. when it was often dark and cold. I tended to doze off again once he got up and awaken an hour or two later. My pattern was to shuffle out to the kitchen to pour a cup of coffee. My hands would be laced around the steaming cup as I carried it back to bed to respond to emails and read the news. The dogs were ready to eat by eight, but I took my sweet time with my laptop computer until then.

My husband worked hard at the supermarket, but the food business was also a fun part of our lives. We both liked to cook, and through food shows and wine events, we stayed up on new trends. Then, in an embarrassment of riches, Rich gave me the trip of a lifetime. He took me to Ireland to explore the land of my ancestors and to document my family's history.

I realized it was the first time in my life I wasn't battling terrible obstacles. Abandonment, poverty, hunger, getting ahead, taking care of my children, pain, and heartbreak had been a daily reality in my life. Without the struggle, my sense of purpose was shifting. My soul was curious and hungry to discover a new way to live. I felt this keenly during a recent conversation I had with a colleague. I was sitting in the office we shared, suddenly incapable of making small talk. We had sat in silence for some time working, when I blurted out, "What was the most crucial moment of your life? How did it define you?"

She didn't pause to consider. She said, "Like a lot of kids, after high school I took a backpack trip around Europe. I didn't speak French. Yet, when I got to Paris, I didn't want to leave. I called my mother and begged her to let me stay. Today, many students can defer their admission and entrance into college and take a year off, but back then, the college told my mother I either started in the fall or I would have to reapply with everyone else. My parents thought it too big a risk. I defied them and found a job as an au pair. I can pinpoint the phone call when I told them they would have to accept my decision as *the* defining moment of my life. I wasn't going to change my mind. Up until then, I had been kind of a goody-two-shoes girl. But now, I was in *France.* The food! The wine! The intrigue of learning a new culture and language!" She clasped her hands, sighed, and rolled her eyes as she made an *it was all too delicious* gesture. She added " And... there was a romance with a *Frenchman.*"

"I am so happy you got to experience all that. You were so brave to do it."

The question that arose in my mind was, what would her life have been like if she hadn't followed her instincts?

We spoke for an hour about the ripple effects of her decision. She speculated she might have stayed in Connecticut and been a homemaker instead of a language teacher and world traveler. She told me she had lived in France for two years where she made friends for life. She was able to travel across Europe and this led her to a love of languages. (She learned to speak three fluently.) Then, she met and married a dashing man.

At the end of our conversation, she confided in me that she and her adored husband were going to ask for a leave of absence from our school and ride motorcycles the length of South America.

She had tears in her eyes. I knew she was my age and he was a decade older. Her passion and courage were as strong as it had been when she defied her parents and stayed in Europe. I didn't know when I had felt so inspired.

I got up and gave her a hug when she went to teach a class. I was left reflecting on my own life. My sons were grown and my finances were stable. What did I want to do now… before I got too old to do it? I had been fortunate enough to travel, but I speculated about what made the difference between a vacation and an adventure. Walking into it with clear intentions? Reclaiming a sense of awe and wonder?

Then, I began to think about redemption. With each decision I made and action I took, I aspired to goodness and examined the consequences of my choices as I understood them. It was a challenge, for I was an efficient woman, someone who liked to complete tasks on time. Interruptions could be annoying. Within hours of making my simple vow, a student approached me wanting to schedule a meeting.

"I'm having a hard time," she said, seeming quite troubled.

Instead of suggesting she shoot me an email, I sat down with her and discussed what was going on.

I became determined to focus on the current moment. In order to do that, I had started the process of letting my boys find their own way. My illness and extended treatment had made me hyper-vigilant, but it was time to relax. Richard, Nathaniel, and John were high achievers and I knew there was really nothing to worry about.

My new interest, our family history, became an obsession. Bernadette had started the ball rolling when she conducted online research and created a family tree that went back hundreds of years. I took trips back to Malachy's in New Jersey to collect documents and photographs. I justified the time I was spending on the project by saying I wanted to write a book for my sons. It was, of course, what I believed at the time.

I had no idea how our trip to Ireland would change my life.

After we arrived, we took a train out to the village of Mallow where we found the heritage center for County Cork. They had prepared a map for me showing farmland my family had once owned. Rich hired a cab to take us out to see it. On a dusty, country, four-cornered intersection, the only structures interrupting the vast acreage known as Killavullen were a church and a graveyard. A priest stood in the open door of the church when we stepped out of the cab. He looked directly at me and I had the sensation he was waiting for us.

I thought to ask our driver his last name. He said Neill and I remarked that my family had been quite close to a Neill family in the 1860s. "Well, if there are any of you left here, our families probably are close still. Nothing changes in this town." He reached over for the money I held out to him and drove away. The most recent census I could find online showed Killavullen had a population of 224 people. I wondered what it had been after the famines and the occupation of the British. Surely, everyone in the area had known each other.

I walked through the gate and down the stone path to the priest and said, "I have come a long way, Father."

"Yes, yes, many of you come for the research. The children will arrive from the school for prayer soon. They won't bother you."

The only sign for the church was built into the exterior stone wall above the double doors. It was in Latin and included the date of 1839. My ancestors were married here in 1861. Their eight children were baptized in this very church and six of the babies lived. The children began to leave for America approximately twenty-five years later, specifically to Englewood, New Jersey, across the Hudson River from New York City. One sibling arrived, and then sponsored the next one waiting to leave, so there was proof of passage fare, a place to live, and the possibility of a job. The church parish of St. Cecelia in New Jersey has the records of all of their marriages with the exception of my great-grandfather. He had married in Ireland and brought his wife and two children to America. The story of why they had to emigrate is the story of Ireland itself.

Cork County, and this includes the town of Killavullen, is nicknamed the Rebel County. Stories were passed down to me of the fighting. Even my own father had had some mysterious dealings with the I.R.A as late as the mid-1960s. My grandfather, Liam Toohey, born in Ireland, but who was a police officer in Englewood for forty years, surely raised money and shipped guns back. I have been to Ireland and, please trust me on this, there is no one who would leave it if given the choice. It is a country that inspires the soul with its unspoiled beauty. Families who were forced off their farms and who relocated to New Jersey are probably the reason for the stereotype of the Irish alcoholic. It is no wonder to me they drank too much.

The priest stood with his arm propped against the building. I ducked beneath it and entered the sanctuary where I was immediately drawn into a swirling vortex of my ancestors' voices. To say I was overwhelmed would be an understatement. I was *overpowered.*

Looking up at the altar, I experienced the sensation of being pushed downward by some unseen force causing me to sink to my knees. Unable to resist, I felt my legs start to give way. Thank God, I thought, it is happening in slow motion. I didn't want the school children to come for their daily prayers and find me prostrate before the sacristy.

I scanned the small space I was in, desperately searching for a place to land on my knees. My senses were utterly filled. I heard the spirits, smelled them, and felt they had also waited for this moment. They were present, these people with whom I shared the DNA of my body and soul.

I spotted a padded kneeler and a railing in front of which rested three levels of large votive candles, traditionally lit by Catholics in memory of the dead. I barely made it to the railing before I collapsed. Rich's presence was suddenly behind me. How much time had passed? I wondered. I asked him to go for a walk and give me the time to pray, so he quietly left.

Added to the voices of the dead were sensory memories from my childhood. The dusty scent of candles, incense, ancient plaster, and old wood. Upon entering the church, I had automatically followed the Catholic tradition of dipping the fingers of my right hand into the font of Holy Water, made the sign of the cross, and touched my fingers to my lips. A faint metallic taste filled my mouth from the oxidation of the ancient font. My fingers sang with coolness as the water evaporated.

Well, I thought, *God is here and so are they. I just hope I survive this.*

My heart was pounding, but not in the way it does when you are frightened. This was no anxiety attack; that much I knew for sure. My head was filled with the Holy Light filtering through the stained glass. I bowed my head and was, perhaps for the first time in my life, in a state of perfect contentment. And then, it was given to me as a whisper on the breeze.

"The last part of your life must be the best part."

The image of a camera came to mind as the entire scene zoomed in toward me. I felt I was in this moment the focus of the lens. The focus of my own life.

When Rich and I returned to Vermont sixteen days later, I called Don in Washington. He had belonged to a family of deep faith; it seemed even as a grown man his faith was unshakeable. I had hoped he would understand and not downplay what had happened to me in the church.

"So, Don," I said after we had talked for half an hour, "I think the message is this: If our life is like a three-act play, we have to work hard to make sure the final act is really the grand finale."

Even though Don had been silent on the other end of the phone while I shared my story, I could tell he loved the idea of the grand finale. When he spoke, it was with complete sincerity, "And Patty, let's hope for encores. Several encores."

Warbling of a Meadow Lark– 2014

It was a lush summer in Vermont. Rich and I made the time·
to hike in the woods with our three dogs daily. It was good for
them, it was good for us, and it gave us a chance to talk.
Sometimes we just listened to the birdsongs. On one memorable
day, we ran into an entire family of martens on a tree that was still
upright, but dead. The mother and children were looking for
insects by digging into the decaying wood. Since there were no
leaves on the tree, we were able to watch them for a long time.
We stood together holding hands in the silence.

Rich's eyes flared with curiosity. He had a talent for observing
animals. I don't take in the details the way he does, and I get
impatient. When we go on his dive trips, I make comments like, "I
get it. There are fish down there. They are colorful." I do
sometimes snorkel, but have only been scuba diving once, while
Rich relishes it all.

Long after we leave the scene of the martens in the tree, he
will tell me what he has absorbed. For example, he asked, did I
notice how long and curved their nails were?

"That must make it easier for them to dig the insects out,"
he'd explained.

Did I notice how their faces were like teddy bears, but their
bodies shaped more like a badger? Wasn't their coloring
interesting? His curiosity was genuine, which made these
occurrences unforgettable.

This is the point in my life when I began to experience many happy days. On summer weekends, we packed up and drove to the Northeast Kingdom to our camp. The term camp in Vermont refers to a place that is a getaway, usually rustic. In our case, it was a four-bedroom (four very small bedrooms) cabin on a lake. The building was not insulated when we bought it, the windows were painted shut, and the exterior was the ghastly blackish color of creosote stain. We weren't in any hurry to fix the place up. We created a priority list and each summer completed another project or two. Slowly, the building began to show the labor of our love.

Down a path through the woods stands a surprisingly well-constructed and comfortable outhouse. I use the bathroom inside the cabin. An old, cast iron woodstove with a big diagonal crack in it supplies the only heat. Water for washing is drawn by a pump directly from the lake and drinking water from a flowing artesian spring a short walk down the road.

We bought this camp from the family who had built it in 1925. These camps were usually passed down generation to generation and it was unusual to have one come on the market. Rich and I assumed the family must have been squeezed for the tax money. Or perhaps it had been inherited by a group of grandchildren who couldn't agree on how to keep it in the family.

The first priority was to have fun when we went to the Kingdom. We kayaked and hiked. Every meal was a ceremony of preparation and eaten outside at a large picnic table that sat right on the edge of the water. We savored every sunset. There was no Internet or cell phone service, and we liked it that way. Our only grudging acceptance of technology was a flat screen television so we could follow our passion of watching feature films. A perfect day was when we found ourselves happily exhausted at sundown, ready to watch a movie, and go to sleep. If one of the kids was with us, I made a fire in the pit outside to extend the day, but when it was just Rich and me, we retired early.

The holiday I am a fanatic about is Christmas, which takes place at our house in Greenfield. My red Waechtersbach Tannenbaum plates go out the day before Thanksgiving and stay out until after New Year's Day. Christmas Eve is the one celebration in our family that is sacrosanct. We do our best to be with family on birthdays, graduations, weddings, and births, too. Between our jobs, the responsibilities and traditions of both our homes, making time for ourselves and our family and friends, life felt full.

There were some blue days, too, especially after John left for Boston. I knew I had to look to myself for the answers, and after John's departure, I started seeing a therapist. What I had not yet realized was now that my sons were gone, I felt safer dealing with all that had happened in my life. Until this point, I had pushed it all down. I think I worried I might fall apart and have a nervous breakdown like my mother, and that was not an option when I had children to raise.

The more quiet and routine my life became, the more I battled with anxiety. A deep well of fear resided in the center of my being. It was like a tidal wave chasing me, ready to swallow me up. When I was younger, I would deal with it by out-running it. I stayed busy; in fact, I was a workaholic. The boys would get angry at me when they wanted to snuggle up and watch a movie together, for I would jump up to change the laundry from the washer to the dryer, grade some papers, or maybe paint the ceiling in the bathroom.

"Mom!" they would chorus. "Can't you sit still for five minutes?"

I couldn't. Not until the day cancer knocked me flat on my back for a year and a half. Even then, I had the boys to take care of and advise. They were the best of distractions. Now, deep in the empty nest, I was alone with my own thoughts. My memories. My heartbreak.

I recognized in myself a longing to be seen and known, but the possibility was canceled out by my fear that if someone really knew me, they would be appalled. In my childhood, I had allowed myself to bond openly with friends. I became much more cautious as an adult. My father had always told us you were lucky to have a handful of close friends in one lifetime. I reckoned I was luckier than most. And, there were the three men who knew me better than I knew myself, Richard, Nathaniel, and John.

Most of my friends think I am entertaining, but I remind them when I am with my siblings I can't get a word in edgewise. We are talkers. During this empty nest period, I missed the absence of conversation for the pure pleasure of it. Nathaniel, the first one, would often say to me, "Let's turn off the television and just talk." We would amuse each other with our ideas. In grade school Deb, Keith, Belinda, Don, Nathaniel, and I would lie in the grass watching the clouds or the stars and verbally scrutinize how we had spent our day. We might compare the shape of our toes. There would be vivid stories passed around about our aunts and uncles. As long as we were being honest, the details of life were fascinating. I longed for that, and to have someone with me who knew me without any explanation.

I still had Belinda. Sometimes. During this period, she had vaporized into one of her disappearing acts. The last time I had gotten her on the phone, she was completely self-absorbed. There wasn't a moment to tell her about my malaise. Instead, I said, "I'm sorry for your troubles, Belinda. Is there anything I can do for you?"

Even after all this time, I still missed my Nathaniel. In therapy, I identified specifically what I mourned was the loss of our friendship. The ease of being together and the lack of judgment. Having a long shared history. I worked to fill in those holes.

I joined a book club and a women's hiking group. I made more of an effort to socialize with my friends. It took a few years, but the happy days became more frequent. I had a great deal to be thankful for. Some days I made a list: Rich, my sons, my job at Three Mountain Valley School, my friends, and the vast resource that is the beautiful state of Vermont.

Early June 2014

Deb called me from Syracuse about details for the reunion. "Are you having crazy dreams?" she asked.

I was surprised. "I thought it was just me." I was starting dinner and could hear her sipping on a drink. "Are you having wine?"

"It's after five," she chirped back. That was all the encouragement I needed.

"Okay, let me pour a glass and we can share cocktail hour."

I was, in fact, having *bizarre* dreams. In one, I was in the hallway of Avalon Park Graded School trying to explain to various people who crowded the hall (they were from all the geographic locations and various eras of my life) that I was a teacher and not a student. Members of the crowd told me over and over again that I had never graduated from high school. Dennis was there. He said I had to come back to finish my courses and get enough credits for a diploma. I began to run down the hallway. There was a dead end. When I looked to my right or my left, I saw a maze of more hallways lined with grayish-green lockers. I sat straight up in bed with a gasp. Although I tried to be quiet about it, I had to change my nightgown because it was saturated with sweat.

"Deb, what kind of wine are you into now?" I asked. I drink more than is, shall we say, recommended. But I am the grandchild of Europeans who are amused with our puritanical effort to be perfect. The more I traveled, the more I heard about it. "You Americans!" they would laugh. "You are always cutting down. You want to cut down on coffee, alcohol, and quit smoking. You don't seem to make the time to enjoy these things at all."

They taught me wine is a natural agricultural product. Way back in the seventies, a major New York City hospital experimented with using it exclusively for pain management because they felt it was healthier than any other drug. And, didn't the Bible specifically mention it was good for digestion? The more opportunities I had to be in Europe the more I understood the relationship between wine and good fresh food. I found the overall influence of it quite positive.

The impact of having cancer upped my intake, I'm sure. Life is too short to deny ourselves the creature comforts. During most of my adult life, I had sipped a glass while preparing dinner and had another splash with my meal. The second half glass I would continue to sip as I cleaned up the kitchen. That was my habit–one and a half glasses a day. Many studies came out to affirm this was actually good for you, though some reports specified four ounces. *What's the point of opening the bottle?* I thought. I went with two glasses a day and the number of ounces was flexible.

Years later, after the fifteen surgeries, the chemotherapy, the countless *procedures*, I began to drink more. In my defense, I want to state for the record that I did first try it the doctors' way. For five and a half years, I repeatedly mentioned my persistent pain and sleepless nights to my doctors. I told them I had not strung together more than four hours of sleep in all that time. They referred me to a pain clinic.

Many, *many* medical scandals ensued. Narcotics were avoided at all costs because tracking them was difficult for the doctors and their employees. Drugs not approved by the FDA were prescribed for the chronic pain syndrome caused by my cancer treatment. Pharmaceutical companies implied these drugs would help, but there was no proof. They had terrible side effects, the worst of which was constipation. I couldn't go. Ever. It gave me blinding headaches. So, I stopped the medications and started sipping more wine. It helps.

The Park in Avalon Park–2014

When I was young, there was an extra baseball field in my town for the overflow games. It was no bigger than a corner lot and the maintenance was minimal. A U-shaped wall of tall trees hemmed the space in. I recall a chain-link fence backstop and some trampled grass. It always looked dry and dusty. A well-worn path through the field extended into the woods, providing a short cut from the older part of town to the newer houses of the Brookside development. After my family moved away, this sad little ball field was transformed into a park, one specifically designed to accommodate special events.

I went online to the Avalon Park Town website and I clicked the *About Avalon Park* link, reading the description of the amenities it offered. There was a gazebo with electricity large enough to accommodate a five-piece band, including a full-sized drum kit. The fine, fescue grass space directly in front of the gazebo could accommodate most standard-sized rental tents. Embedded in the gardens that bordered the tent-ready areas were outdoor power outlets suitable for use by catering services. There was even a half-wall housing propane tanks for grills. Paving stone paths tastefully crossed the gardens and planters were at the ready to contain the annual blooms of spring bulbs, summer geraniums, and autumn mums.

At the entrance to the park were stone pillars with a cast metal archway. Abutting the pillars were the back cobblestone walls of the women's room (to the left if you are headed into the park) and the men's room (to the right). The doors of these facilities were unexpectedly impressive. Craftsmen, affiliated with the town, had been encouraged to submit their designs and had outdone themselves.

Party businesses were listed on the site. Their advertisements made arranging an event seem easy. It was all there: tents, a sound system, tables, chairs, food, and even a liquor store that walked us through the process of obtaining a liquor license. The nearest hotel also had a link, as did many referrals for wedding and party planners. As a committee member for the class reunion, I made note of the block-room rate and a generous cancellation policy. All we had to do was select a price point and a date. Most dates were already booked, but when we sent an email asking to book our reunion on June 29th, we received a swift response. The deed was done.

Invitations and inquiries began to go out by the miracle of Facebook, email, and our cell phone contacts. I quickly became sentimental about the friends I might see again after all this time. The football players from our grade school class were silent, and for Belinda's sake, I was grateful. But the music and theater "kids" were quick to contact Deb, some of them wanted to ask friends from other classes. The children who attended St. Agnes and Avalon Park Graded School knew each all their lives and were especially close. We attended elementary school from kindergarten to eighth grade together. When we moved up to high school, we made other friends and they, too, were clamoring for an invitation. This was not going to be the stereotypical reunion that re-enacted the high school pecking order, I realized.

The small group of us, who at a very young age had started giving plays at the local church in the summertime, was thrilled about getting together. I have always found it easier to ask forgiveness rather than ask for permission. Unilaterally I had made the decision to include kids from a few grades above us and below us. I was sure Donald Hampton's name had drawing power, so I asked him to write the posting.

He laughed. We had always gotten on well.

Bergen County Youth Theater North

At loose ends for the summer, some friends from Avalon Park looked at each other and said, "Let's put on a show!" Four weeks later, "A Man for All Seasons" premiered to a sold-out crowd. There was no air conditioning, some of the lights were held in place with twist-ties, and no one had thought to print programs. But, it turned out to be magic and something fantastic was off and running.

When we were a little older and rehearsals had ended, we would head for the reservoir. Who can forget the music floating across the summer air? For many of us those evenings were a rite-of-passage.

Hard as it is to believe, we started that little theater group forty-six years ago this July. Many of us are reconnecting now on the Internet; catching up on kids and careers. For some of us, though, the Internet isn't quite cutting it; some of us think what's needed here is some face-to-face time. So, in the same "let's-put-on-a-show" spirit, conversations have started about actually getting together.

The Avalon Park Graded School and St. Agnes Academy have hosted reunions together before. The classes of 1969 are now having their 45th Reunion at the Park in Avalon Park on Saturday June 29th. They have agreed to extend invitations to all members of our theater group including actors, student directors, musicians, dancers, artists, tech people, and crews, regardless of age or grade when you graduated from high school. If you want to come, we want you there! It is now a: **45ish** *Class Reunion.*

Please contact Patty Toohey at _pattyt55@gmsvt.net_ *for information.*

Those were some wonderful summers, and it would be amazing to spend some time again with the people who made them so. Please give this some thought and let us know soon. We can't wait to see you!
Many thanks,
Deb Guianti
Donald Hampton
Patty Toohey

It turned out to be a good thing we combined groups. I told Deb, the self-appointed reunion organizer, I hadn't intended to step on toes.

"No, no, there are no toes," she said. "I only jumped in because nobody else was doing anything about the 45th."

Deb was actually thrilled to have two other people helping her and we soon we had exactly the number of attendees we needed in order to make down payments and break even. We knew many would wait until the last minute, but it felt right to have covered our nut as it were. Don and I were both highly motivated and agreed this was the very party we wished we had created for ourselves in high school.

Nathaniel emailed me almost immediately:

Great news about the reunion. Where do I send the check?

It wasn't five minutes later when Belinda called to firm up our travel plans.

"So we will drive down together? And you understand that I need my own room?"

The decision to include more people changed any preconceived notion of what our reunion would look like. The rigid protocol normally surrounding a school reunion had been tossed out the window as people began messaging each other. The kids considered "cool" back then weren't coming, and it became evident it was morphing into an epic party for the *rest* of us. Most agreed that kids in the sub-cliques prove to be far more interesting over the long haul of life.

Don, who had recently been divorced by his wife of thirty years, said this reunion was just what he needed. I suspected she wanted to be single when her elderly parents died and she came into her inheritance. This was a phenomenon I had observed with a few couples who knew money was coming down the pike.

Additionally, Don was still recovering from surgery to have a cervical tumor removed from his spine when his wife had left him– trapped in the recliner of his home office. Two days before, a surgeon went in through the front of his neck to access the vertebrae, and he had been advised not to lie flat for a month. Even the shallow angle of the reclined position of the chair caused him to have a claustrophobic choking spasm. Every small movement caused him pain, but when he gasped, he would wildly thrust himself upright in an attempt to swallow. The abrupt effort precipitated a stabbing sensation that took his breath away and forced a whine out of him at the same time.

After one particularly vicious episode, the phone next to his chair rang. With great effort ("The telephone seemed to weigh as much as a barbell," he told me), he picked it up and carefully brought it to his ear. Seemingly coming from another dimension, he heard his wife's voice, "Did you even *notice* my clothes are gone? Did you even notice I'm not in the house?"

He said he had flushed red with embarrassment because he really had no idea. For the first time in his life, he was helpless. And, for the first time he could ever remember, he was utterly alone.

I assured Don it *was* the perfect time for a reunion.

When Nathaniel's check arrived in the mail, I noticed he paid for just *one person.*

The Morning of the Reunion
June 29, 2014

Don, Belinda, Deb, and I ordered room service for brunch. We had created a nest for Don on the chaise lounge with three giant pillows and a purple throw. The chaise was turned so it directly faced the side of the bed. I had ordered each of my friends to come to my room in lounging attire and to bring two pillows and a blanket with them. We girls made nests on the king-size bed, positioning ourselves by alternating feet and heads.

Don tried to get into the spirit of things by putting his feet up on the chaise. We could tell he felt stiff at first and a little out of his depth. He had rarely seen any of us since he moved out of New York City. Although his wife had left him, he admitted to having a fleeting thought she might be upset to see him in a situation like this. The way the four of us were sprawled around could be perceived as the beginning of a pornographic movie. Well, perhaps not a porn movie—after all, we were fifty-eight and Don's physician had specifically told him he was seriously out of shape.

As for the rest of us, Belinda had gained a great deal of weight since Don had last seen her. Deb looked pretty great for her age, he had to admit, but he never been particularly attracted to her. Don knew what had happened to me and he didn't really believe I would be wantonly shedding my clothes any time soon. Still, it was obvious there was a familiarity that made him uncomfortable.

I wanted to break through his tension. "What's the point of getting old if we can't have fun?" I asked him. I glanced around the room. "We did this when we were young, remember the choir trips? It felt so easy to be together then. I think we deserve to have as much fun as we used to. I certainly hope one advantage of getting older is we no longer have to worry about gender roles and sexual tension."

There was a knock on the door and two trays of food were brought in. The wait staff raised their eyebrows as they surveyed the hotel room and the old folks lounging around.

"There," I said after I had signed for the food and closed the door behind me. "We have created a *scandal* and I for one am delighted."

"A *scandal*," Don said. "I don't think I have ever *created* a scandal." He had the most adorable silly smile as he dug into his pancakes. The rest of us giggled like schoolgirls. For the first time in many years, I laughed so hard I had to lay back and hold my stomach because my muscles hurt.

Once we calmed down and finished breakfast, Deb announced how much time we had to kill before we would have to dress for the party. "I'm going to need a full hour just to do something with my hair," she said.

No one moved. We had been out late the night before and today promised to be a long one, as well. After ten minutes of silence, I assumed my roommates had gone to sleep. I've never been able to nap during the day, but it felt wonderful to rest. I stared at the ceiling.

With her eyes still closed, Deb asked, "Are you guys asleep?"

Everyone laughed.

I took hold of the situation. "I have an idea. I'll throw out a question. Let's start with Don and move clockwise around our circle. Belinda, you'll speak next."

Belinda smiled. "Can you tell she's a school teacher?"

We burst into laughter again.

I said, "The question is, what is the next big thing you would like to do in your life?" No self-editing allowed. Absolute honesty. It goes no further than this room. Don?"

The three of us rested our elbows on the mattress and framed our faces with the palms of our hands in mock anticipation. Our expressions were deliberately animated and we batted our eyes. Don knew we were joking, but I could tell he was still flattered by our attention.

"Okay... well... You all know I love to vacation by traveling to photography seminars. My family and friends have been complimentary about my work. When I post a new photo, I get all kinds of great feedback. I really want to know if I am any good."

After a few seconds of silence, I asked him, "What would have to happen in order for you to know that?"

While Don prepared his thoughts, I had a sudden insight. Belinda had been uncharacteristically quiet during our lounging breakfast. I perceived she was interested in Don, and now I waited for her to encourage him with praise. To my surprise, she remained quiet, and seemed groggy.

Don continued, "I have some ideas. There are a few magazines I could submit work to. And, there are websites for photographers to sell photos. That would be validation enough for me."

When we were sure he was done, we gave him a round of light applause. A good-for-you tone had been set.

Belinda was next and her answer was surprisingly simple. "I want to travel. Not around the world even. I have a client and she owns a cottage on Long Beach Island overlooking the sea. I would love to rent it for a week and drive down there."

Belinda had told me about the cottage the summer before and she had asked me to go with her. It was a long drive and I was loath to leave Vermont in the summer, which is its most perfect season. Belinda could also be volatile and I worried about feeling trapped for a week. Money was also an issue, as she could be generous when she had some, but she often didn't. When she let it slip she had already invited her current boyfriend, then our friend, Don, and another woman friend before asking me, I let go of any feelings of obligation.

Don spoke up, "You've mentioned this before Belinda. What has prevented you from going?"

The question stumped her. She pursed her lips and her eyes stretched open with the effort of thinking about his question. I could watch the wheels turning. After what seemed like a long time, she said in a quiet voice, "I'm not sure."

We grew quiet again until Deb said, "Maybe you don't have an answer right now. Maybe a seed has been planted here today."

We all nodded our heads in agreement.

After a few moments, Don squinted his eyes pointedly at me. "Patty? You're up next."

As soon as the words came out of his mouth, Belinda jumped up and said she had to use the bathroom. Something about the impatience in her voice sullied the moment. I resigned myself to self-reflection rather than taking the opportunity to address the group. The moment Belinda settled back in, Don returned me to the spotlight, asking me again to give my answer. I was grateful.

"Belinda?" I turned to my oldest friend, "Do you think it's fair to say I always finish a project once I have started it?"

"Absolutely!"

"I have been writing since the day I was diagnosed with cancer. That was almost twelve years ago. I thought with all that has happened to me, there must be a reason for it. I am honor bound to tell the story. I just can't seem to finish the book. So, that's my goal… to finish the damn book."

Deb made a sharp movement with her head. "Oh God, I'm sorry! I just saw the clock!" She was slightly panicked. "I know it sounds silly, but I'm a little nervous about this reunion. I feel if I just do my hair right, it will give me some confidence. I have to go and take a shower."

"Go!" Belinda said, releasing her from any further obligation. Everyone went into action and decided to get cleaned up, too. Don picked up his pillows and blanket. He asked me if he could help stack the dishes on the trays. Belinda, on the other hand, blew out of my room like a tornado, leaving the mess behind.

We agreed to meet in the lobby in ninety minutes.

The Big Day—June 29, 2014

The core reunion group showed up two hours early for the party. There were ten of us, including the four who had been in my room, for our brunch. We thought there would be last minute things to do, but the professionals we hired were very good at their jobs.

With almost two hours to wait, Don and I lollygagged our way through labeling name tags. I had argued against having to wear a self-stick piece of paper on the brand new dress I had bought for this occasion, but the others had overruled me.

The Park looked festive and elegant. We were all pleased. A bartender who was setting up his table was kind enough to allow us sodas and water as we puttered about. It was warm, but tolerable, by Jersey standards. I could hear Belinda telling the story she repeats at her twelve-step meetings. Her grogginess had been converted into something approaching mania.

"I am a recovering addict and alcoholic," she said. "I once woke up five thousand miles away from my home and no idea how I got there." I asked myself, "Why does she think it's a good idea to reintroduce herself to people with so many labels? She hadn't seen them in years." My judgment felt like a large bubble inside my brain that was about to burst.

Little did I know at the very moment she was declaring herself twenty-five years clean and sober, she was actually under the influence of drugs. Belinda wore a beaded pouch with a strap that crossed over her shoulder and draped between her breasts. The pouch itself nestled onto her left hip. In it was a red pack of Marlboros, a bottle of tranquilizers, another of amphetamines, and an old Tylenol bottle packed full of black market Oxycontin.

I could feel my jaws clenching in disapproval as she droned on. My rule of thumb is before you disclose your mistakes to someone, they must first have earned your trust. And… yes… by the way, this is a *party*; we are supposed to be having a good time here. Nobody gets a prize for having had the worst life. I knew from experience that I couldn't stop her diatribe, so I walked far enough away from the sound of her voice that I couldn't hear the actual words she was saying anymore. It was just a steady rhythm now of and… and… and.

I'd had enough of Belinda during the car trip down from Albany. She complained that I was controlling. She bellowed at me to slow down, and blamed her temper on her anxiety problems. She asked repeatedly why it was taking so long. We had to stop frequently so she could smoke a cigarette. When, at long last, we reached the hotel, she took to her bed. We were already an hour late to meet friends for dinner when I decided to call her. We had adjoining rooms and when her phone rang, I could hear her screaming like an angry toddler. Having rationalized her bad behavior over forty-eight years, I finally acknowledged in that moment that she was impossible. Instead of mellowing her, age had made her more difficult.

I was locking my door when she emerged from her room in a state of suspicious calm. Her eyes were blurry, but she announced she was ready to go. We arrived at the restaurant just in time to say good-bye to our friends. We stood on the sidewalk outside catching up, and by the time we got back to the hotel, I was starving.

So, suffice it to say, that today, I was in no mood to listen to her war stories about her drinking years. I saw a wood and cast-iron bench under an ancient tree with the branches spreading an enormous canopy over the area. I walked over and sat down, glad to have a few minutes alone. A breeze rustled the leaves. I gazed out onto the scene where our party would be taking place in a few hours. It was exactly the way I had imagined it. The band was setting up in the gazebo, which abutted the large white party tent. The sides of the tent were rolled up and tied with red and blue ribbons. Party lights adorned all the vertical stakes used to support the roof. A wooden dance floor covered a third of the space. Round tables and white chairs were placed in a semi-circle around the floor. I watched the bartender in his separate tent polishing glasses.

The breeze shifted and then Belinda's voice floated into my consciousness once more, interrupting my reverie. She said, "I could never have children because my high school boyfriend... you remember Keith?... got me pregnant and wouldn't take responsibility. It was horrible. I was just a teenage girl. I was bleeding heavily and my mother took me to the emergency room. It was terrible to see the look on her face when the doctor told her what was wrong with me. He was my boyfriend and, after that procedure, he turned his back on me. I was devastated. Apparently, the scarring from the abortion was terrible because when I was ready to have a baby, I couldn't get pregnant. I tried for years." A shocked moan went up from the circle surrounding Belinda.

She was working especially hard to ensnare Don in her tale of woe. I had expected her to verbally pounce during our room-service brunch at the hotel, but Belinda evidently needed more of an audience. On the drive down from New York, Belinda told me they had chatted online and this had led to phone calls. She had ticked off the ways Don would be a good catch for her. He was very successful... meaning he made a lot of money. His children were grown... meaning she wouldn't have to raise any kids. His divorce was his wife's idea so that would be over soon. She pointedly said while I was driving that she had never had children, and let the statement hang in the air. I didn't respond, as I didn't know where she was going with it. She stared straight ahead, then said, "My vagina and breasts are still firm."

I started to fume, hating the tone of the one-sided conversation. After all, I had had three nine pound babies. She continued, "Someone is going to snatch him up and it might as well be me."

I finally responded, "In the entire world, there are no two people more different than you and Don."

I was determined not to take the bait and confront her. Don is an extremely intelligent man, I reasoned, and he can certainly figure out what he wants. Who knew, maybe he was up for a good fling? The less rational side of me desperately wanted to warn Don about what I knew Belinda was selectively editing to her advantage. However, this was none of my business. There was no good that could come from me filling him in on Belinda's checkered past. Even though they had not been friends, I was sure he had some idea of what went on during the Studio 54 years. He would discover all that he needed to know in his own good time.

Belinda's voice was again dominating the space around me, and I could feel my old anxiety that occurred during her indiscretions kicking in. Another statement about Keith ruining her life floated back to me. Does she think she is in a therapy session, I wondered? I thought about walking over to the group and attempting to redirect the conversation to a safer topic. I could see the cluster of people around her, who were riveted by her storytelling, but I also knew the topic of Keith would be polarizing.

Poor Keith! He would be showing up for the party soon and, unbeknownst to him, there were at least five people who knew a dark secret about him that may or may not be true. It was like being back in high school again; only the stakes were much higher. As for me, I decided to pretend I didn't hear any of it. I had managed to stay friends with both Belinda and Keith all these years and I simply was not going to get involved.

I switched my attention to Deb, who was at a small folding table with name tags, a checklist, and a small metal box for money. I wandered over to see if I could help. She greeted our classmates, checked them off her list, and I handed over their name. I quickly realized Deb had been right about the tags. Many of our classmates were heavier, lost hair, or aged so much I would not have recognized them without one.

Within the hour, I felt like a supermodel of the Class of 1969. I weighed three pounds more than I had when I was eighteen and I had all my own teeth. My hair was a shorter and a more fragile version of the waist-length mane I carried around when I was young, but I still had it. I had also inherited my father's pigment, so I'd never gone completely gray; instead, it had simply darkened with age. It was rumored my paternal grandfather died with jet-black hair. In my new summer frock that covered all my scars, I felt pretty good about myself.

I heard another car door slam and glanced toward the parking area. I saw a vintage red convertible Volkswagen Beetle with the top down. The Tomato! My heart leapt. Next to the driver's side door stood a rather bloated older gentleman with brassy blond hair. The hair color seemed wrong, more like something meant for a doll. It was too thick for someone this man's age. I already knew Nathaniel was quite sick and I expected him to look frail, but whereas I got skeletally thin and wore my baldness openly during my cancer treatment, he was extra thick around the middle and wore a wig.

The desperate bulk of hair stood out in grotesque contrast to his gray skin and faded eyebrows. I watched as he slipped on a suit jacket and an expensive and large-framed pair of sunglasses. His body was now encased in what was surely a custom-made suit. With his eyes covered, he had managed to disguise the dying man and transform into an affluent doctor.

Nathaniel, yes, *my* Nathaniel, walked up the short pathway to the table where Deb and I stood. I tried to draw a breath as he came near. When he came closer, my hands began to shake and I stuck them in the pockets of my dress. I was sure I was still wearing the generic smile I had on my face before I saw him. My mouth had suddenly gone dry, and my top lip, due to the intense parchedness, stuck to my front teeth. It would neither slide up nor down. I hastily took a swig of my bottle of water and turned to lick my teeth and spread some of the moisture around.

Nathaniel spoke to Deb first. He shook her hand and accepted his name tag, "Thank you so much for organizing this event. I must apologize that I haven't been any help at all. I hope you understand. I look forward to catching up with you later, but right now I need to speak to Patty." He walked around to my side of the table, stood close to me and held my eyes. "Could we have a few minutes before all this gets into full swing?"

I welled with tears. I was grateful he *wanted* those few minutes. I took his arm and led him to the bench where I had observed the party preparations. We sat. I reached up briefly to touch his face, convincing myself I wasn't dreaming. We talked as though no time had passed since our last conversation. We didn't speak about the minutia of our everyday lives. There was no specific mention of children, spouses, or careers. We talked instead about ourselves, and what we had observed about life over the many years we had been apart. We spoke in the private language we had developed when we were still children.

I revealed myself to him. "What was God thinking?" I asked. "If you do a really good job as a parent, your children grow up to be independent and they don't need you anymore. All the sacrifice, all the expense, all the time. If they are healthy adults, they move out of your house and you are lucky to get a phone call. What kind of system it *that?*"

He laughed and nodded in agreement. "I worked so hard to learn to communicate," he said. "Everybody said marriage is about communication. So, when I finally learned to listen I found I was actually troubled to hear what my wife had to say. I realized I don't want to know what she's thinking. I found it was better for both of us if we moved forward on a very superficial level."

I let out a little whoop when I heard this and slapped my leg. "I know, I know! Never ask your spouse what they are *thinking*, or worse... if something is *wrong.*"

We laughed until my face ached and we were delighted with ourselves. Although we had lived an entire adult lifetime apart, *we* hadn't changed at all.

Once I adjusted to Nathaniel's wig and extra weight gain, I began to notice other things about him. He clearly exercised as his arms and shoulders were more muscular than I had ever seen them. His skin, while ashen, was still his. And, I found his hands fascinating. He gestured with them when he spoke and, much to my horror, I found myself suddenly and completely aroused.

I was extremely annoyed to be blushing like a young girl. I waved my hands as if fanning my face and blamed it on a hot flash. He slowly leaned back and put one arm across the bench while I scooted as far as I could to the edge in order not to be too close. He sat in repose, and glancing over at him, I was sure I wasn't imagining the smug little smile that appeared and disappeared.

I wanted to bring the conversation back around to our life lessons. "I've learned no one is indispensable," I said. "For years, I would not allow myself to miss a single day of work. No matter how sick I was, I assumed my students needed me. The first time I allowed a substitute teacher to take my classes, I was stunned when the kids told me how much fun they had had."

"You know, Patty. When we were young, I felt known. Everyone took me exactly as I was. I've never experienced it since. Once we graduated from high school, I found myself constantly trying to measure up to what someone wanted me to be. "

"Like the only real friends you make are when you are children."

Nathaniel agreed sadly. "Like it was the only time you get to be loved as you are."

We nodded in synch and it was a wonderful feeling to be understood. I could have spent the entire afternoon with him discussing whatever came to mind, but when we noticed Belinda waving furiously and beckoning to us to come join the group under the tent, we had no choice. The look on her face was accusatory and we both felt suddenly embarrassed. Reluctantly, we brushed ourselves off and went to join the party. Only now, when we were walking side by side across the grass did I feel any awkwardness. The intimacy of our conversation made me acutely aware of the spouses we had both left at home. I was positive he felt the same.

We entered the tent and headed toward the small group Belinda had been entertaining earlier. Belinda, speaking in a stage whisper, tried to enlist their help.

"Keith's here! He's here! I can't believe he has the balls to face me!"

The group was expanding by the minute, curious about the melodrama going on.

Keith was on the bandstand visiting with the musicians. He is the most handsome man of Puerto Rican ancestry I have ever met. When we spoke on the phone, he told me he was turning into an "*hombre gordo*" as he grew old, but the truth was time had been kind to him. He was also charming.

From the years we were in Manhattan together, he had played in professional bands. He had loved touring, but grew tired of sleeping on couches. I learned from our conversations he was now an engineer by day and played music two weekends a month.

I watched Keith and the drummer talk. Then Keith turned and spotted all of us across the dance floor. Agile as someone half his age, he jumped off the stage and strode over to a small group beside me and opposite Belinda. The smile that lit up his handsome face was slow to leave, for it took him a few seconds to recognize and absorb the dead silence that greeted him. I understood he had to reorient himself. Most of the group members stared at the ground, obviously uncomfortable. Keith's face crumpled into an expression of bewilderment and dismay.

"What's going on?" he asked the group directly.

Don, God bless him, took matters into his own hands. As a divorce mediator and collaborative attorney, he was used to handling difficult situations. He drew himself up to his full height and exhaled.

"Keith. Nobody wants any trouble here. We have come a long way to attend this event and we just want to have a good time. The truth is Belinda does not wish to speak to you. I'm going to ask you to honor her request. Please join a different group and we'll all just go back to the party."

I could not have been more impressed with Don. He had managed to say what most of the group was thinking *and* he made it sound like a reasonable choice.

However, Keith was incredulous. He stared at Belinda, his eyes displaying his innocence. "Why?" he asked. "It can't be because we broke up. We were just kids... I mean, that was forty-two years ago."

Deb, full of nervous energy, as always, could no longer stand the growing tension. Her eyes bulged a bit when she spoke. "You got her pregnant! She had to have an abortion and you abandoned her. The only thing she ever wanted in her life was to be a mother and you destroyed that dream. She had terrible scarring! Her parents found out and humiliated her. The entire family was traumatized."

I could hear her energy wane with each frenzied statement. Her voice grew quieter as her conviction wavered. Her last sentence was said in a whisper with her face showing regret. I will say this about Deb in that moment—despite the high humidity—her hair looked fantastic.

Keith grunted in disbelief. He was clearly knocked backward by Deb's outburst, and seeing me, he grabbed my arm for support. I, too, was stunned because I knew Belinda had had two abortions in New York City in her twenties. On one of those occasions, I know she was furious about being pregnant and couldn't wait to be rid of the baby. I had many reasons to be indebted to Belinda, but this conscious action to destroy Keith's reputation was cruel. It struck me that she was extremely unhappy at this time in her life and she was on the prowl for someone to blame.

Keith took a moment to compose himself, then shook his head as though still in disbelief about the accusation. Even in anger, he was striking. His pore-less skin made him appear as if he had been carved out of beeswax; his gorgeous high cheekbones flexed, his jaw clenched. His dark eyes glowed. We couldn't take our eyes off him.

I have always found the truth has a ring to it. We know it when we hear it because it is instantly convincing. I had never seen stronger proof of that than what Keith uttered next. "Belinda, you and I have never had sex," he said.

Our gazes switched from Keith to Belinda. The defiant look on her face faltered and her jaw, which had been thrust forward in rage, was now trembling.

Keith, acting neither cruel nor superior, addressed her in a clear voice. "You were pregnant when we started dating. You wanted to get an abortion because you didn't know who the father was and you came to me for help. I did help you, even though I knew I wasn't responsible for the baby. I have never told anyone about it, *never*, even after all these years. I'm pretty devastated right now." In ending his speech, he allowed himself a modicum of bitterness. "I don't understand why you would do this to me."

A floodgate of shame had broken open inside Belinda during Keith's disclosure, an emotional hurricane that swept her out of the tent. One moment she stood with her haughty face sucked in across from me, sneering at Keith, and the next she was halfway across the green space. I thought, and this is actually how my mind works, there should have been a sound effect at the ready for such an exit. Nathaniel agreed when I later talked to him about it. We debated what that sound should have been.

Schwoosh?

Thrwoom?

Zzzuummiiiinng?

Visually, it would appear in the air as bold text like a comic strip. Belinda, with her exaggerated looks and style, had come to resemble a character in a Marvel comic.

Intuitively, I knew she was headed for the copse of trees at the back of the park and to our old short cut. I ran—actually ran—in my almost-high-heeled shoes, to catch up with her. It was my knee-jerk response to Belinda's panic that sent me chasing after her. I was forced to slow down when I reached the narrow, root-covered path, and had to duck slightly when I stepped into the woods.

I heard her ahead of me thrashing through the tree branches and prickly bushes.

"Belinda! Slow down," I called to her, but she didn't respond.

I saw patches of her as she moved through the dense green leaves. I sent up a silent prayer to be delivered from the poison ivy, which I am deathly allergic to. I slapped at the buzzing insects around my hair and neck. Of course, I am also severely allergic to bug bites. Again, I prayed, this time not to be bitten in the corner of my eye. It's not a great look when your eye swells shut. I tripped on my stupid heels and then caught the right one on a tree root sending me flying. When I righted myself, I saw the front of my calf was bleeding. A few more minutes of stumbling and I remembered the trail would soon open up when we reached the tree fort. I was rewarded with the sight of Belinda standing on the far end of the clearing with her back to me, gasping.

Sunlight streamed down in thick, steamy rays at an angle in front of her, casting her into a shadowy silhouette. She was overweight and she had large breasts. Belinda had struggled with her weight as she aged, fluctuating between obesity and an overall plumpness. Today, she was wearing calf-length black leggings and a graphic, brightly colored tunic over them. The tunic was at this moment stuck high on the top of her butt. She yanked it down and smoothed it over her rear end and thighs.

Half bent over from the exhaustion of running, we both inhaled and exhaled deeply trying to slow our breathing.

"Geez," I said, laughing, "I didn't think you would ever slow down."

As soon as I said it, her body still a contoured shadow, froze. Her posture abruptly changed in a manner that was disquieting to me. She just didn't look... right. Her demeanor made me squirm. Letting my eyes examine the clearing, I saw the tree fort from our childhood, but it was bigger and more gentrified. A plaque on the tree announced it was now an official community project. Nearby was a small stack of lumber left over from the construction project. Judging by the greenish color of the wood I surmised it was pressure treated.

Belinda squared her shoulders, arched her back, stuck her butt out, and then tossed her hair at me. She flexed her neck this way and that. In the alternating profile, I saw her superior expression. She turned slowly toward me with a snicker on her face. I recognized her sucked-in cheeks and imperious manner though she was now cast in deep, dappled shadows. She stared at me, inviting confrontation with a *blink, blink, blink* of her enormous butterscotch eyes glowing in the relative darkness.

My fight-or-flight instinct was now fully shrieking. I felt like I was staring into the eyes of a stranger. The blinding light and contrasting deep shadows still obscured many details. I tried to calm down. I told myself to stop overreacting and my hand flew up to shade my vision in an attempt to better focus on her. Blackbirds called and crickets roared as the seconds passed. The odor of a charcoal fire was pungent in the humid air. Then, I was only aware of us breathing.

Finally she drawled at me. "It's not like *your* love life has been perfect."

I responded reflexively because as much as my body signaled a warning, my brain was trying hard to make sense of her peculiar behavior. "Obviously, Belinda, I was divorced."

Ignoring me, she said, "You make so much out of the past, Mary Patricia. Ohhhh, Nathaniel this and Nathaniel that, as if you two had the perfect love."

A foreboding silence lay between us and I was aware of one heartbeat and then another. Adrenaline was already making my head pound.

"He didn't love you as much as you like to think. It wasn't the way you remember it." She had a sly sneer on her face belonging to someone I didn't know at all.

I moved toward the lumber pile, upon which rested a four-foot long two-by-two. My sweaty palms itched for the feel of it. I watched her rear up and stretch her spine like a pin-up girl from an old movie. She was clearly having fun.

Blood roared in my ears when I asked her, feeling somewhat foolish as I said the words, "Who *are* you?"

"I'm one of the Belindas," she responded. "She calls me Brigitte, like Bardot, but I'm just one of us."

"Have we met before?" I asked her, curious despite my chilling discomfort.

"No. But she has talked about me."

I was astonished to realize this was true. Belinda had talked about a part of herself that arose when a man was around. I thought she was describing herself as Brigitte Bardot*ish* because of the way she acted. She had always said she hated that she became another person with men. I never believed it was an *actual* other person.

I said, "I thought you weren't supposed to know about each other. I mean, if there are two of you inside the same person."

She glared at me as if she had a bad taste in her mouth and said, "That's only in the movies. Of course we know all about each other. We're not *insane.*"

When she used that word, every hair on my body stood on end. I felt nauseous as she continued, "We are so tired of you. We are more intelligent than you are; some men even think we're more beautiful. Yet, everybody admires Patty. Oh yes, everybody likes Mary Patricia. Our teachers believed her to be the smartest. She's always one of the guys, although they are all secretly in love with her. It gets so old. You have children. You even got your husband back. You have everything I ever wanted. I would kill for your life."

The word "kill" hung heavy in the air. Fear coursed through me making my hands and feet sweat. Yet, I also felt deadened and detached as if I were watching the whole scene from above.

"I had Nathaniel in the tree fort," she said, waving her hand about her head. "He wasn't very good. As tall as he is you'd think his package would be bigger."

She turned away from me, dug into her pouch, extracted a cigarette, and lit it. I watched her as she inhaled with deep satisfaction. It was a post-cataclysmic moment, one she had the power to inflict on me.

I didn't believe she'd had sex with Nathaniel. Not for one second. It was impossible for me to imagine him lowering his standards to have sex with the girl she was back then. And, too,

Belinda often lied. Why would I believe it?

"He made the strangest noise when he got off," she said calmly. She again had my full attention as she continued, "It was like a demented horse whinny." She imitated him, "Whooooo haaaaaa haaaaa, whooooo haaaaa haaaaaa."

Her performance only lasted a couple of seconds, but my understanding of the truth had turned on a dime. As my mind swirled in a full circle, my body did, too. At the tail end of my pivot, I leaned over to pick up the piece of wood; in a second graceful movement I swung it over my shoulder like a baseball bat. Belinda still had her back turned to me as she dramatically flicked her cigarette to one side and behind her in my direction.

"Where was I when this happened?" I asked her simply, and she answered with a shrug,

"At your aunt's house."

I took a stance to ready myself for an imaginary pitch across a pretend home base. With one arm, I pointed the wood into the crowd of forest trees to call the spot where I would hit my home run. I wound my arms to aim and walked toward her. With cold cunning, I repositioned my stance several feet behind her, but slightly to her left. My swing into her shoulder blades had perfect follow-through as I shifted from my right foot to my left front. I harnessed all the adrenaline flowing through my veins. It hit with all the power and force of a grand slam, actually lifting her off the ground. She went flying head first into a cluster of skunk cabbages.

Brook Street

The tree fort marked a halfway point from the old part of town and the cul-de-sac where my childhood home was. The style of the house was center hall colonial; an architectural reproduction I thought was a cliché even when I lived there. I much preferred the antique homes set in the older section of town with their mature trees and narrower streets with sidewalks.

Our house was situated in a now almost sixty-year-old development called Brookside. The trees were varied and even exotic, like the Japanese maple in our side yard, but they were too small to give any significant shade. For reasons unknown to me, the developer had made the streets really wide. There were no sidewalks, so I concluded that it was paved to both walk on and drive down. When I was young, the dark expanse of asphalt offended my aesthetic sensibilities. Walking these roads made me feel vulnerable and exposed.

The only advantage of the area was it was fun to play on during a hot summer day. The tar bubbled up to the surface in the heat, and we thought it was fun to pop the bubbles with our big toes, causing scorching water to spray over us as we ran away laughing. At least, that was what we believed it to be, though I suspect it was a chemical leaching out of the tar. What is asphalt made of anyway? No wonder I got cancer.

After letting Belinda have it, I wanted to see my house again. I hurried down the path. The light ahead of me was brightening, indicating the trees would soon give way to open sky. Belinda was far behind me. I could barely hear her shrieks. When I left, the cries she was emitting sounded more like she was having a temper tantrum rather than wailing in physical pain. I fought an urge to run back and hit her again.

I emerged from the woods into the blasting summer day. I glimpsed down at my feet as I walked, trying to dodge the piles that dogs left behind. That's when I saw Nathaniel sitting in his vintage convertible. The top was down and the radio was playing.

"Is she all right?" he asked me casually.

"I hope not," I said, my hands on my hips.

My tone apparently startled him. He blinked and asked, "Why?"

"Because she selected this moment in time to tell me she had sex with you. I picked up a piece of wood and hit her with it. Knocked her to the ground."

He sat there in his open Bug, leaning back with one arm up on the window frame. He retrieved his pair of expensive sunglasses from the dashboard and put them on. He had taken his jacket off, revealing a short-sleeved sporty shirt. He was chewing gum in that sexy way only boys from New Jersey can do. Finally he said, "Jesus," without much inflection.

He wasn't giving anything away; he was going to bide his time and see where this conversation was headed. His mouth and cheekbones remained locked in a deadpan expression while he chewed. I stood frozen, staring at him. He broke the silence that lay between us by popping his gum at the corner of his mouth.

"I was at my Aunt Sheila's house, Nathaniel."

"What is that supposed to mean?" He tilted his face back as though he was ready to sunbathe. I knew him well, maybe better than anybody, and I knew he was avoiding my eyes.

"That's it!" I yelled, and started to stomp away from him and down toward my old house. This was the street I had lived on for almost eight years. I thought I knew it like the back of my hand, but the cool canopy of trees lining both sides of the road suddenly disoriented me. The gardens were beautiful. Every lawn was of a uniform turf that simply wouldn't survive out in the country, certainly not in the state of Vermont. Each narrow blade of grass was a shade of green that had been blended with the slightest hue of blue. Wouldn't it feel cool, I thought, to lie down on the soft ground?

The great weight of Belinda's disclosure made me want to sink to my knees and take a nap on one of these lawns, but I willed my leaden legs to keep moving. Each time my foot hit the ground, it made a booming sound inside my ears. Yet, I was still aware enough to be shocked by the neighborhood with its large, well-kept homes. It seemed only vaguely familiar, like something I had seen in a magazine.

I heard a crunching gravel sound as Nathaniel slowly turned the car around to follow me. I continued to walk with the thundering in my ears. He drove alongside me in silence, with the car's engine and the road grit crackling beneath the tires breaking the silence that hung heavily between us.

Finally, I couldn't bear the tension. "I was at my Aunt Sheila's house!" I said again.

It was a primordial howl from deep inside my gut, so deep that it nearly knocked me over backward. I tried to steady myself.

"Uh… okay…"

"It was Sunday dinner. It's not like I was away for the whole summer. It's not like I *moved*. I was gone for a couple of hours." I stopped talking because I felt a sob coming up.

I will not cry!

I will *not* cry.

I will not *cry.*

I forced myself to keep walking. My heart felt like it was swelling. It seemed enormous and started to beat so slowly that a fright came over me. I wondered if I was having a heart attack. I had survived two different breast cancers and now I am going to keel over face first into the asphalt? In New *Jersey?*

I tried with all my might to maintain my dignity. The crunchy, gravelly sound continued as Nathaniel slowly drove down the street beside me. I felt the blood rushing to my head. I had never experienced such rage.

He can't even get out of the car? I thought. Quickly changing my mind, I realized if he got out of the car, I might hurt somebody else today. The Bug was close enough for me to feel the heat coming off its hood.

Crunchyroll, crunchyroll.

The sound irritated me to the core.

Crunchyroll, crunchyroll.

I turned on my heel in a fury. I lost my balance again and so I planted my feet wider, facing him. Nathaniel. Yes, *that* Nathaniel. The *first* Nathaniel.

I heard him put the car in park. He stared impassively at me from behind the dark glasses. Eventually, but I have no idea of the time frame, he opened his door. At first, there was a jolt of triumph because I had won. He had made the first move to break the tension between us. Then, out of the clear blue sky, I started pulling in deep raggedy breaths. My exhales became a terrible sound to hear, even to myself. Nathaniel made his way around so the car was between us, but he could face me.

"Look," he said. "It's really hot out here. I want you to try to calm down for your own sake."

"Always the *doctor*," I spat at him.

Nathaniel winced with the layers of my meaning. "Patty, I don't want to make you angrier than you already are, but this thing with her happened over forty-three years ago. I was a teenage boy. I was wrong, but I was just a boy."

I asked him, "Is it possible you were the father of Belinda's baby?"

My eyes never left his face, but his skittered around me, down to the ground, and finally up to stare into my eyes as he let out a huge sigh. Then, he stood with his hands in his pockets staring at the clouds. He released a second sigh before he suddenly moved in my direction. My legs were shaking so badly that I was unable to walk away. He came closer and closer, testing whether I would bolt or not. Eventually, he was near enough for me to smell his cinnamon-milky-vanilla scent. It had mixed with his man sweat as the sun beat down on us. I nearly fainted when he put his arms around me.

I wish I could say my extreme reaction was an exaggeration. I would have loved to discover his power over me was not in any way like I remembered it. But, never has an embrace brought more relief. We clung to each other until we both began to shake. When I finally pulled away to look at him, I realized we were crying. A whispered moan escaped from him, "I am sorry, Mary Pat. I'm so sorry. I'm so sorry."

Time must have passed. It seemed suspended, but that doesn't really happen, not in real life. I know it was enough of an interval to grieve the loss of us so many years ago and what we might have become together. Somehow, we had shifted from deep regret about our past to *this* moment in this place. Across the almost six decades of our lives, we had both learned a great deal about grief and how to move forward. We drew upon that knowledge now.

I needed to say it out loud, "We really did love each other, didn't we?"

"Oh, Patty!" He seemed exasperated. "I was just too young to realize it. How rare it is, how seldom it comes along, I... oh, Jesus..." He rubbed his eyes with the heels of his hands. "I wouldn't have thought I had any tears left," he said, and we both started to laugh.

"Back then, I had a plan for my life which included medical school and money. Lots of money. I thought I was in *control.* If I knew then what I know now." He paused and turned to me. "But then, I wouldn't have left you, which means I might not be a doctor, wouldn't have my son. I might have had other children with you, but not the son I love so much."

That said it all.

I would never trade the events of my life either, for the exact sequence had brought my three sons to me. *Wouldn't give nothing for my journey now. Nothing for my journey now.* The old spiritual ran through my head. Mary Patricia and Nathaniel did what they did, and it could not have been any different.

I heard voices and saw people were watching us. One woman made a big gesture in our direction. I suddenly grew alarmed at the possibility Belinda might stagger out of the woods any minute covered in dead leaves and maybe even blood. Were that to occur, she would surely be howling like a spoiled child.

I said to Nathaniel, "Let's get out of here before somebody calls the police."

I got into his car. It seemed certain to me this would be the last day I would ever see him. He was very ill and I, too, was lucky to still be alive.

As we sped back in the direction of the party, I leaned my head back and felt the wind and sunshine on my face. Feeling washed clean, I stole a glance over at Nathaniel. He was bone tired. He was old and bloated from the medications that he had to take. What once upon a time was perceived as exceptional confidence for someone so young had long ago decayed into arrogance. Beneath the sunglasses, there permanently resided an expression of self-importance. I weighed the measure of the man before me against the boy I once knew. How long and far had I carried a different image of him flash-frozen in time? Memories from thirty, even forty, years ago, handpicked and then crystallized in my mind. It made me think of a poem I sometimes read to my science students:

"Amber, the freezing gold, that is not hot and is not cold
Has caught within its dreaming arms,
the insects and the flowers charms
Time has kept as still as death, holding instant, every breath
Now from out our fading past, a scene which can forever last."
~ Garry Platt

Amber hardens over time. It is, at first, a fluid resin created inside a tree that slowly secretes out when there is a wound on the bark. Some insects are repelled by it. Others are attracted and even get trapped on its sticky fluid surface. Protecting the tree's gaping wound, the resin continues to flow out and over the living creature. The insect may wind up memorialized in rare precious stone. Petrified, the little creature in the amber is fascinating when held up to the light. We can project feelings onto the bug and speculate over what it might have been thinking when it was covered. The truth is, though, that even before the insect became entombed, it had already died.

I talked to Nathaniel as we drove back. "You and me, me and Belinda, we were fused together by emotional shocks that got hardwired into our brains. We were so loyal to each other that we experienced a whole lot of first times together: our first time away from our parents at camp, our first movie without adult supervision, first drink, first sexual experience, and all these experiences create a powerful bonding. I hang on to Belinda because I feel if I can just repair our friendship, my childhood pain will be fixed, too."

He nodded a silent yes several times. Despite the sunglasses, I could tell he was thinking very hard about my amber metaphor. He said, with one hand on the steering wheel, the other gesturing to me, "I once saw an entire flower, stem and all, preserved in amber. It was in a museum."

His pensiveness encouraged me to continue. "I have idealized the love we had, Nathaniel. We were such good friends, I could literally tell you anything. We had that because we grew up together. You protected me when we were young, so, naturally, I always feel safe around you. If I had met you when I was thirty, you probably would be like any other man. At times unkind. Me always trying to interpret the monosyllabic responses you gave me across the dinner table. No one has ever told me marriage is easy, not one person."

We remained in contemplation the rest of the way.

Nathaniel dropped me off in the parking area near the tent. "Please say goodbye to everyone for me." Our eyes met. "Seeing you again has taken its toll on me." He shifted his gaze to the rear view mirror for a few seconds before making a disgusted face and pushing it away. "I look like shit. I feel like it, too. The heat only makes it worse."

I knew he must be serious because he had impeccable manners; it was unlike him to consider driving away from his classmates without making the rounds to say goodbye. We hugged one more time, and then, I tore myself away before I started to cry again. I reached for the door handle and heard his final words to me, "You might as well know I slept with Deb, too. The summer after my first year of medical school."

I opened the door and said over my shoulder, "I could have gone the rest of my life and not have needed to know that, Nathaniel."

I sauntered toward the tent, and realized I looked damn good in this purple dress that covered up all my scars. I knew Nathaniel was watching my still fine ass as I took long strides away from him.

I ducked into the tent and never looked back.

And Yet It Was Fun

The band's regular drummer stood on the sidelines drinking a beer and watching Keith play his set. His head bobbed up and down to the rhythm and it was obvious he admired Keith's skill. I was surprised by how good Keith's chops still were. From our periodic phone conversations, I knew he played out perhaps twice a month. His performance tonight told me he had to have practiced a lot, and for the first time, I wondered if he was heartsick about having given up his music career. We all knew he had been devastated when his wife, who was younger than the rest of us, died of cancer four years ago.

The band took a break and Keith walked over to the bar, and ordered a glass of wine for me. "Thank you. I could really use this," I said.

He said, "Hey, I love you."

"I love you, too."

We didn't need words. He put his arm around me.

"Nathaniel's gone. He doesn't feel well."

Keith nodded and said the band wanted him to play guitar on the following song.

"Do it!"

He went back to the bandstand and over the next hour owned the entire crowd, switching from guitar to lead vocals and back to drums. Everyone was going crazy, dancing in a kind of ecstasy because the band kept on delivering.

I walked over to Don and whispered in his ear, "Is this part of the grand finale we were talking about?"

In response, he put an arm around me but never took his eyes off the stage.

During the last song, a New Jersey anthem of my generation called *Badlands;* Keith put on a pair of sunglasses and played the saxophone. We were screaming and jumping up and down pretending he was the celebrity, "The Big Man," and not an impersonator. I danced to every song.

Keith staggered off the stage and whispered to me that he was exhausted. I handed him a glass of water. He was the star of the night and the most beautiful women at the party clamored to be near him, and he let himself enjoyed it.

While the band took a break, we played taped music — Elvis, big-band music, and Doo Wop. Don had not once stepped off the sidelines during the rock and roll classics, although he still danced in place and threw his arms up in the air the way he used to at the reservoir. However, when an iconic Bee Bop tune, *Jungle Fever,* was played, he grabbed my hand and escorted me to the dance floor. In an exceptionally well-executed and complicated jitterbug, Don astonished everyone as he led me through the swing dance. At one point, he had us back to back, our arms linked, and in a great swoop rolled me up and over. I had a moment of panic that I might rupture a disc, which made it all the more fun when I landed with no harm done.

The song ended and Deb cut in for a dance. It seemed every woman present wanted a turn at dancing the jitterbug or foxtrot. I was surprised by Don's stamina. He wrote to me a few months later to say when he returned to Washington; he joined a dance club and met "a very nice woman" there.

At five o'clock in the afternoon, the party was winding down. Don, Keith, and I went to the microphone to thank Deb for her hard work. Someone had started a collection to pay the band for another set of music, which was well worth the money. No one wanted the afternoon to end. It turned out that the group was playing a gig just down the road that night. We all went out to dinner and then returned to the hotel for a little nap. At ten o'clock, we met at the roadside bar. Belinda was nowhere to be found and I wasn't looking.

Fortunately, for the rest of us, Don, who doesn't drink, declared himself the designated driver. The rest of us got a little crazy.

The Fourth of July 2014

The Northeast Kingdom of Vermont is known for its many glacial ponds and lakes. On this summer morning, on one particularly remote body of water, the morning mist was just starting to be warmed by the rising sun. The mist lifted and formed twirling columns of white.

At daybreak I had thought it was raining, but Rich assured me we were "just socked in; it won't last." By the time great patches of fog had burned away to blue sky, we were halfway across the pond. A bald eagle flew high above us, waiting to fish. Rich was in his big, blue kayak and I paddled along in my smaller red one. We circled our paddles on one side and then the other, barely making a splash. Nearer to the far shore was an island where a pair of nesting loons lived. We wanted to find out how the hatchlings were progressing. And, if we were very lucky, we would see Mama Beaver taking her litter of kits out for a swim under a protective cedar bough.

The kits sound like puppies; in fact, they resemble a bunch of them trying to swim. We had started out early enough; Mama and her babies should still be outside the lodge. On each of our kayaks was clipped a holder for our to-go cups (Oh, how we loved our custom dark beans.) Approximately forty feet from the island, we stopped and put our paddles down to sip our coffee. We sat in complete silence, assessing the water and the shoreline. What was left of the mist, loosely spiraled long threads of white, spun and danced around us. Though the morning air was still cool, the sun on my face warned it would be a hot July day.

We snuck in closer to the beaver lodge and heard a rewarding chorus of whining, "ahng, ahng, ahng." Their coos are similar to a newborn baby. There in the shade of the low-hanging tree bough were the bobbing little brown heads. The mama swam back and forth in front of them to keep them in line, I suppose. If we ever got too close, and we really tried not to, she would swim out to us and slap her tail on the water as a warning. We stopped again. Silently sipping.

When we arrived back at camp, Rich went for a swim. Every hour or so, a car would pull up and jockey around trying to find a place to park in the small space in front. Malachy, and his wife, Isabel, waved. They had come all the way from New Jersey. John showed up later with Richard, and Nathaniel pulled up in a truck he had rented at the airport. Our niece and her family brought Rich's mother, Arlene. Rich, having finished his swim, began the process of slow cooking multiple racks of ribs. Three large coolers sat in the shade, filled with potato, chicken, and pasta salads I had made. The radicchio and endive coleslaw was in the refrigerator. Beans were baking in the oven inside with strips of Vermont maple-cured bacon on top.

Once all five of the boys arrived (including Malachy and my niece's husband), they began to assemble their arsenal. They had been collecting fireworks all year. It became a little scary the older they got and the more disposable income they had. Camp dwellers around the pond made a game out of shooting the great arches of light over the center, challenging the others in competition. My boys planned their attack. One of them hit upon the idea of baiting the other camps by shooting off smaller cheaper, bottle rockets.

The largest cooler was filled with beverages. While there was a tremendous stash of water and sodas, I would be lying if I said an extraordinary amount of beer wasn't consumed during the holiday. I started a fire in the circular stone pit around six o'clock. It would take a few hours to get the coals hot enough to roast corn, and by then, the sun would be sinking low toward Bald Hill Mountain.

I walked out to the far end of the long, floating dock, my terry robe wrapped around my damp bathing suit, and listened to the bonfire starting to crackle and pop behind me. Thin, wide, fair weather clouds shifted in color from silvery pink to purple, with red rimming some of them, as the lake prepared to swallow the sun. I rubbed my forearm across my nose that itched and caught the scent of the pond water on my skin, as pristine as it was divine. A Holy Water. I blessed myself, and in my deep pocket felt for an object at the bottom.

Not long ago, a box had arrived at my house unceremoniously on a brown UPS truck. The driver rapped quickly twice on the door, but didn't wait to see if anyone was home. When I swung it open, directly in front of me sat a little brown box. I brought it into my kitchen and slit the packing tape open with scissors. The contents inside were wrapped in newspaper and sealed with scotch tape. I cut through the tape, unwrapped it, and found myself holding a brownish-gold piece of glass the size of my palm. I bumbled around searching for a pair of reading glasses. My heart thrummed as I put them on and looked again. Was it authentic amber, or a symbolic replica? I thought the former. Inside a flower bloomed, reminding me of a small white iris, perhaps even an orchid. I felt my hand shake, the memory of my last time with Nathaniel still crushing.

Nathaniel and I attended three proms together when we were in high school. I went with him to his junior and senior proms, and he went with me to my junior prom. My parents refused to let me buy two different dresses because the events overlapped. I couldn't understand why this was so important to them, especially because I was paying for the outfits. After some creative thinking, a girlfriend and I rotated our formals. When Nathaniel came to pick me up, he presented me with a floral wristband. This was the custom of the day and considered a much cooler alternative to the corsages old ladies wore at weddings. Each time he gave me a white orchid. When I came home from the parties, I had placed the corsage in the refrigerator so I could carefully study them the next day. While the petals are waxy and exotically shaped, the heart is simple. A seed-producing ovary is tucked safely beneath it, while on a central column sits a lush cap of mustard-colored pollen. I would take the orchid out of the fridge and set it beside me as I did my homework. Just looking at it brought back some of the dreaminess of prom night. Eventually, the flower would begin to wilt on the edges. At that point, I pressed it into my diary where it dried to parchment.

I knew there was still a hole deep in my very core. It was the place where Nathaniel, like a key into a lockset, had fit perfectly. To this day, and I am no longer a young girl, I wish it were not true.

In the early evening sunset, a cool spread of air came off the water. I pulled my robe tighter around me and retied it at the waist. Once again, my hand went deep into the right pocket and found the piece of amber Nathaniel had sent to me. It was the exact size of the palm of my hand, flat and round. With an intense pleasure, one I had rarely experienced, I arched my arm, and with a flick of my wrist, hurled it across the water. The pink and purple sky was reflected across the surface of the pond as the amber hopped across its shimmering water. With one, two, three skips... it stopped and fell, then dropped into the clear, spring-fed waters. The amber was laid to rest on the sand and boulder bottom of the Newark Pond.

Finish the Book!

I went to Rich and told him I wanted to finish my book.

"This is the first summer break I don't have graduate courses," I said. "I didn't take on any tutoring students. The only big event I have is my high school reunion. Once I get back from New Jersey, I can bear down on the writing."

I wasn't asking his permission. I was letting him know what my plans were. I felt a little embarrassed whenever I mentioned my writing to Rich, but I said it anyway because I was letting him know that, while it may be a pipe dream, it was still *my* dream.

Rich could always tell when I was working on some creative project because I would become absorbed in it until it was completed. When I was designing our house, I spent hours on the land watching the sunrise and sunset. I would try to talk to him about how the breezes blew across the property and how the light would one day slant into each of our windows. Rich worried I was obsessed as I filled sketchbooks with interior views of the house that were in my head. It consumed hundreds of hours of my time.

One of my siblings had long ago been diagnosed with Obsessive Compulsive Disorder, and Rich actually worried I might one day step across that line in the middle of one of my projects. I discounted his concerns. "I love the old saying that what makes us good makes us bad," I said. "I am a detail person." I never felt more alive than when I was making something.

Rich was busy at the store that summer. The tourist business was up. It seemed climate change was working to Vermont's favor in that more and more people came north to escape the heat. I cooked dinner most nights because he was working and I wasn't. I found time to exercise with my close friends, and when Rich wanted to hike the dogs each day, I made myself available. If he wanted to go to camp, I went with him. He had nothing to complain about, but there was a part of me that I knew was absent from his life psychically, if not physically.

At the dinner table, I sometimes talked about my writing. "A landmark event like my 45th reunion makes me reflect back on my life. When I reminisce about the past fifty-nine years, I think about how only a few people really got me. *Really* got me. Most of them were the friends I made as a girl. Why is that? Isn't it true for you, as well? Your two best friends are guys you knew as a kid. What changes, as we get older? What happens to us?"

It made Rich nervous when I turned my introspective questions toward him. It made him feel cornered. His answer was invariably the same, though I knew he tried to stop himself. "I don't know. What you want me to say?"

I was exasperated. "I don't want you to say anything in particular. I'm just trying to explore your thoughts. I wonder if what I am telling you resonates with you."

"Resonance is a scientific phenomenon. An object free to vibrate tends to do so at a specific rate. It has to do with frequency, not feelings. You know I'm not entirely comfortable with emotions. I sure as hell don't like talking about them."

I knew him well enough to change the subject.

Rich told me later that he felt guilty when he heard me call my brother while I was cleaning up the kitchen. Apparently, after a brief description of my observations, I had exclaimed in a relieved voice, "I know. *Right?*"

He took me aside later, "I realized that you needed some kind of validation. Malachy understood what you were trying to tell me. I feel like I let you down. I want you to know that I care, even when I can't always give you what you are looking for."

The summer I decided to write my book, I took over one of the boys' rooms upstairs. I made it into a comfortable office where I could change positions by moving from chair to chair. My friends tell me I talk about my pain factually, which doesn't sound like complaining. Sitting becomes painful quickly, as does standing. The typing was an ordeal with my neuropathy, so I installed a program that allowed me to dictate to my computer. It helped, though the program made many mistakes. I learned to measure my good minutes using my hands against what I needed to say in the book.

I would turn to Rich and say, "Okay. Do you need anything? I'm going to go up and work on my book."

Behind the closed door, Rich would sometimes hear me laughing out loud. Other times, and this was the hard part, he would hear me cry.

It's Always Something–July 2014

Many tangents presented themselves as I worked. Nathaniel sent an email.

Subject: photos
From: Nathaniel Hayes drhayes#1@aol.com
Date: July 21, 2014 8:00:05 PM EDT

I have some photographs of you I have not been able to bear parting with. They were taken in a studio and are large archival prints. Maybe I could have some copies made of them and send you the originals. As I said, I have carted them all over the world. Considering my health, I think the right thing to do is to give them back to you.

Subject: photos
From: Mary Patricia Toohey <pattyt55@gmsvt.net>
Date: July 21, 2014 9:20:46 PM EDT
To: Nathaniel Hayes drhayes#1@aol.com

Thank you so much for offering to return the photographs. After I got your message, I found an old letter in which you asked me, many years ago, to send you pictures. I then compared the date of the letter to my journals. At that very time, I was studying photography. I set up the studio and lights myself. If you can't see my hands in the photographs, I am using a long cable release on my large format camera. In the photos where you can see my hands, I had a friend trip the shutter for me. I processed the film and paper myself.

They are self-portraits long lost to me. I am certain my children would love to see them, especially my Cannes-winning director-cinematographer-animator-photographer son by the name of Nathaniel.

MP

Hoping to enrich the details of my story, I decided to dig out *all* the letters I could find from my childhood friends. I wished so much that I could discuss the gushing up of memories and feelings with Belinda, but she was in lock down. Just a few days before, she had called me to announce she was in California in a court-mandated rehab facility. This was the first time we had spoken since I struck her by the tree fort. In the end, we didn't even talk about my assault or of her disclosure about Nathaniel.

Instead, Belinda told me about a peculiar adventure.

After our altercation, she had made her way back from the woods to the reunion. In the parking area, she ran into an old friend who many people had avoided due to her religious zealotry. Without any prompting, she started pulling Jesus pamphlets from her purse and thrusting them into the hands of her perplexed classmates. Floating from one small group to another, she dominated the conversations as she described her love for the Lord and all the ways in which He was her best friend. Within the first hours, we all politely, but firmly avoided her. It was uncomfortable. She left early.

Apparently, as the woman departed, she saw Belinda and handed her a pamphlet. Belinda hugged it to her chest. "Awesome. I love Jesus. Do you want to see me do my Jesus face?"

Of course the woman wanted to see it, but she wasn't sure how the expression Belinda mimed for her had anything to do with her Lord and Savior. Belinda remained unequivocally positive. "The Holy Spirit has personally saved me. It is a miracle I am alive."

Mrs. Evangelical was put off-kilter as they launched into a lengthy discussion about miracles, a topic where she had long been accustomed to holding forth. "Are you putting me on?" she asked.

Belinda was outraged by the question and insisted she witnessed miracles every day in the rooms of AA and NA. The other woman was interested, but had a hard time reconciling her religious training with the doctrine of Alcoholics Anonymous. It was here Belinda's memory began sputtering blanks. She told me this same woman who had been married for thirty-eight years to a *minister* somehow wound up in bed with her. Belinda remembered waking up beside her, but thought they must still have been in New Jersey at the time. Extrapolating from the charges brought against her in California, and the tickets and extradition charges from other states, Belinda thinks they headed west in the minister's wife's car.

The minister's wife came to visit her at the rehab. At first, Belinda thought the woman had made a terrible mistake; as far as Belinda was concerned, she was a complete stranger. However, when the woman described their journey together, some foggy images emerged. The wife said Belinda had convinced her she must see the Pacific Ocean. Until the night they spent together in New Jersey, Mrs. Evangelical had never had an orgasm. For her, it was a continuation of their long conversation about miracles. That *was* a miracle. She had full faith at that point in Belinda being able to move mountains. Belinda knew secrets and held the answers to questions she had carried for so very long. The wife was like a baby chick that had pecked its way out of the shell and was newly imprinted on its mother. She would follow Belinda anywhere.

When Belinda suggested they smoke crack cocaine, it didn't seem outrageous to Mrs. Evangelical, not compared to the lifetime she had spent holding back her sexuality. They stopped at strategic truck stops along the way, and when the dealer approached the driver's side he asked, "What do you want?"

Belinda, who always insisted on driving the wife's car, would answer, "The best you got."

The drugs they smoked were varied and had their bodies bouncing between speeding up and slowing down.

In the first few days, they lived off the wife's cash and credit cards. As the money ran out and her cards maxed out, Belinda got creative. In remote areas, she simply stole gas and drove away. It was relatively easy to do the same with food in small towns with many miles stretching between them. However, the legal record shows Belinda was losing it, making a U-turn across a highway island in Utah that caused a three-car collision involving children. Cameras recorded her running several red lights in Kansas, and then Nevada.

When Belinda and Mrs. Evangelical crossed the border into California, it was not so easy to skip out on payments. The erratic substances they were using stupefied the women. They were ever more emboldened by the fact they had not yet been arrested. Although they had only had sex once, Mrs. Evangelical held hope against hope it would happen again once they were settled in near the sea.

She never did get to see the Pacific Ocean. In Stockton, the ladies got it in their head that it would be easier to hold up a store than to try to shoplift. Security officers had them on the ground spread eagle almost as soon as they got their threats out of their mouths. Video footage shows them looking pretty frightening though, as they were both high as kites.

7/24/14

Dear Nathaniel,

Belinda is in jail. Well, point of fact, she was in jail and was then moved to rehab. I worry that you and I are to blame for it. Her downward spiral started at the reunion. It's a long story and I really feel she should be the one to provide details when she is ready to tell you about it.

I never got a chance to explain to you that I decided to write a book. I am two hundred re-drafted pages into it. This is not as out of the blue as it may sound. The balance where I have found happiness in my life is family, creative work, and lastly, my teaching career. I love real estate projects; I paint, and was a touring musician on the weekends for many years.

When you mentioned you had old photographs of me, I was inspired to dig out my boxes of old letters. I thought they would be a great resource for the book. I filed them by person, and in some cases, by date. Today, looking for clues as to the girl I might have been, I read all of your letters in chronological order.

I am struck by how star-crossed we were. How ill-fated our young love was. Obviously, I knew how our story would come out, yet I still found my heart racing as I came to the end of your thick stack of letters. It really was distressing; we were youngsters who were so earnest in their attempt to find some kind of future together and the sheer hope we mustered in the effort.

I know this is asking a lot, but could you have any letters I sent to you at that time copied? It would be a great help to me in establishing vivid descriptions.

It is a beautiful Vermont summer day. I hope the same is true for New Jersey and that this note finds you and your family well on this Sunday.

Thank you for considering my request.

As always,
Patty

Rich was away golfing at a tournament with his friends. When he called to check in, I talked about the dogs instead of Belinda's arrest or reading the old letters. I felt very much alone, like I was caught up in a time warp only my classmates from Avalon Park could possibly understand. All three of my sons received a phone call from their mother on that Saturday afternoon. I had never been more interested in their lives, and asked the kind of questions they were happy to answer. My wiles were poured on, so when each of them hung up the phone, they thought, *I should talk to Mom more often.*

I even called my mother-in-law. "I just wanted to make sure you are all right," I said to Arlene. "Rich is out of town and I wondered if you might need something."

When my dogs snuggled with me on the couch that evening, I played with them instead of making them settle down. Rich got home on Sunday night to find his favorite meal waiting for him. Rich is the most delicious-smelling man I have ever known, and when he came to bed, I was intoxicated by the scent of him. I quickly moved in to inhale all of him, every inch. He was amused by my ardor and I was profoundly comforted by his presence.

From: Nathaniel <drhayes#1@aol.com>
Subject: Letters
Date: July 25, 2014 2:05:26 AM EDT
To: Patty Toohey <pattyt55@gmsvt.net>

Patty,

Belinda is in jail? What the hell happened?

I love the book idea, and I'd love to help if I can find any old letters. I am very touched you saved mine.

When we get back home from Tuckernuck Island in a week, I will send the photos for sure. Any letters will be harder to find, as I was not as organized as you were. But I will try.

Fondly,
Nathaniel

Nathaniel never sent me the pictures or the letters.

And, as it turned out, Belinda once again became a model member of the AA and NA communities once she was in jail. She was offered a chance by the court to complete a long term rehab and she took it on with very serious intent. After the first month, she had earned some phone privileges and she called from the West Coast as her program ended for the day, but before her dinner was served.

Across the continent, my phone would ring in my kitchen somewhere between eight-thirty and nine at night. My day began at 4:45 a.m. when our coffee machine was tripped on by a timer and started making steamy sputtering sounds. Then Rich's alarm clock exploded on full blast at five. He would get up, take the dogs out, and shower. I usually lay in bed trying to doze off until I heard his car tear out of the driveway. So by nine at night I had taught my classes, sat in on meetings, graded papers, walked my dogs, exercised, completed house chores and projects, and made dinner and cleaned up the kitchen. The extra time I had I worked on my book. I was tired by nine o'clock and, I will confess, had a few glasses of wine.

Three thousand miles away Belinda was trapped in an institutional schedule. She wasn't allowed to have her cell phone. Every other day, she could use a calling card at the pay phone in the lobby. An attendant timed the phone calls; fifteen minutes tops. Other women waiting for their turn surrounded her. It was sometimes difficult to hear her, but she was so anxious that she talked non-stop. I would grunt an affirmative response now and then as she described her living conditions. Belinda was fighting for her own life. She knew this would be the last time she would be offered paid treatment for her addiction.

"Everyone in group keeps turning to me like I know the answers because I put together so many years of sobriety," she said. "If I'm supposed to be the expert, then we are all in big trouble. I keep telling them you have to be vigilant. Addiction is a monster waiting out in the dark to attack you when you least expect it. You must be aware at all times of how vulnerable you are to a slip. You have to be mindful. I got complacent and the next thing I knew, I was being arrested in California."

We both laughed at her deliberate exaggeration. Yet, the truth was plain. Belinda was terrified and it haunted me. The phone call ended when the staff at the rehab told her dinner was being served West Coast time or when she was ordered to hang up.

September 14, 2014

I had the day off and I was upstairs at my desk working. Malachy called while I sitting there staring at the pages I had just printed out which comprised the third draft of my book. It was done and I hated it. When I picked up the phone he asked me, "What are you doing?"

"I'm just sitting here filled with self-loathing."

"So, you are writing. Do yourself a favor and take a break. Put it in a drawer and walk away. A month from now you are allowed to open the drawer. You'll have a totally fresh perspective."

As an escape, I made Rich take me to the Fleming Museum at the University of Vermont in Burlington. "I would give a million dollars right now to stand on the streets of Manhattan," I had said. I don't miss living in the city. What I miss is the profusion of cultural opportunities. Art, whether visual or performed, energizes me. I walk into a venue as one person and walk out a better, improved version.

At the museum, I went through a room, turned a corner of one long hallway, and ran into the four pieces that comprise *The Scream of Nature* by Edvard Munch. It was a traveling exhibit, and I had no idea it was there. There was no time to emotionally prepare, and I began to weep. Rich came around the corner and saw me. He seemed ready to defend me as his eyes swept the room back and forth trying to locate the invisible offender.

"What happened?" he finally asked.

I managed to sob out that it was the paintings. Somehow, they were magnifying my fears about Belinda's disease, and my empathy for her valiant attempt to save herself.

Rich was puzzled. "The *paintings?*"

While I sat on a bench silently trying to take in the full power of the pieces, he held his hands behind his back and began to read every bit of information about them. It appeared he was trying to memorize the plaques and posters, but I never once caught him appreciating the art. Other people came around the corner in the same clueless manner I had. It was as if they had entered a vortex and were pulled into *The Scream*. One woman let out a groan. She was as surprised by the volume of her noise as everyone else around her. Another man leaned on his friend for a moment of support. But Rich just read on, learning and trying to remember what the museum said about Munch.

When we walked away, Rich spoke to me very casually. "Huh, I didn't know there were four of them."

"What do you mean?"

"Four screams. I didn't know there were four of them."

The comment hit me squarely in my funny bone. I laughed so hard I knew Rich was offended. "I'm sorry. But remember how surprised you were to learn that I didn't swim? Or when we built our first house and you assumed I could make curtains? I guess you only then realized I couldn't sew. When you were growing up, every woman you knew made her own curtains. That's how I feel right now about the art. These pieces and their history are something I thought everyone learned in college." He had an annoyed look on his face, but he remained next to me as we wandered around and viewed the various displays.

Later, we went down to the basement level to use the toilets. When I walked out of the ladies room, I started to walk in the wrong direction. Rich was incredulous, yet he knows for a fact that I have no sense of direction at all. So, in my own defense, and to turn the tables on him I asked him why he has to read every line of text at a museum.

"You just pointed out that I had no education in painting and art history. Maybe I'm trying to learn something."

"I think it's because you paid for us to get in and you want to get your money's worth."

"What's wrong with that?"

"Do you actually see the art? I mean do you think about how it was created, how he executed a particular brush stroke or mixed a certain color?"

"Mary Patricia. I don't know anything about how to mix a color. That's your department."

I reached my arms out and put them around him. "It's a good thing that you aren't an artist. Left to my own devices we would be penniless and starving. Your talent is for business. Thank the Lord one of us knows how to make money. I mean look at this book I'm writing. The hundreds of hours I have spent on it. Someday I will publish it, but who will care?"

He hugged me back and we kissed. He drew back and stroked my cheek. "You will care," he assured me gently.

Everybody Wants to Write a Book–2014

I suppose I didn't realize how many hundreds, if not thousands, of inquires book editors must get every year. So, I chose to be naïve when I was struck with curiosity. I had just read the most interesting book on the *New York Times* Best Seller list. I Googled the editor and landed on a website. There was a link to contact her.

Impulsively, I sent an email.

From: Mary Patricia Maddin pattyt55@gmsvt.net
Subject: Re: From Vermont
Date: December 20, 2014 10:09:46 AM EDT
To: Carol Slater carolaslator@gmail.com

I am writing to you from Greenfield, Vermont where I am a math teacher and my husband's family has owned the local supermarket for seventy-five years. This is a town so small that there is no traffic light. Our residents regulate the one-lane covered bridge that connects land on either side of the Mad River. We take turns. If it is clear which car pulled up to the other side of the bridge, we simply let them cross first. If not, there will often be windows rolled down and voices saying, "You go ahead. It's all right. I'm not in a hurry today." Whenever there is talk of putting a light in, it is squashed on the grounds that our method has worked for hundreds of years.

Yet, life happens here just as it does everywhere else in the U.S. I was adjoined to a chemotherapy machine when a plane hit the twin towers on 9/11. A tube was snaked into my neck, crammed down my jugular vein and into my heart. I was helpless but to watch every second of the news. Ten hours later, I walked into my kitchen and the phone on the wall was ringing. My mother had just died in New York. The next day, I would have to travel into the eye of the storm.

I have written a book about living beyond common, yet devastating tragedy. It demonstrates how pivotal events such as a 45th class reunion can galvanize healing and change. This is a fictionalized memoir and a slice-of-life piece.

What I am most concerned about is when it is done, it will be the best book it can be. Someday, my three sons will turn to each other and ask, "What *happened* to Mom?" This is what I will leave to them as an answer.

I am looking for a development editor to help me. It could be redrafted and ready to be read by January.

Do you have time?

Mary Patricia Toohey

It took two hours to teach my next classes. The students were tired and it was hard going. After it was over, I did what I always do and clicked on the icon to check my email.

From: Carol Slater carolaslator@gmail.com
Subject: Re: From Vermont
Date: December 20, 2014 10:15:48 AM EST
To: Mary Patricia Maddin pattyt55@gmsvt.net

Dear Mary Patricia,

I'm not really taking on new authors at the moment, as my schedule into the foreseeable future is extremely full. Yet, I like your query. If you'd like to send the first 25-35 pages of your book to me, I'll read them.

I know Greenfield. I used to ski there in the 70s when the only store was near the covered bridge. I do hope it hasn't changed too much.

Best wishes,
Carol

From: Mary Patricia Maddin pattyt55@gmsvt.net
Subject: Re: From Vermont
Date: December 20, 2014 12:09:46 PM EDT
To: Carol Slater carolaslator@gmail.com

The store you are describing belonged to my husband's grandfather. When Rich's father took over the business, he built a larger building down the road. My husband added extensions on it as he added new departments. Still, it isn't like a big-box store. Greenfield remains a small town.

Please find attached the pages you asked for.

If you come up to ski again, please let me know that you are in town.

MP

From: Carol Slater carolaslator@gmail.com
Subject: Re: From Vermont
Date: December 23, 2014 1:15:48 PM EST
To: Mary Patricia Maddin pattyt55@gmsvt.net

Dear Mary Patricia,

I loved the first pages. Can you send me the full manuscript?

Carol

Belinda's A Hero–February 2015

The winter had been brutal so far, with a record-breaking forty-one days below zero. Since my school had a February break, Rich and I were leaving for a short vacation in Mexico. It would be a respite from the extreme cold and the almost constant anxiety plaguing me.

Within the next week, my book would be published. When we got back, I expected to find a carton of hardbound copies in the pile of mail. My apprehension about revealing myself to the world at large was consuming me.

I had already lived a long and complicated life before I ever put a pen to paper and wrote about it. In order to tell my story, I needed the emotional distance of many years, which provided a buffer for me between my troubling memories and the safe, comfortable world I now inhabited. Having reached this vantage point, I examined the events of my life.

My editor, Carol, had asked for further changes to my book, and that was excruciating. As she shredded my book apart, I sometimes felt like I was torn, as well. It was as if she expected me to sever my connective tissue and then reattach it according to her instructions. I had to admit the changes she asked for worked well, but was I strong enough to withstand the personal revelations?

I was just starting dinner when the phone rang. The caller-id showed a California phone number. When I picked up, I heard a match strike and then an inhale of smoke a moment later exhaled with choking and sobbing.

"What happened?" I asked Belinda.

"My roommate tried to kill herself last night."

"Jesus!"

"I am calling from the phone outside the hospital."

"They let you leave rehab?"

"I saved her life." It was said so matter-of-factly.

"Tell me what happened."

"We go to meetings in town. When we get back, it's late. She said she didn't feel well and didn't come with us." Belinda took a drag off her cigarette and I waited. "It was dark and she was asleep when I got home. I tiptoed across our room and slipped into bed. I took my bra off intending to sleep in my T-shirt so I wouldn't wake her making noise going through my drawers. I didn't even brush my teeth. Even so, it seemed weird she didn't hear me. I expected her to turn over or something. I got out of my bed and put my hand in front of her nostrils. Her breath seemed faint. My hand rested for a second on her pillow. It was wet and sticky and then, I smelled the vomit."

"Belinda!"

"I ran out of my room down to the nurses' station. I wasn't even wearing pants. They were busy with paper work and said they would be down in a minute to check. I could tell they didn't really believe me. I ran back and turned the light on. My roommate looked blue. She was clearly unconscious, so I picked her up, believe me, it was difficult. I carried her back down the hallway screaming at the top of my lungs."

She took a break to let out a sob. After a few minutes, there was another drag on the cigarette. "The next thing I knew, they told me to shut up, and they said a doctor had been called. I had a feeling this was very bad. There is a hospital about a city block from the rehab. A giant parking lot lies between us and the entrance to the Emergency Room. When they told me we had to wait until a doctor was available, I walked out the double front doors with her."

I sat stunned, listening.

"You hear stories about the power of adrenaline. I am here to tell you it really does happen. I saw the hospital in the distance and I started running. My arms and shoulders are killing me today, but at the time, I didn't feel anything. I burst in to the ER and… oh, Jesus!"

The sobbing was back. I took a breath in and then out. In and out. In and out. Belinda could only tell the full story in her own good time. "I don't know why, but there was a local television crew in the emergency room. I guess they started filming us from the second I carried her in. No pants! No bra! I was yelling directions at everyone as I crossed the room. Then, I put her right down on top of the front desk. You never saw people move so fast. A stretcher was brought out and the doctor asked me if I wanted to go with her. He's treated me as a colleague ever since. He told me she would have died if I hadn't done what I did. I've been here since last night." Belinda barely got the last word out when she started crying again.

"Are you all right? Have they fed you anything? What are you wearing now?"

"Scrubs."

She sounded pitiful. I wept for her, too. I hoped there was someone on the other end who could bring her tissues. As hard as she was crying, the tears must have been drenching the top of her shirt, and I didn't want to think about the snot running down. I heard small spasms of air entering and exiting and I knew she was slowing down.

She said, "A few minutes ago, a nurse told me the film was going to air on the news tonight. The local station already has 8,000 hits on its website. They are thrilled it might go viral. I haven't seen it yet. God, I don't want to, I'm sure I looked like a madwoman."

As I was absorbing this, Belinda asked me to come out to California.

If I decided to go to Los Angeles, Rich would ask me why I would sacrifice our vacation. He would remind me this was the same woman who had betrayed me. He would reminisce about her history of disappearing out of my life for months on end. He might recite an insult she had cast at me. He would definitely quote me back to myself, as I had told him many times I never wanted to go through it again. This would not be easy.

"I need to ask you something," I said.

A gasp of air followed.

"Shoot."

"No, I'm sorry. Maybe this is not the time to bring this up. So much has happened to you. I'll ask you later."

"Well, now you have to say it. Listen, whatever it is it will get me out of my own misery for a couple of minutes."

Some seconds elapsed while I struggled with embarrassment. "Do you *love me*?" I barely squeaked the words out. I sounded like a small child. Tears streamed out of the corners of my eyes.

"Of course I love you. Why would you even ask me that?"

"You are always running away. One minute we are fine and then you disappear. For me it feels like the Apocalypse."

"When they brought me in here, they did a psychiatric evaluation. One of the things they asked me was if I lost periods of time. That's what they call it. *Losing time.* Apparently I am prone to dissociative amnesia. "

"So, now we have a name for it?"

"Yes, so please stop calling it my disappearing act. It's not an act. It's a real thing."

" Okay, okay. But Belinda, there is the little matter standing in our way here. You seduced the boy I loved."

"It was the drugs, Mary Patricia."

"I am not accepting that as a blanket excuse. It's not really an apology. It's like you are saying you had no choice in the matter."

"I understand. I suppose I'm so appalled at my own behavior that it's hard to get the apology out. There are times when I make the worst choices a person can make, yet it's hard to stop myself. It's like I'm compelled to use a man sexually the way I have been used. It kinda takes the power away from them. For a little while anyway, it relieves a terrible pressure inside of me."

"But *Nathaniel*?"

"He was male. I was high. It happened and I am sorry. I think I actually blocked it out of my mind for many years. If you had found out, I was sure that would be the end to our friendship."

We both spent the next few minutes sniffling. "Patty, I love you as much as I can love another person. I know that love, even friendship, is not my strong suit. If I stop to think about it, besides my brother and sister, you are the only long-term relationship of my life. And, you pay witness to me and the life I have lived. You see me, both the good and the bad. So, when you see something I am ashamed of, I run. Your presence makes my mistakes seem so real."

She dissolved again into tears. "Well, I love you too, Belinda. But..." I had entertained the idea of ending our friendship many times. I was standing in my kitchen trying to decide if there had been more good times than bad. We always showed up for each other during the really difficult moments of our lives, obviously we did that. Yet, other friends sometimes advised me our relationship was toxic. After forty-nine years, I had to face the truth. It was too late to bail now; we *had* to remain friends.

I told Belinda Rich and I would try to put together a plane ticket out of our credit card miles. "I need to call you back later tonight with the details. Go to the nurses' station. They can either give you their phone number for me to call in directly or retrieve your cell phone from the safe at the rehab. Remind them they are getting a lot of media attention too. Have them bring their security in on this. The rehab is going to bend over backwards for you now that you are the hero. Please tell them you want to schedule some private sessions for you and me. It's my only contingency, Belinda. I feel like we're caught in a hopeless cycle. Now that I know it's part of your disease, let's make an effort to see if they can help us. Make sure they feed you, too. Stay at the hospital until you hear from me. Then we will make a plan."

"All right, but I have a contingency, too, Patty. Stop using that superior tone with me. I can just picture the look you have on your face right now, your nose crumpled like you smell something bad."

We both laughed.

Hard.

By the time my plane touched down the next day, the video had, indeed, gone viral. When my cab pulled in front of the rehab, there were reporters waiting outside. A member of the pack shouted to me, "Are you here to see Belinda?"

I ducked inside the doors that were now guarded by a security detail. The crowd grew so large the administration was forced to bring in a media consultant to prep Belinda for a press conference. With her striking looks, the cameramen loved her. But, I don't think the reporters were prepared for how articulate and intelligent she was. That night, the spot played on every national news show.

At eleven thirty, Belinda fell into her bed, physically and emotionally drained. I slept in the chair next to her and awoke the next morning with a stiff neck. A staff member walked into the room about eight a.m. and took pity on me.

"Hi. My name is Jean. Wednesdays are for families. It would be wonderful if you could stay for a couple of days and participate. Listen, I don't usually do this, but I have a guest bedroom. You can walk to my apartment from here."

"That's so kind of you, Jean, I would be happy to pay you."

"Well, maybe just to cover utilities, toiletries, and what not. I don't exactly make a fortune working here. That's not why I do it. How about ten dollars a day?"

"I'm giving you twenty. If you don't want the extra money, I know you will put it to good use."

When the entire group gathered for family day, Belinda was asked to introduce me. She said, "This is my best friend of almost fifty years, Mary Patricia. She just wrote a book and it will come out soon. I don't want to say that any character is based on me, but you might want to read it." She winked at everyone.

For once, I made a concerted effort to keep my mouth closed and listen to everything they told me about Belinda's disease and how she had suffered. The program also generously provided us with three private counseling sessions. Uncharacteristically, I encouraged my friend to do most of the talking.

Nine days later, when I hugged her goodbye, most of my usual judgment and anger had given way to something akin to compassion. Belinda held me close and finally said, "Call me when you get home. I don't care what time it is. I have to know you made it safe and sound."

Jean took me to the airport where I made a quick morning connection to Chicago. But once there, I had a three-hour layover before the flight to Burlington, Vermont boarded. Since there was no hurry, I lazily rolled my carry-on along, window-shopping and people watching. I turned from a shop's display of snacks toward the airline gate across from it, where about half the molded seats were full. A man there appeared to be hearing voices. He screamed and gesticulated wildly as if he were having a heated argument with a ghost. When I saw him reach up to his ear and adjust something, his actions made more sense. He was wearing a headset and talking on his cell phone. Most of the other passengers were hunched over theirs, texting, seemingly lost in electronic prayer. However, one handsome woman was reading a book, and I found myself riveted by the cover. Although I felt quite shy, I walked right over to her.

"I'm sorry to disturb you, but I was wondering where you got that book."

"Excuse me?"

I pointed. "That book. It's mine. I wrote it. I'm Mary Patricia Toohey."

She turned the book around so she could see the cover, then she stared up at me. "Well, for heaven's sake!"

"It's just been released and I haven't held a copy yet. How did you get it?"

"Oh my, I just Googled *book with a heroine over fifty* and a link for Amazon came up for *The 45th Class Reunion*. I'm going to have my fiftieth high school reunion this summer, so the title was intriguing to me. Look, I'm half way through and really enjoying it. Did you actually work for the Chicago Mob?"

"Yes I did. May I... this is going to sound really strange, but may I hold it?"

She marked her place and handed it over without question.

The heft of the bound copy in my right hand was rewarding as I stroked the artwork on the cover with my left. I grew suddenly emotional, so much so that I surprised us both by collapsing into the seat next to her with a great thud. I held my book against my heart for several minutes and tried to steady my breathing. Instead, I embarrassed myself by crying, and that is when I felt her take my left hand in hers. When I looked up into her deep, brown eyes, I saw the resemblance; they were pools of sparkling empathy.

I told her, "You look like someone I used to know. Someone who made a great difference in my life."

"Really? What was her name?"

"Sister Mary Vincent."

"Sister Vincent? A nun?"

"I hope you aren't offended."

"No. Not at all."

"Are you Catholic?"

"I'm not."

"Well, I'm sure that's why you aren't offended. But Sister Vincent had true gift when she was working with children. I believed her when she said she had a calling, that she had a vocation. She loved us with the purest kind of love."

"I'm so honored I remind you of her. It's funny. I'm a teacher too. Mary Patricia... if she were here with you today... what would she say?"

"She favored an old Irish saying. When we were children, no matter what mistakes we made, no mattered what had happened, she would tell us, '*If there is a way into the wood, then surely there is also a way out of it.*'"

I squeezed her hand and the muscles of my face flexed as I fought back my tears. I gasped a few times before I could speak again, "In fact, she would probably tell me I was put on this earth to say there is a way out. Very soon, I will be sixty. And this has turned out to be the best time of my life!"

Acknowledgements

Many thanks to:

Tom Mehuron, my husband who, thank God, is not an artist. By default, he is then charged with holding the fort down while I spent hundreds of hours writing and chasing my dreams. I have known no greater act of love.

Mike Best, my baby brother, who treated me like a real writer long before I was one. Your talent inspires me, and your friendship, along with your wife, Michele's, keeps me steady.

Bruce Hyde, Jr., Jonathan C. Hyde, Thomas Mehuron, III. My children. I don't know who or where I would be without you. It is especially gratifying that as grown men you actually enjoy my company.

Special thanks to my dear friend of almost thirty years, Carol Wheelock, who is a role model for how to live life to the fullest and the best cheerleader anyone could hope for.

Janet Hubbard. Editor extraordinaire, author of many published books, teacher of writing, friend of nearly thirty years.

My exercise friends who were forced to listen to the development of this story and suffer through the many drafts of the manuscript. Trapped on our trekking loop of mountainous dirt roads, they patiently encouraged me across hundreds of miles. Extra gratitude to Chuck Martel who challenged my original ending.

The Green Mountain Valley School that took a chance on me when I was coming back from cancer treatment. In particular, Jen Robillard, Alice Rodgers, and Dave Gavett.

The adults who took an interest in me as I was growing up. Your encouragement kept me on the relative straight and narrow, and may well have saved my young life. God rest your souls, Gloria and Ralph Omstead, Sister Vincent, Mr. McGill, Mr. Grew, Mr. Goba, Ms. Ceru, and Ms. Gogarty.

My grandparents and great grandparents who are the shoulders I stand upon. They sacrificed all to get us to the United States, and in their memory, I wish every immigrant family the same chance to achieve the American dream.

Questions and Topics
for Discussion

1) Many children suffer physical and sexual abuse, which causes some predictable and often negative outcomes. How do you think Mary Patricia's childhood affected her later life? What about Belinda?

2) What are your thoughts on Mary Patricia's character? Was she made stronger or more vulnerable by her religious upbringing?

3) Mary Patricia was born mid-century to a culture that no longer exists. A lack of technology contributed to her isolation in Milwaukee and San Diego. What has been invented since 1973 that might have helped her?

4) How are Belinda and Mary Patricia alike and how are they different? What held their friendship together for almost fifty years?

5) Do you understand the betrayal Mary Patricia felt when told that Nathaniel and Belinda had had sex back in high school? Would you have reacted in the same way?

6) Do you think the success of Mary Patricia's three sons has to do with their mother's illness?

7) Were you pulling for Rich when he reentered Mary Patricia's life in order to help get her through the cancer?

8) Mary Patricia idealized her childhood friends; it is as though her feelings for them were frozen in time and covered with amber. What realities was she ignoring?

9) Are you surprised that Belinda becomes a hero? That Mary Patricia goes out to California to help her? That Rich lets her go?

10) Do you think Mary Patricia was wise to respond to Nathaniel's emails?

11) Discuss how illness changed both Nathaniel and Mary Patricia?

12) Did reading about Mary Patricia's various treatments and procedures empower you to ask questions if ever placed in the same situation?

Excerpt from *Even Now*

by Mary Kathleen Mehuron

Vermonters call November "stick season," referring to the time of year when the maple trees have shed their magnificent red and orange foliage, and even the birches have sloughed off their feather-shaped yellow leaves. A cold, pervading dampness sets in that lasts for weeks, and settles into the joints. I observe its effects in the checkout line at Rich's grocery store, as a customer waiting to pay bends his legs in a plié several times trying to alleviate the stiffness in his knees. I could set a metronome to his movements. The middle-aged cashier waiting on him sits on a stool, complaining about her achy hip.

"It's raw out," she says.

"Brutal," the customer replies. "Just brutal."

Some late autumn mornings, the cloud cover is so thick and low that I question if the sun has risen. The opacity remains throughout the day, and by four in the afternoon it feels as if night has already descended. We pray the daylight savings time change will help. It doesn't, and it will be awhile before the first deep snowfall, which will launch the holiday and ski season. We know a good Nor'easter will transform the unspoiled countryside and the fresh air, while bracing, will be invigorating. In the meantime, we endure.

Rich came home in early November 2015 and suggested he take the entire family on a trip for Thanksgiving, which was only ten days away. I looked at him to see if he was joking, for that was one of the busiest times of year for his store, but he assured me he was serious. I began researching resorts that would match our varied interests and our budget. We had, at one time or another, dreamt of going to Turks and Caicos, but it had always felt beyond our reach. Rich wanted to take all three of our sons and my mother-in-law on vacation. The prices I was quoted for the six of us took my breath away.

At first, I couldn't find any information about the area because Rich kept referring to it as Provo. While on the Internet, I stumbled across resorts on Providenciales, the most populated island in the Turks and Caicos Islands, which are east of Cuba, south of the Bahamas, and north of Haiti and the Dominican Republic. The island's first large hotel and casino complex, a Club Med, opened in 1984 and became such a success that many hotel chains followed. I prepared three different trip proposals at leveled price points. Certain he would balk at the cost; I started planning a return trip to Mexico.

Rich, who had already shocked me with his spontaneity, told me to keep looking in Turks and Caicos. A place named Bohio kept popping up on my computer, located on Grand Turk, a short flight from Provo. I read, "Warm sunny days, crystal clear blue water, white sand beaches, a great atmosphere, and some of the best scuba diving in the world." It seemed perfect for us. Rich was passionate about scuba diving, as were Richard and John. Nathaniel would dive a few times, but was keen on sailing on a Hobie Cat. Eighty-five-year old Arlene could sign up for yoga classes, and work on her celebrated tan. I dreamed about having four hours of uninterrupted writing time each day in a tranquil setting, far from the damp achy gloom at home.

I called the number listed, and within an hour, we were booked. Rich said it would be a "once-in-a-lifetime" adventure, and I nodded, but had no idea then just how special it would turn out to be.

Rich, Richard, Arlene, and I drove to a park-and-ride hotel in Boston on Friday, where my youngest son, John, joined us. By noon the next day, we were touching down on the island of Provo. As soon as we landed, we stripped down to our t-shirts. We would board the puddle-jumper in two hours. In the waiting area, I asked a gate agent how I could call the hotel owners to let them know our arrival time and he reached into his pocket for his cell phone and handed it to me.

"Are you sure?" I asked.

He shrugged. "It's a local call," he said.

When I turned to hand it back to him, he had disappeared. Twenty minutes later, I spotted him and ran up to return his phone.

"Oh thanks," he said casually.

I found my family among the waiting passengers and explained that Cabman Jack would be picking us up. The four of them simultaneously leveled a questioning look at me with slightly raised eyebrows, as if to ask *who*? I laughed. "That's what the owners called him. Cabman Jack."

An ominous question occurred to me, where was Nathaniel? I thought he was departing from Los Angeles, but Richard was certain he had said Philadelphia. The gate agent, who had offered his phone, checked the list of passengers and said there was no Nathaniel Maddin on the reservation list. I started to worry, and said I didn't think we should leave without him. My concern that my globe-trotting son couldn't manage on his own set me up for ten minutes of teasing remarks from his father and brothers. I could tell Arlene was tired, evident from her face and the color of her skin, so for her sake I agreed to board without Nathaniel.

We climbed up to the fifteen-passenger propeller airplane and discovered that our seats were directly behind the pilot and co-pilot, which made me feel like we were embarking on a carnival ride. They had weighed each of us, and our suitcases, then distributed us out to create some balance. It made me nervous to think the weight of our luggage alone could make the plane crash. Once aloft, though, it was a smooth ride as we gazed down on the turquoise sea. Turks and Caicos are comprised of forty islands and cays, and only seven of them are inhabited. They form a ragged paisley shape, and from the air you can see that they are connected by the underwater coral reefs. Each island is jungle green, but outlined with wide sand beaches. The water above the reefs is lighter than the deep ocean and it reflects every shade of blue-green, from cyan to teal.

We descended the steep narrow steps of the airplane and walked out onto the crushed white-shell tarmac, then paused to look around. John suddenly exclaimed, and pointed. "Do you think that's Nathaniel?"

We followed his gaze to a helicopter that had obviously just landed, and watched a young couple emerge. The woman was holding a clipboard, and the guy peered over her shoulder at something she was showing him. He gave her a slight hug goodbye, saluted whoever was behind the windshield, and bounded over to us. He was wearing a little hat that even I knew was cool, although if pressed to say exactly why I couldn't have done so.

"Hey, everybody!" We stared at him as though he were an apparition.

"Last minute shoot," Nathaniel said a little breathlessly. "I was editing a commercial in Buenos Aries. He launched into an explanation about the studio agreeing to pay for most of the exorbitant helicopter bill, and that hiring it was a no-brainer because it arrived at the same time as our flight. We exploded in laughter. A family joke was born. From then on, whenever we made a purchase, we would defend our choice by calling it a no-brainer.

We entered the airport, and while waiting for our luggage someone called out hello, then started shouting our names. "Mary? Rich? Richard? John? Welcome to our island!" Cabman Jack was wearing a grey uniform, and was animated and obviously quite a character. I waved and as if on cue, music filled the room. I followed Cabman Jack outside, with my family trailing behind, and stopped at the sight of a three-piece band.

It was my introduction to an instrument called a ripsaw, partially created out of a common variety handsaw. The musician played it with the finesse of a classical violinist. Intrigued, we formed a semi-circle around the musicians to listen. Cabman Jack broke the spell by saying during a break, "Let's get you to the hotel. I'll have a rum punch in your hands before another hour passes."

On the way to the hotel, Jack told us he was sixty-nine and had lived on Grand Turk since he was five, when his parents moved there from Haiti. His cheerfulness was genuine, and contagious. He drove with the windows down, slowing down to shout greetings to locals as he passed.

He pointed out the grocery store and a short time later we drove between the stone pillars of Bohio, and on down a stone-paved road, with the Caribbean on our left. Ahead, I saw an oasis of tropical trees and flowers. Cabman Jack pulled into a circular drive and stopped in front of a Bahamian-style building where the doors and windows were thrown wide open. Two men greeted us, then took our suitcases, and led us through an impressive glass double door with sidelights and transoms.

By the time we unpacked and changed into summer clothes, it was already cocktail hour. We met at the Ike and Donkey Beach Bar, a small building named for the hurricane that almost destroyed it and the wild donkeys that roam the island. Multi-layered decks surrounded an open-air bar that looked out onto the ocean. The sound of waves lapping against the shore was hypnotic, and we reminisced about the trip we had just taken to get here while looking out to sea.

Everyone, that is, but Nathaniel, who was still in work mode. "I have a conference call at six."

We all groaned.

"Look you guys," he said, "I'm at a totally different level now. My career is on the fast track. The laws of social convention don't apply to me right now. Directors have a short shelf life. I have to make the most of this *right now.*"

When his cell phone rang, it was obvious the reception was poor, for Nathaniel stuck a finger in one ear and said repeatedly in a louder and louder voice, "You're breaking up, man." He angled his chair in a different direction to see if that made a difference. His back was to the ocean. He next scooted his chair away from the table, arched his back, and began leaning to one side to optimize the signal.

"Honey!" I called to him.

Thinking I might be on the verge of reprimanding him, he glanced over at me, and said, "Mom! This is important!" He held his index finger up for emphasis as he silently mouthed the words, "Rules don't apply." All the while, he continued to inch his chair back and dramatically stretch his body to one side until he had reached the edge of the deck.

None of us said a word as we watched him fall over backwards ass over-teakettle. His cell phone bounced off his chair and broke into two pieces that flew in opposite directions. I stood up slowly and leaned over the railing.

"Apparently, the law of *gravity* still applies," I said.

Once they were certain he wasn't injured, his father and brothers guffawed loudly. They began imitating the expression on Nathaniel's face when he realized he was going to fall. He had landed on his back in the sand and he lay there for a few moments in abject humility. Then, he rolled around moaning, working the situation for comic effect. Finally, he gave a wave of his hand to acknowledge his folly, and John jumped down to help pull him up, and then set the chair aright.

Two waitresses had witnessed the entire episode, and they, too, were giggling. Not wanting to be rude, they tried to cover their laughter with their hands. Nathaniel made one further attempt to conduct business. "Do you have internet here?" he asked one of the waitresses.

She shrugged and said, "Sometimes."

He sat down and slid the pieces of his cell phone to the middle of the table. "The hell with it!" he said. "I told my crew we were in a remote location. People in LA can't imagine being off the grid. Well, I am, and they will just have to deal with it."

We raised our glasses in a toast. Nathaniel was finally with us.

A band started to play softly, and I noticed guests making their way to the tables. The chef spread out hot coals to start the barbequing process. Richard and I were fascinated by the musicians and spent the time between sets guessing their various nationalities that ranged from Cuban to Nigerian. After the welcoming three-rum punch and a long day of travel, I found myself mesmerized by our setting. Rich was suddenly next to me and he whispered into my ear, "If you can guess what I have in my pocket, you can have it."

The next thing I knew, he was kneeling before me, and we were pretty much eye to eye. His mouth wasn't smiling, but his eyes were. Rich's mouth, in fact, was trembling a little. I started to feel self-conscious. I looked at my sons who were gathered around the long table, the drinks in front of them matching their personalities. A microbrew for John, a Manhattan for Richard, and a glass of Grenache for Nathaniel. Rich's mother who rarely drank had ordered a piña colada. All of them were smiling.

"A ring?" I asked.

Rich pulled a beautiful little box from his pocket and handed it to me.

"Open it," he said.

It was a princess-cut diamond set in platinum, and it fit me perfectly

When I kissed him, the crowd in the restaurant applauded. As if on cue, a tall man in a dark suit stepped out from the inn and gestured for Rich and me to stand together on a platform facing the ocean. One of the innkeepers appeared with a bouquet of tropical flowers and put it in my hand. I burst into tears and hid my face for a moment behind the flowers. Rich put his arms around me, and we rocked back and forth.

"It's time," he said.

It had been twelve years since we divorced, and though I had moved back in with him during cancer treatments, we had not remarried. A waitress brought a napkin to me, and I wiped away the tears. The sun was setting as the Justice of the Peace walked us through the short and simple ceremony. When he joined our hands at the end, the band struck up a lively tune. They played it in the Turks and Caicos style with a steel drum and a ripsaw. Something about the song sounded familiar yet out of place. I caught Richard's eye and mouthed to him.

"The Drifters?"

My eldest child rolled his eyes upward and spread his arms out in agreement. My gaze shifted to John who nodded a simple, but firm, yes. It was the 1960 American hit, *Save the Last Dance for Me.*

Led by our innkeepers, the other guests toasted us with a glass of champagne. The low angle of the sun cast an orange glow, which was flattering. A photographer began taking pictures, and for a fleeting instant, I wished I had washed my hair at the hotel in Boston. My sons and mother-in-law embraced us as the upper rim of the red sun began to disappear over the horizon. We all stood together and watched when, unexpectedly, dramatically, almost unbelievably, the final rays of the setting sun turned to columns of bright green light that flashed up and out into the night sky. The crowd stood and cheered.

Author Jules Vern once described this optical phenomenon, Le Rayon Vert, or The Green Flash as "… the true green of Hope."

Hope.

Take it in. Take it in. *Take it in.*

Biography

Mary Kathleen (Kathy) Mehuron is a career math and science teacher with an artistic side; she has also been a professional musician, photographer, and artist. Kathy has reached a point in life that she has the time to write every day and she does. She lives in Vermont with her husband and dogs, Sydney and Tasmania. She has three grown sons. This is her first book.

Contact the author:

kathym55@gmavt.net

Mary Kathleen Mehuron
P.O. Box 59
Waitsfield, VT 05673

Made in the USA
Middletown, DE
27 January 2016